SWIPE

EVAN ANGLER

SWIPE

THOMAS NELSON
Since 1798

NASHVILLE   DALLAS   MEXICO CITY   RIO DE JANEIRO

Published in Nashville, Tennessee, by Tommy Nelson. Tommy Nelson is a registered trademark of Thomas Nelson, Inc.

Cover design by Jay Smith, Juicebox Designs.

Tommy Nelson® titles may be purchased in bulk for educational, business, fund-raising, or sales promotional use. For information, please e-mail SpecialMarkets@ThomasNelson.com.

Page Design by Mark L. Mabry

Library of Congress Cataloging-in-Publication Data

Angler, Evan.
 Swipe / by Evan Angler.
   p. cm.
   Summary: In a world where everyone must be Marked in order to gain citizenship and participate in society, a group of youngsters who questions the system struggles to identify the true enemy—while pursuing a group of Markless teenagers.
 ISBN 978-1-4003-1836-0 (pbk.)
 [1. Science fiction.] I. Title.
PZ7.A5855Sw 2011
[Fic]—dc23

                                                                    2011026611

Printed in the United States of America

12 13 14 15 16 QG 8 7 6 5 4 3 2 1

For my family,
who makes it possible

CONTENTS

CONTENTS

THE FRIENDS
IN THE DUST

THE MOON WAS THE COLOR OF BLOOD, AND THE clouds moving past were pale like bone. Blake sat atop the slide in the starlit playground and noticed this, waiting.

Two of his friends ran and yelled below him, chasing one another around the wooden castle, jumping and doing flips off the swing set until one fell on his face and cried, "New game!" while his nose streamed moon-hued rivulets and the other said, "I've won, I've won, I've won." Farther off, a girl and boy sat on the ends of a teeter-totter, balanced, motionless, suspended, and ready.

It was fast approaching midnight, but not one of these teenagers worried about curfew or bedtime or accountability. Not one of them thought of families calling them home or of parents grounding them for bad behavior. They were alone. And the Dust played by its own rules.

In his way, Blake looked forward to these playground nights, grim as they inevitably became. This one had been a long time coming, and the flustered butterflies of anticipation taunted and amused him.

He squinted to see. At the edge of the park, a small girl had appeared, groggy and in pajamas, walking as if still in her own nightmare.

It was her.

She had come.

All at once, the five kids on the playground went still and silent. All five watched as the girl ambled through the grass and shadows, still holding a tattered half of their invitation in her hand.

Blake slid down the slide and balanced on the wooden lip at the edge of the cedar chips.

"Meg," he said.

She nodded. Under her left eye was a green and brown bruise stretching from ear to nose, and it shone painfully in the twilight. But the rest of her was sturdy and thick, and coarse blond bangs framed a square face that was brave and defiant and anything but fragile.

The Dust encircled her slowly while Meg stood and stared them down one by one. But she trembled slightly, and it was too warm a night for that. Blake saw this and frowned.

"There's nothing to be afraid of," he said.

But when Meg turned to run, the kids behind her proved Blake very wrong.

Her struggle was brief. But there was nothing gentle about the way the Dust blindfolded Meg, and tied her hands, and dragged her clumsily into the shadowed woods beneath the quiet cover of night.

ONE

LOGAN LANGLY, BOY
WHO CRIED WOLF

1

THE LAST THING LOGAN WOULD WANT YOU TO know about him was that he was afraid of the dark.

But Logan *was* afraid of the dark, and if you ever asked him about it, ever brought it up to his face and maybe teased him a little even, he'd stop you right where you stood and tell you it was for a very good reason.

It was because Logan Paul Langly was being watched.

He didn't know who, and he didn't know how. But every night, when Dad pulled up the covers, turned out the light, and shut the door behind him after demanding sweet dreams and tight sleep, Logan Paul Langly found himself on the wrong end of a spyglass.

So when Logan awoke with a start—even in the comfort of his own bed, even in the warmth of the late-summer evening that was anything but dark and stormy, the weekend before his first day of eighth grade—it was with well-worn urgency that he sat up, rubbed the sleep from his eyes, and scanned the room for signs of intrusion.

Tonight, there was only one. His window rested an inch above its seal, and a breeze dried the nightmare sweat from his forehead.

Logan couldn't remember if he'd left it open, but if you'd asked him in that moment, he would have told you he had not.

Had his father? Had his father walked to the window during their conversation that night? Maybe for some cool air in the midst of their heated discussion? Logan replayed the scene in his head.

He had been focused on his breathing, controlled and steady to keep himself calm. He had pulled the covers back but was standing a few feet away from the bed, just in case someone was under it, waiting for an ankle.

I'm too old for this, he thought, and he shook his head with just a little bit of shame.

"Whatcha doin', bud?" Mr. Langly said in the doorway behind him, and Logan jumped as if the words were a spider falling down his back. "Imagination got hold again?"

Logan nodded but didn't turn around. Instead he crawled into bed and pulled the covers high up over himself, curling up and facing the wall. He could feel his father sit beside him, hunched over and looking at his hands, folded and resting on his lap.

"You know," Mr. Langly said, "I think school's gonna be awesome this year. I think school's gonna be its best yet. You've got that government class ninth period—I know you're gonna love learning about all that stuff, and you've got gym and art and technology and—"

"Dad," Logan said, and his dad stopped abruptly. "I'm not worried about classes." The two were quiet for a minute. Mr. Langly wondered if he should take the opportunity to ask what Logan *was* worried about, and Logan wondered if he should say. But Dad pretty much knew the answer.

"The Mark, right?"

Logan stiffened at the sound of the word. Finally he said, "We're all turning thirteen this year. Everyone's getting it. It's just a matter of time."

Logan knew that if he was going to talk about this with anyone, it had to be Dad.

You did not talk about the Mark with Mom.

"Look," Mr. Langly said. "This year . . . is going to be . . . it's going to be great." But he frowned and sat still for several breaths, and Logan believed him less with each one.

. . . three.

. . . four.

. . . five.

"I remember when I got the Mark," Mr. Langly said, finally. "Just after you were born, when the program began. They give you a spoonful of nanosleep, so it doesn't hurt. You just go in, answer some questions . . . sit back, and before you know it, you're Marked and on your way. It's nothing. Honestly.

"And then it's great! It's like playing your first hover-dodge game, or getting your first tablet, or going off to school, or . . . I mean, you're *free*! With the Mark, you're free. You can get a job, you can shop for things . . . if you want more juice, you can just go out and get a carton yourself. You won't even have to wait for Mom or me to come home—"

Logan rolled over and pulled the covers away from his head to look his father in the eyes. "*Juice?*"

"Or something." His dad smiled. "Why? What would *you* get?"

Logan refused to think about it, refused to allow himself even the slightest excitement over the Mark, so he and his dad had a little unspoken staring contest instead. They did this from time to time, just reach a moment of disagreement when Logan would stare, and Mr. Langly was a good sport, so he'd always stare back.

"You can't pretend it didn't happen," Logan said. "You can't pretend it didn't kill her."

And Logan's dad sighed.

That pretty much ended the staring contest that night.

2

In all of it, Logan couldn't remember his dad opening the window, couldn't remember the draft coming in and animating the blinds' soft *rat-a-tat* against the pane, as they did so ominously now.

So who had done it? Who had touched the window, and when? There had to be a reasonable explanation, but Logan couldn't think of one.

Why could he never think of one?

For years, it had been this way, off and on. He'd walk home from school on the familiar sidewalks of his town, looking over his shoulder the whole way. He'd finish homework on his lap with his back to a wall, his desk beside him empty and gathering dust, so as always to keep an eye on the room he was in. He'd brush his teeth at night transfixed by the door behind him in the mirror, his eyes trained on the knob that at any time could betray him, could turn or jump or jiggle. A quiet moment was one spent listening for footsteps, for leaves rustling in the fall or snow crunching in the winter. Time alone was time spent watching the movement in the shadows.

Being underage, Logan couldn't see a doctor without a Marked guardian, so at his moments of highest desperation, when his parents had had enough and didn't know what else to do, his dad would take him—drag him—to the Center. Logan would sit in the examination room, prodded and scared, while Mr. Langly said to the doctor things like "We don't know what's wrong with him . . ." and "Ever since his sister . . ." just exactly as if Logan wasn't there, wasn't sitting *right there* and crying silently as the doctor shone lights at him and shook his head coolly and clicked his tongue, saying words like *traumatized, paranoid, delusional.*

Over time, Logan learned to carry his fear. He learned to swallow it, deny it, live with it. His accounts of faces in windows and footprints on floors, of sounds at night and doors opening and closing on their own, of being followed or tracked or who-knows-what-else, had all been brushed off so many times by his parents and teachers and adults of any kind that sometimes Logan wondered what was real and what was imaginary.

But his sister *had* died. That *happened.* And ever since, Logan was about one floorboard creak away from certainty that someone, somewhere, was out to get him too.

∃

His parents didn't know it, but Logan kept a flashlight hidden under his pillow. The switch to the ceiling light was all the way across the room, and he would have had to get up out of bed to turn it on. That was unacceptable. So Logan sat, now, back to the wall, covered in blankets up to his neck, and his hand braced the flashlight against his cheek to steady the beam of light as he swept it around each corner of the room.

There was nothing immediately out of the ordinary, except for the opened window. No mud on the floor, no stuff out of place . . .

He turned the flashlight around, pointing the unlit end of it away from him, and flipped a switch along its handle. The main light turned off, and out of its other end, the violet haze of a black light began to glow.

Black lights were useful. They revealed lint, smudges, blood, traces not seen by the unaided eye . . . and most importantly to Logan, they showed nanodust. There wasn't a Marked person around who didn't leave a cloud of it behind.

Tonight, though, like every night, Logan saw nothing—just the single small trail left by his father, an empty room with an unpleasant draft, and a window slightly ajar.

Time to check the rest of the house.

Logan tiptoed to the corner of his room and called for the elevator, which arrived promptly and took him to ground level.

Like many private residences in the town of Spokie, Logan's house had just one room to a floor, with an elevator connecting them and an open-air spiraling staircase outside in case of emergency, or for use during the nice summer months. Each room had panoramic windows and doors in two of the corners—one to the elevator and one to the outside staircase. The height of these houses varied widely and could reach higher than twenty floors, but Logan's had only eleven. This was good. More would have taken longer. Because every night, without fail, after his parents had tucked him into bed and gone to sleep themselves, it was Logan's job—self-appointed—to look thoroughly through each floor, bottom to top, flashlight in hand for signs of even the slightest suspicious thing.

Paranoid? To Logan, it was practical. These were simply the habits any boy might develop if he were certain that someone was out to get him.

The first floor was the foyer, lined with pictures of the family and hangers for coats and not much else. Nothing unusual this evening, so Logan double-checked the front door's dead bolt and moved on.

The second floor was the kitchen. Knives were all in place. That was a good sign.

The third floor was the dining room, only ever used for holidays and entertaining guests, and tonight it was as empty as expected.

Fourth floor was the bathroom, but no one lurked in the shower tonight. Floor five was the living room, cluttered but hardly suggesting a break-in. Six was Mr. Langly's office, and the holograms of his latest architectural projects glowed untouched. Seven was Logan's bedroom, which he skipped for now.

Eight was a rec room that no one ever used. It had been Logan's room up until five years ago—right *there* was where his bed used to be—but he'd moved down a floor when his sister passed away. Because she had lived on the ninth, and because every night while she was alive she'd tap a rhythm for Logan to hear through the floorboards. *Shave-and-a-haircut*, it went, and Logan would throw both shoes up at his ceiling. *Tap-tap*, they went. *Two-bits*. That was how they always said good night. When Lily died, it didn't take more than one tapless night for Logan to know that he couldn't live under that ceiling anymore.

Lily's room, nine, was a floor frozen in time like a museum of her last days, like one big held breath. It was Logan's least favorite to visit. A chill ran through him each time he did, and his eyes watered and made it hard for him to see, but still he never skipped it—nine was the perfect place for an intruder to hide. Tonight, though, like each night, there was no one there, or at least no one Logan could find, and he wasted no time stepping back into the elevator, knocking a soft *tap-tap* against the wall as he did.

Ten was his parents' bedroom, which Logan didn't need to check, so he moved straight to Mrs. Langly's study on eleven, filled to the brim with screens and meteorology tablets and satellite dishes, though no spies or burglars or murderers. It was beginning to look as if Logan would wake to see another day.

On the roof was the Langlys' yard. It was too small to play football up there, but it had a nice view. The grass shook gently in the evening wind, and having now checked each floor, Logan relaxed and allowed himself the drowsiness leading so pleasantly to sleep. He took the elevator down to his room on seven and crawled back under the covers, relieved to have made it through another night.

Except!

There! On his desk! The picture he kept . . . had it moved?

In its frame was the last snapshot taken of Logan and his sister, on the eve of her death, smiling over presents with the blur of family celebration behind them. Logan always kept this picture positioned so he could see it from his bed. Now it rested ever so slightly pointed away, his view of it not quite straight on, the desk space in front of it just slightly wet with water that should have been in the glass beside it.

Who had been there? Who had snuck in through the window? Who had tipped the glass and knocked the picture askew?

No one.

No one, Logan told himself. *You're being insane.*

. . . Right?

And Logan's heart snapped in his chest—so hard that it hurt—when across the room, the door to the outside stairway clicked quietly shut.

TWO

ERIN ARBITOR AND THE
GOVERNMENT WORK

1

ERIN ARBITOR WAS AWARE OF HER FATHER'S voice beside her, but she couldn't have told you what he was saying. His chatter filled their magnetrain compartment like a bored conductor's while her mind wandered further and further away, past the blur of unfamiliar tracks, past cities and towns, over mountains and across rivers, all the way back to Beacon City, her city, half a continent away and nothing like the humdrum destination she rode to now.

Spokie, she thought. It would never be home.

"—don't know why we couldn't have caught an earlier train," Mr. Arbitor was saying. "Soon as we get in we'll have to register you for school; then I need to get straight to the office and set up while you unpack at the apartment."

"Fine, Dad," Erin said. She held her pet iguana up to the window so it could see an oily and polluted Lake Erie off in the distance.

"It's just a lot to do in one afternoon—"

"I know, Dad."

"—and you and I are both gonna need to hit the ground running tomorrow." Mr. Arbitor shook his head. "Not even there yet and we're already behind. Kept saying we should have left on Friday . . ."

Erin rested Iggy on her lap and emerged reluctantly from her daydream, caustic and angry. "If only there could have been some way for us to stay with Mom in Beacon instead of uprooting our lives for no good reason." She shook her head, feigning sympathy. "Then you wouldn't be suffering such a *terrible* inconvenience."

"It was your mother's decision not to come with us," Mr. Arbitor said forcefully. He ignored Erin's tone. "She knows how important this job is. And not just to me—to the Union."

Erin sighed, caught square in the middle of a standoff between two strong-headed, working parents.

Just two months ago, Mr. Arbitor had surprised his family with the announcement that he had received a promotion at work, and that they would be moving to Spokie to accommodate it. Erin's mom, a top economic software analyst on Barrier Street in Beacon City, had told him precisely what he could do with that idea. Of course, Mr. Arbitor was certain it was only a matter of time before his wife gave in and found a way to keep the family together, but so far, she had not, and Erin was left with no choice but to get used to a new town a thousand miles away while her dad played a game of spousal career chicken and her mom continued enjoying life in the Big City back east.

"Well—anything for the Union," Erin said sarcastically, and her father rolled his eyes.

"I mean it," he said. "I took this job with good reason. You'll feel better about it once your mother's out here with us."

"She's not *coming* out here with us, Dad! She's waiting for you to come to your senses and tell DOME you can't just uproot your family because some bureaucrat's offering more money to copy and paste documents in Spokie than in Beacon!"

"That's not what this is, Erin."

"What about Mom's career, huh? What about my education—"

"This is what's best for *all* of us," Mr. Arbitor said, in a tone that suggested he'd been through this enough times with his wife already. "When we are called upon, we make sacrifices. Some things are more important than—"

"Than what? Than your family? How important can it be when you won't even tell me what you're needed for? I mean, maybe if I had some sense of what you were doing out here, at least I could wrap my head around—"

"Government work, Erin. Government work."

"'Course, Dad," Erin said. In all his years at DOME, Mr. Arbitor had never once talked about the specifics of what he did. When friends asked, Erin said what she was told to say, which was, "Government work," even though she had no idea what that meant. Somehow it just summed it up, said it all. If anyone pressed, she was supposed to say, "DOME, Department of Marked Emergencies." But no one ever pressed. The weight of the first two words was enough.

Frankly, Erin couldn't understand what her father was doing at a desk job in the first place. When she was younger, he had been a Beacon police officer, and a good one at that. In those days, when they'd play games together, he'd swoop her around the room with one hand. She'd hug him at night after his long days of patrolling the city, and it'd knock the wind out of her, every time. She loved that.

Now, sitting beside her in the plush, DOME-reserved train car, Mr. Arbitor was balding, and what remained of his hair was too long and unkempt. His face was lined from stress, and he'd become soft and fat. Looking at him, there were hints at some of the strength he'd kept—the definition in his forearms, the width of his back—but nothing that would grab a person's attention, nothing to terrify a criminal in pursuit, and Erin resented him for it. Why he'd given up life as a hero, as a *known* hero in the greatest city on the continent, for anonymity at DOME doing who-knew-what for higher-ups too selfish to mind transferring a family man halfway across the country, Erin would never know.

"Been a nice ride, anyway," Mr. Arbitor said, after hours of silence, and despite herself, Erin had to agree. She'd never been away from the coast before, hadn't ever ventured far beyond the closest suburbs of Beacon. There'd never been a reason to, and anyway, long-distance travel was tough ever since the airline and auto industries collapsed. A plane ticket from Beacon to New Chicago would have cost several times Mr. Arbitor's annual salary, and private cars were mostly a forgotten luxury. Intercity magnetrain lines were just recently becoming reliable enough for cross-country travel, and even this trip was only really made affordable by the tickets DOME had supplied.

Erin had to admit she liked the feeling of it, of the smooth, silent tracks, of seeing the countryside pass and change. The Beacon Metrorail trains were different, slow and loud and rough enough to make you sick, and none of the lines went far enough out of Beacon for a change of scenery, anyway.

On the magnetrain, the world transformed before her. The vast metropolis spreading out from central Beacon gradually thinned. Buildings shrank in both size and height, and city blocks eventually gave way to towns, which gave themselves, in turn, to wasteland.

A satellite photo of North America at the time would have looked much like a grim, sepia-toned shooting range. Three enormous bull's-eyes dotted the browned and dusty continent, and Erin was making her way between two of them now. The first and most prominent would certainly have been Beacon, which was the largest of America's cultural epicenters, its rings extending up and down the eastern coast as well as westward, their faintest influences reaching all the way out to the Allegheny River.

The second bull's-eye would have been New Chicago, much smaller than Beacon, but very dense, and stretching far north to create a long oval, marred only by the Great Lakes, and extending well into an area once known as Canada.

The third and final bull's-eye of the American Union would have been Sierra City, the youngest and least developed of the Union's urban capitals (it had been within Erin's lifetime that the old western coast was destroyed by the earthquake), but sprawling and lively nonetheless. Recently the city had celebrated its growth into territory as far as what had once been called Mexico (before it all just became the A.U.), and Erin was often told that if you could stand the heat, Sierra was a great place to live.

Outside of these urban areas, though, North America was mostly uninhabited, and while Erin had long known this to be the case, it wasn't until today that she could visualize what "uninhabited" truly meant. Along the ride, Erin had seen a few vistas still dotted with houses, and a couple even covered with them, but those were rare sights. Mostly, these days, following so many years of environmental disruption, the country was desolate, its old cities and towns long abandoned and forgotten, occupied by only the most occasional and intrepid of settlers still willing to risk its climate of hurricanes, tornadoes, floods, wildfires, heat waves, blizzards . . .

Consequently, the sky between cities was open and infinite, unobscured by a single skyscraper or overpass (except the occasional ruin), and it seemed to Erin that it might swallow her whole if she didn't hold on tight to her seat.

As they rode north through the suburbs, fifty miles out from New Chicago's city limits, the development returned. But it was hardly the bustling urban life she'd grown up with. This was small-town, and everything about it was unfamiliar. The buildings stretched only ten, maybe twenty stories off the ground. The streets were quiet and humble, scattered with pedestrians, but hardly any rollersticks or electrobuses. There were no treads on the sidewalk for automatic moving. No trams. No crowds. The buildings' sides were vinyl or glass or brick, and none were covered with the ground-to-sky advertisement and news screens from back home. Intersections didn't even have stoplights here. No one moved fast enough to need them.

"You're looking at it!" Erin's dad said as the train came to a stop. "This is Spokie."

Half an hour into their walk through the quiet streets, Mr. Arbitor wasn't so jovial. Sweat pooled in the crevices of his shirt as he lurched and dragged an oversized luggage carrier behind him. Droplets beaded and ran down his forehead. He huffed and spoke very little.

Erin refused to help.

"It has to be somewhere around here," Mr. Arbitor said. He wiped his face hopelessly on the collar of his shirt.

They passed Erin's new middle school three times before either of them saw it.

2

"I hate this," Erin said, standing at the edge of a large, empty field sandwiched between tall buildings on either side. "I can tell already."

The field was carpeted with plasti-grass, lined with bleachers, and big enough for any variety of outdoor sports. At its edge was a track for running, and by the sidewalk was a small sign announcing the school's presence: The Spokie School of Middle Development.

"Middle of nowhere," Erin said, and Mr. Arbitor walked with the luggage to a glass booth at the field's corner.

"I guess this is the entrance," he said, and they opened the booth's door and descended the long escalator into the school below.

The halls of Spokie Middle were bright and warm with a natural light, surprising for a place so far underground. There weren't windows in the traditional sense, but the walls were indeed lined with glass, behind which were simulated, three-dimensional video projections of vistas from all over the world—a reminder to the students of how things once were. Erin was impressed in spite of herself. Her school back in Beacon had hallways named for their subjects of learning: the math wing, the English wing, the science wing . . . but Spokie Middle's seemed to be known by their views. There was the Amazon Wing, with its "windows" looking out at ground level through the virtual trees of a rain forest from long ago; the Sahara Wing, with a "view" of the sand dunes of northern Africa; the Pacific Wing, re-creating with startling accuracy the sensation of walking below the old ocean's surface; the Arctic Wing; the Beach Wing . . .

Erin walked with her father through what must have been the Moon Wing, rendering its view of Earth from Tranquility Base. The school's main office was just beyond the lunar module.

Behind the front desk, another "window" looked out into an endless expanse of computer-generated stars and planets. A small woman with short black hair sat facing away from the door, staring into their infinity.

"'Scuse us," Mr. Arbitor said, and the woman jumped and spun around. "I'd like to register my daughter for class here. I believe you got my message last week—"

"Mr. Arbitor! Oh yeah, sure, I remember." The woman spoke in an old-fashioned Midwestern accent that made Erin feel farther from home than ever. "Pleasure to meetcha. Nancy Carrol." She extended her tiny hand to shake theirs. "From Beacon, aren't'cha! Oh, sure, that's a long ways."

"It is," Erin agreed.

"And what brings you to Spokie, now?" she asked as she pointed to a Markscan on the desk.

"Business." Mr. Arbitor shrugged, and he and Erin swiped their hands under the scanner.

Ms. Carrol read the back of the Markscan and wrote some things on her tablet computer. "And what is it'cha do?" she asked, but before Mr. Arbitor could respond, the answer popped up on the screen she held in her hands. Ms. Carrol's eyebrows lifted well into her forehead. Erin couldn't tell if the woman was impressed or afraid. "Government work," she said.

Mr. Arbitor smiled politely. "That's right."

And everyone knew that was the end of that conversation.

∃

For lunch, Mr. Arbitor suggested they stop at a Spokie diner for "some local flavor," and while Erin had no desire to know what that was, they were soon looking over the menu in their corner booth.

Beside them, a television frame flashed world news at a low volume, and their table displayed snippets from the local paper, which could be expanded and read by tapping on the glass surface.

Erin was skimming an article on a recent Spokie kidnapping when her father directed her attention up to the frame.

"Seems Lamson and Cylis are close to a treaty," Mr. Arbitor said, and they watched on television as the general in chief of the American Union met with the European chancellor overseas.

Erin nodded. "It'd be good for us, right?"

"Best thing possible," Mr. Arbitor said. "Anything to avoid another war." He swiped his Mark against a scanner on the table and tapped his order into its interface. "Besides, the chancellor's ideas are good. His E.U. policies make sense. Practically every speech Lamson gives, he's singing the guy's praises . . ."

"Everyone is. Mom can't say enough about how great it's been over there recently."

"I'm aware." Mr. Arbitor rolled his eyes. "She certainly visits enough to know."

"She has to, Dad—it's her job."

"And yet I'm the bad guy for bringing us to Spokie."

"Let's not talk about it," Erin said, and she swiped her own Mark to place an order.

"You know, your mom's not the only one 'forging unity' these days." He waved his hand dismissively as he said it.

"Okay, Dad."

"What do you think we're doing out here, anyway, huh? What do you think 'government work' actually means?"

"I don't *know*, Dad. You won't *tell* me."

"You think your mom's algorithms would do any good if there weren't people like me to——"

"Dad, *drop* it."

There was a pause. A waitress came by with Erin's grilled soy cheese sandwich and Mr. Arbitor's tempeh burger.

"*Enforce* it," Mr. Arbitor said quietly.

But Erin didn't respond.

The truth was, Erin's mom *was* gone quite a bit. Ever since she'd had Erin, Dr. Arbitor had worked increasingly from Europe, facilitating the merger of A.U. and E.U. economies as the Americas adopted Cylis's Mark program under the encouragement of General Lamson. Now that a treaty was in the works to merge governments too, Dr. Arbitor was overseas half of each year.

"Will Lamson still be in charge?" Erin asked, watching the news on the wall.

"Of the American branch, sure." Mr. Arbitor was absorbed in his sandwich.

"What about Parliament?"

"They'll still be around. Like how it used to work with state governments in this country." Mr. Arbitor wiped his mouth on his sleeve. "Why, you gonna run for office?"

"What'll they call it?" Erin asked.

"Call what?"

"The new country." On the television, Chancellor Cylis was smiling and waving to the cameras.

"It probably won't happen for a while yet," Mr. Arbitor said. He pushed his plate away and stood up to leave.

"But when it does."

Mr. Arbitor smiled. "The Global Union," he said.

"And then there won't be any more conflict?" Erin thought back to the earliest years of her childhood, of how scary it had been, hearing bombs fall at night and gunshots each day, seeing bodies on the street, learning of family members who weren't coming back. The four billion people dead or AWOL. Gone for good. And that was already after the worst of it, after General Lamson had come along and turned the tide.

Those were distant memories now, brushed under the carpet of ten peaceful years without American borders or divisions. And yes, under Cylis, the situation had improved in Europe, and in Asia and Africa too. But somehow, the idea of a totally unified world, East and West together . . . it seemed too good to be true. Worth fighting for, sure. But possible?

"It's possible," Mr. Arbitor said, swiping his Mark against the table again and punching in a percentage for the tip. "And this right here"—he touched his own wrist and pointed to the Mark on Erin's—"this is the start of all that. This is the symbol. This is what I'm in Spokie to protect."

"Okay," Erin said, not knowing at all what that meant.

They thanked their waitress on the way out.

4

After returning from the new DOME office where Mr. Arbitor had taken her that afternoon, Erin spent the night unpacking, alone in an unfamiliar apartment on the seventeenth floor of a complex at the edge of a town she knew nothing about. It would have had a nice view if the small skyline hadn't looked so lonely to Erin. The lights weren't even enough to wash out the stars, and to her it looked as if no one was home, anywhere. She stared out the window and thought of the starscape in her new school, of the Moon Wing in the administrative hall, of the secretary at the desk.

"Government work," she'd said.

"That's right."

And the look on her face that followed . . .

What was it Erin didn't know about her father's job?

She turned to fill the shelves and closets and tabletops with tablets and clothes and mementos from Beacon, but looking around the apartment now, Erin couldn't help but notice that the place her father had chosen was really only big enough for the two of them and the lizard. So instead Erin said good night to Iggy, turned off the heat lamp above his cage, and placed a family album frame by her bed to watch its slide show. She sat above the covers for a long while, thinking sadly of her mother back home, knowing that she wasn't on her way, knowing that it wasn't just a matter of weeks, and wondering honestly when they'd see each other again.

In that moment, Erin was reminded of quiet summer evenings like this growing up, when, like now, her father would stay late with work.

Except those nights were never so lonely, because always, Dr. Arbitor would be home too, reading to Erin while they waited for Dad in the late hours. She would read Erin anything, not just children's stories, but news articles and editorials and classic literature, insisting that the world was ready for Erin, and that Erin was ready for it, whether or not she still sucked her thumb. This made Erin feel like the luckiest kid in the world.

One summer, years ago, Erin and her mom even plowed through the entire works of Shakespeare, acting out all the parts in their pajamas over the course of the passing weeks. And every night, by the second or third or fourth act of a given play, Mr. Arbitor would return home and take his share of the spotlight— usually making up his own parts and speaking in silly voices and fully derailing the story as he did—much to his wife's chagrin and his daughter's delight.

But those memories were far away now, impossible even, and with a small sigh, Erin rolled out of bed to turn off the picture frame so she could finish moving in without distraction.

It wasn't until halfway through emptying her last box that she finally got a call from Dad.

"I'm gonna be late at work, sweetie," he said.

"It already is late," Erin told him. "I'm practically done unpacking."

"That's great! Maybe you could empty some of my stuff too? Just lay it out for me? Don't stay up too late or anything, but just some clothes and essentials for tomorrow?"

"Sure, Dad," Erin said, seeing no advantages to a refusal. She lifted the top few boxes off his pile without complaining, but soon found herself running a hand over one that caught her eye. "Hey, Dad?" she asked, just before ending the call.

"Yeah?"

Erin chewed her bottom lip. "When are we gonna be a family again?"

In her tablet, Erin could see her dad smile sadly. "That's up to your mom, Erin."

"Then we're not going back, are we?"

Mr. Arbitor sighed. "Someone's making a mess in Spokie,

Erin. And the Department of Marked Emergencies thinks I'm the best man to clean it up. If I can do that quickly, we'll go home. If not . . . well, listen . . . I really think you're gonna like it here."

"What's the mess?" Erin asked. "Just tell me already. Give me something to believe in."

Mr. Arbitor pointed to his Mark over the connection and winked.

"You're not going to tell me, are you?" Erin said. She was tired of her father's deflections, and for the first time, she had a reason to care.

"Government work," Mr. Arbitor said. And he ended the call.

Erin stared at the box under her hands. "DOME," it read across the top. "CONFIDENTIAL." Erin knew it was not hers to open. She knew it was strictly her father's, his documents from the Department, which at any other time would be locked away in so remote a corner that Erin wouldn't even think to look. And yet, in the haste and chaos of the move, here they were, right in front of her, separated from Erin by only a thin layer of cardboard and some tape.

Under ordinary circumstances, Erin wouldn't have dreamed of opening the box. Under ordinary circumstances, she couldn't have imagined anything inside being of any interest. But Erin was angry, and lonely, and far from home. She wanted, she *deserved*, to know why. So Erin peeled the tape from the lid.

It took her several minutes to remove the strip without tearing the cardboard underneath. She knew there could not be a trace of what she had done.

Her heart pounded. In all his years with the Department, Mr. Arbitor hadn't once brought home a story, hadn't once shared a single interesting thing he'd done that day. What could anything inside this box possibly reveal? She hadn't a clue.

And in fact, even if she had, it would not have prepared her for what she found.

THREE

FIRST DAY, NEW FACE

1

THE FIRST DAY OF SCHOOL AT SPOKIE MIDDLE was always pandemonium. Logan stood in the Freshwater Wing and noticed how the white-water rapids in the windows bore such close resemblance to the students crashing down the hall.

"I forgot how to read!" someone boasted as he walked by with a circle of friends.

"I can't hold a stylus anymore!" shouted another, waving one around as if he'd never seen anything like it.

The laughter and yelling of reunions in every direction were rough and unforgiving; Logan twisted and spun as the student body flowed violently past.

Everywhere, people compared tans, new clothes, dropped voices, Marks . . . each worn like a badge of honor. Logan decided to skip the parade and head straight for class.

"Hey, Logan, where you runnin' off to?" said a voice somewhere behind him. It was Dane Harold, Logan's best friend and life preserver in the turbulent social waters of Spokie Middle Development.

"Dane!" Logan said. "How ya been?!"

It had been weeks since the two had seen each other, since Dane had spent most of the summer with relatives in downtown New Chicago.

"I'm good, man, I'm good. Not looking forward to computer science, though. I hear we're getting into compiler construction this year. I barely even remember how to quicksort."

"First period?" Logan asked.

"Yeah, right now."

"Me too, man. That's awesome!" So the two of them made their way to the Old City Wing.

"Hey, it's Tom," Dane said, pointing the class president out across the hall. "Tom! You look awful! Didn't anyone tell you we were just on summer break?" It was only friendly teasing, but Logan couldn't help noticing Dane was right. Tom looked like he hadn't slept in days.

"I'm Pledging tomorrow," Tom said. "Been prepping all weekend."

"Right on, man! Good luck!" Dane said. And he and Logan pushed onward down the hall. "I turn at the beginning of next month," Dane told Logan. "Then I can finally start getting paid for my gigs. Stop relying on my stupid parents. First thing I'm gonna buy are some new wailing mitts."

Dane was a cyberpunk rocker by night, lead singer and mitt wailer of his band, the Boxing Gloves. Even now he wore reminders of this alter ego—pants with a few wires coming out of them and a shirt that changed color with the temperature but always remained some shade of black. The look was out of style, a holdover from the late pre-Unity period and flashier than the modest, practical (*boring*) clothes worn these days, but Dane liked how it made him look different from the other students at Spokie Middle. His own quiet rebellion.

"November for me," Logan said. "Can't say I'm very much looking forward to it, though."

"Why not?" Dane asked, kicking another kid's leg.

"Hey, watch it!" The kid swung around, but his expression immediately brightened when he saw it was Dane. "Dane! How ya been? Find me at lunch, okay?" Logan didn't know the guy, but it never ceased to amaze him how much everyone liked Dane.

"You got it," Dane said. Then he turned back to Logan and continued their conversation as if uninterrupted. "Why wouldn't you want the Mark?"

"Well . . . you know . . . my sister," Logan said, and Dane stopped dead in his tracks.

"I forgot," he said sincerely. "I'm sorry." It was moments like this that made him such a good friend.

Dane elected to stay in the hall another few minutes, joking around and teasing girls he thought were cute, but Logan was eager to get to class. Even in school he worried about being followed, and in the hallways it was always too crowded to tell for sure who was watching. Logan hated crowds.

Being the first one in, he had his pick of seats, so as usual, Logan chose a back row desk in the corner. He liked to be able to see the whole room in front of him, with his back to the wall. More comfortable that way. Safer.

The rest of his classmates arrived in a trickle at first, like a leak from the flood of students outside, but by the time the bell rang, the room was buzzing with the same crowded energy as the halls, and Logan thought of this as a cruel trick of osmosis. He was glad to have no one behind him.

"Hello, world," Mr. Arty said, just as Mr. Arty had every morning for twenty years.

"Hello, Mr. Arty," the students said in a lackadaisical attempt at unison.

It was only their first day of school, but all of the kids in Spokie Middle already knew Mr. Arty well, as he'd taught each of them since the first grade. Mr. Arty was famous in Spokie, known well by parents and students as the best computer programming teacher around, and that was in large part because Mr. Arty was a computer program himself.

Not one to waste time with small talk or tangents, Mr. Arty launched straight into the day's lesson, appearing in holographic form on everyone's tablet computers simultaneously, each instance of him discussing with passion the intricacies of how one might go about passing the Turing Test.

2

The rest of the morning was a blur. History this year would focus on the period leading up to the States War and the founding of DOME following the success of the Mark Program in Europe. Mrs. Henry began with a speech trying to personalize the subject for her students by asking any who'd gotten the Mark over the summer to raise their hands and share a little bit about their experience.

"I got a job at the supermarket," one boy said. "It's nice to be eligible for work."

"I'm looking forward to voting," a girl admitted, and the teacher nodded.

"That's right," she said. "Parliamentary elections this spring. Certainly couldn't have come at a more fascinating time in politics. Has anyone here been following the story between General Lamson and Cylis? Would anyone like to share their thoughts about that?"

Logan raised his hand not once throughout the discussion. Somehow, he couldn't imagine Mrs. Henry much wanted to hear about his family's experiences with the Mark Program; something about his sister's story didn't quite seem to fit with the day's lesson plan.

In math, they learned about imaginary numbers. In art, they drew holograms. In English, they analyzed the themes and common symbolism of modern post-Unity literature.

At lunch, they discussed the new girl.

It wasn't often that Spokie got a transfer student from another town—there might have been one new student a year, *maybe*— and whoever it was invariably became the topic of all September and early October gossip.

"You met her yet?" Dane asked, taking a bite out of his sandwich before he interrupted himself with a look of mild disgust.

"What's the matter?" Logan asked.

"*Quorn*." He held it out. "I'll trade you."

Logan scrunched his nose and shook his head. He knew full well that meat was hard to come by since the A.U.'s rapid environmental decline, and that vegetarian alternatives had become increasingly popular in its place, but that didn't make Logan a sucker. "I'll stick with my peanut butter, thanks."

The two of them sat on the sports lawn with the rest of the eighth graders, who made small clumps around the field and picnicked with their lunch bags, despite the sweltering midday heat.

"Whatever," Dane said, throwing his sandwich back in its bag.

"I hear she's from Beacon." Logan shrugged, talking again about the new girl. He always seemed to have interesting gossip; being paranoid had its advantages.

"Oh yeah? I bet she hates Spokie."

"Apparently her dad's a government guy."

"Anything interesting?"

Logan frowned. "Standard. Government work. Who knows? Her mom's a big-shot financial something-or-other, though, on Barrier Street."

Dane frowned. "Well-bred."

"Looks like it," Logan agreed.

"Hey, guys . . . happy, uh, lunch break," Hailey said, creeping up behind them out of nowhere.

"*Man*, Hailey, do you have to do that, always? Act so weird all the time?" Dane turned around, pretending to be annoyed. Hailey laughed but didn't look up from the ground.

"Hi, Hailey," Logan said, and Hailey waved. She still didn't look up. "You have a good summer?"

"Yes, you?" Hailey kicked idly at a clump of plasti-grass.

"Fine. Hey, we should have hung out more."

Hailey paused. "What'd you do, Dane?" She eyed his outfit. "Find any time to wash those clothes?"

Dane sneered at her. "Mostly rehearsed with the Boxing Gloves, actually, when I wasn't in New Chicago."

Hailey shrugged.

"You know, *my band*?" Dane said. "We're playing a concert at the end of the month. *Man*, you're weird. Why are you so weird, Hailey?" Hailey shrugged again. Dane kept talking. "Rode around on my new rollerstick some too. Oh, hey, Logan, did I tell you I got a rollerstick?"

"No. Don't you need a Mark for that?"

"Well . . . fine, it's my dad's, technically. But it'll be mine soon enough! Just four weeks 'til—"

"Your Pledge. We know." Logan rolled his eyes, and Dane made as if he were going to hit him, playfully.

"Guess that's the other thing I did this summer," Dane said. "Studied. Quick, ask me anything! Ask me about the Inclusion!"

"Let's not talk about it," Logan said.

"Mm-hm." Hailey nodded. No one had anything more to say. "Well, I'll see you, then." Was it possible Logan saw her wink at him before she walked away? But that was too weird to be true.

As late as fifth grade, Dane, Logan, and Hailey Phoenix had been inseparable. They spent weekends together, they studied together, they played sports together . . . Two years in a row they'd been champions in the Spokie Elementary hover-dodge league, and Logan had been pretty sure it was mainly due to the fact that the three of them had such good communication. A wave of the hand or a nod of the head was all he ever needed from either of them to know exactly what they were going to do next. At night, the three of them would often message one another on their tablets at exactly the same time. On holidays, they'd send identical electronic greeting cards. It was just that kind of friendship.

They'd spent summers together too, at that hippy-dippy sleep-away camp, Underbrush Woods, up north. This was before Lily died, before Logan became afraid he was being followed. Back when he never worried about anything.

They had all liked it there, because the rules were loose, and the three of them could spend their days halfway into the small, thin patches of what remained of A.U.'s northern forest, looking up at the leaves and clouds and talking about how they'd be friends long after each of them was Marked and married and raising grandchildren . . .

Then between fifth and sixth grade, biology played a mean trick. Gradually, Dane realized, much to his alarm, that he might someday like to be more than just friends with Hailey. And that *would* have been fine—a manageable emotion, at least—except for the twist that came one week later, when Hailey approached Dane to admit that *she'd* fallen for *Logan*, and wasn't it funny, and what she really needed to know now was what Dane thought she should do about it.

Logan never did hear about the epic argument that erupted between Dane and Hailey that day. Neither of them told him about the feelings and jealousy Dane admitted to, or of the embarrassment Hailey felt, and Logan never did understand why the relationship between his two closest friends went so suddenly cold in the final weeks of that summer. He assumed it was just natural when Hailey quietly faded from the two boys' lives the following school year; that it was just the course of things when she started spending more and more time with other girls, or when she fell in with those elusive "cooler kids" last year at whom Hailey hinted every once in a while, when the three of them made awkward conversation at lunch or on the way home from school.

And Dane, for his part, buried his feelings as best as he could, protecting himself and saving his friendship with Logan in the process.

"She is so weird," Dane said to Logan now, though Logan

couldn't help but notice him staring at Hailey 'til she was out of sight.

"Cool about the rollerstick, anyway. I've always been terrified of those things." Logan shrugged.

Dane nodded, accepting the change of subject. "Hey, is 'at her?" he asked, and Logan squinted across the field.

It was the first time he saw her, Erin Arbitor. She was sitting on the plasti-grass, eating corn bread, alone.

And Logan said, "I don't know," though he was somehow sure that it was.

"What's she doing? Looks like she's talking to herself," Dane said.

But Logan didn't notice that. Instead he noticed her hair, straight and copper all the way down to the small of her back. He noticed her eyes, shining cobalt blue in the sunlight. He noticed her clothes, which couldn't possibly have come from Spokie. Kids from Spokie wore local fabrics, mostly drab shades of cotton, wool . . . but hers were loud, bright, and synthetic. She was foreign, somehow. Different. Better. She was beautiful.

"Talk to her," Dane said, seeing the look on Logan's face. "I dare you."

"I don't know," Logan said, but Dane laughed and gave him a good, hard push in the right direction, and somehow Logan's feet just kept right on walking after that.

⌐

Halfway across the lawn, Erin sat, totally inside her own head, playing through what she'd discovered the night before.

My dad. My dad is a . . .

She felt the words form on her lips but didn't speak them aloud. This was her secret. Not even hers, in fact, but her father's and her father's alone . . . if it was anyone's at all.

The box had been filled with papers, a whole stack of them, the most she'd ever seen at once. Nothing was ever written on paper anymore, since everyone had switched to tablets, and yet here was a boxful of it, yellowed, handwritten, one of a kind, confidential. In an age of infinite digital documentation, paper was the last safe place for secrets. Not to be copied and pasted with the stroke of a stylus, not to be sent around the world at the press of a button, not to be recorded and stored forever in a million irretrievable pieces across cyberspace and time, paper was intimate . . . fragile. Her father wrote of things she never knew existed, of the Eyes & Ears Bureau where Mr. Arbitor worked within the Department of Marked Emergencies, of missions he'd been on, surveillance he'd taken, people he'd locked away . . .

My dad is a spy. Erin now found herself reassessing every perception she'd had of her father. His career move from the Beacon police department finally made sense. The stress he was under, his humbled nature, the seriousness with which he took his work . . . even his effort to blend in, physically, over the past few years . . . all of it fit, once Erin had the context.

And then there was the paper at the top of the box, the most pressing memo of all—Agent Arbitor's current assignment. The one that brought him halfway across the country, the one that uprooted Erin's life and tore her family apart: *Peck and the Markless threat in Spokie.*

A real-life mystery. A whole slew of unsolved crimes. Ongoing. Dangerous. And her father was the detective.

She had just begun to wrap her head around it when out of the corner of her eye she saw a short, skinny, jumpy boy with dirty-blond hair approach and heard him say in a quiet voice, "Hi. I'm Logan. You're Erin, right?"

But in that moment the class bell rang across the field, and Erin did not answer, and Logan went red and hurried away.

4

"No luck, huh?" Dane ribbed Logan as they walked the halls to their next class. "Maybe she was just overwhelmed by your confidence and your masculine good looks."

"Shut up," Logan said, but he was laughing. "I didn't exactly see you walk away with her number either."

"I was just playing hard to get," Dane said. "Chicks dig that. *Don't they, Hailey?*" he yelled, and Hailey looked confused and caught off guard across the hall. "See what I mean?"

Science & tech lab would have been beyond boring if Dane and Logan hadn't been joined by class president Tom Dratch, who fed off Dane's sarcasm and turned the two of them into an unstoppable comedy duo intent on getting Logan detention for laughing.

It turned out Hailey was in the class too, as was her friend Veronica, and from across the room they quickly became the source of Dane and Tom's comedic material for the day.

Having grown up just a bit bigger and stronger than the other girls at Spokie, it seemed that every semester Veronica tried a new sport only to become the best at it. So far she'd been Spokie Middle's MVP in soccer, field hockey, tennis, lacrosse, and softball.

She was taller than any of the boys in their grade, had coarse black hair and wide shoulders, and always dressed in a sports uniform. Before class started, Dane and Tom asked her if she planned to join the boys' football team this year. Tom said they needed a new quarterback. The boys all laughed, but Logan got the impression that Veronica was genuinely interested.

Logan didn't know Tom too well outside of Tom's friendship with Dane, but Logan did know he could count on Tom to begin bugging him about the school play, and Tom sure didn't disappoint. This year, it was *Mark of a Salesman*. As class president, Tom saw it as his job to stir up interest in all the school's extracurricular programs, and years ago he'd pegged drama as Logan's one true calling. (It wasn't.)

"I just think it would get you out of your shell," Tom said, having no idea how condescending that sounded. "Besides, it's a classic. You'd make a great . . . what's his name? You know, the brother character."

And Logan said, "We'll see," even though he knew he wouldn't, just before Ms. Dirkin began boring the class with the practical details of New Chicago's nuclear fusion plant.

Logan's last classes of the day were gym, government, and economics, and in each, he swam in a sea of anonymity. In fact, the only familiar face whatsoever was Veronica's in gym, and all that meant was that Logan would never win a game.

Yet the moment Logan entered economics, he had the feeling it was soon to become his favorite period of the day.

Why? Because there, right there, two rows from the front

and three desks in, sat the new girl, Erin, right beside an empty seat. Maybe it was time for Logan to change his back-row-only policy.

5

It was five minutes from the end of the day, and Erin Arbitor had yet to learn a single thing. Computer science had been a joke—judging by the syllabus, she could have taken the final exam that morning and aced it. English looked like it'd be the year of rereading, since her school in Beacon covered modern post-Unity lit in the sixth grade. Government she was already an expert on through her father, and economics she knew inside and out just by listening to her mother chat about work. None of this bothered Erin, though, since to her, all it meant was more time to contemplate her father's secret case, *Peck and the Markless threat in Spokie*, which she was increasingly determined to crack.

Erin was so distracted by last night's revelation, in fact, that she didn't even hear the final bell ring. It took that nervous kid bothering her again—again!—just to snap her out of it.

"You're new here, right?" He'd certainly wasted no time in approaching her.

"Sorry?" Erin said.

Logan cleared his throat. "Hi again. I'm Logan. I heard you're from Beacon."

"Yeah," Erin answered flatly. Her mind still hadn't left her father's box of papers.

"I've always wanted to visit Beacon. My dad's constantly talking about it," Logan said.

"Oh yeah?" Erin gathered her things and began making her way toward the door.

"He's an architect, so I guess he's interested in it from a civil engineering perspective."

Erin could not have cared less about civil engineering, but she managed to say, "That's neat," before exiting the classroom and escaping down the hall.

Logan followed her through the Pacific Wing, where a pod of computer-generated dolphins swam by. "Hey, I bet he'd love to pick your brain about it sometime," he said, trailing behind Erin, who simply could not understand why this kid wouldn't leave her alone.

"Maybe," she said.

"Where do you live? I'm over on Wright."

"I don't know where that is," Erin said. She tried walking a little faster.

"Just a few blocks from here."

"Well, I'm on Vital Lane. It's a pretty far walk." Erin was glad to have an excuse to get rid of the boy, who so obviously liked her and whose enthusiasm bordered on pathetic.

"I'm right on the way!" Logan said. "I'll walk with you!"

Erin rolled her eyes, but Logan couldn't see.

So this is life in Spokie, America, she thought. *Boring classes, long walks home, and desperate boys.*

Erin couldn't get back to Beacon quickly enough.

6

"Space is at a premium here, since we're so close to New Chicago, and we need to save space for farming 'cause so much of the land farther out's gone bad." Logan shrugged, trying to fill the empty air on his walk home with Erin. "I guess in Beacon they just have hydroponic farming, but we don't have that out here yet. So to leave room for everyone after the Unity, Spokie said any private lot couldn't take more than four hundred square feet of ground space." Logan pointed to the examples as they walked past along the sidewalk.

"'Course, you can buy more than one lot, but for most people that's too expensive, and the zoning's usually restrictive. That's why a lot of public buildings, like our school, are underground. And that's why all the homes here are so skinny . . ." Erin didn't care. But it was easiest just to let the boy speak until they made it to his house. ". . . and why most people just build up and up. Mine's eleven stories, but it's just one room to a floor, so it isn't actually that big. Some houses have twenty or more."

Logan went on to talk about the days when almost everyone in the Corn Belt lived in houses that were wider than they were tall. And you could still see examples of them, he said, in the few that remained among the buildings in Old District farther across town. But only the very wealthiest citizens could afford a home like that, since there were so few left, and since no more were being built.

"But you live in an apartment, right?" Logan asked. "All the buildings on Vital Lane are apartments, I think."

"Yeah," Erin said. "It's an apartment."

"That's cool. You have more space to spread out that way," Logan said, "since it's not a private lot. I bet your floor's pretty wide."

Erin stopped him. "Well, here you are." Wright Street was just up ahead. "It was nice meeting you . . ."

"Logan," Logan said.

"Right. Thanks for taking—"

"Oh, I don't mind. I'll keep walking with you."

And Erin couldn't help but laugh.

"I see you got the Mark already," Logan said, clueless and trying to keep up with her accelerating strides. "Must've been recent—it looks dusty, still."

Erin glanced down at her wrist without stopping. "I guess so," she said. In fact, Logan was right. She'd Pledged for the Mark just last month, and fine nanodust—enough to notice even without a black light—did trail off it as she swung her arm, though she hadn't noticed until Logan pointed it out.

"It's nanotech ink, you know," Logan said. "Not sure why they can't just use normal ink, but I guess they don't."

"I wouldn't know," Erin said. "Those details don't make their way onto the test."

Logan was quiet for a moment. "I'm kinda nervous about the whole thing, to be honest," he said.

Erin frowned. "That's stupid. There's nothing to be nervous about."

"Mm-hm," Logan said. "Everyone keeps saying that. No one likes to talk about the kids that don't make it through."

This got Erin's attention. She stopped short and looked Logan in the face. "That's a myth. And it's absurd. There's no such thing as flunkees."

Logan frowned. "It's not a myth."

"Come on. Flunkees? There've been, like, two."

"More than that," Logan said. "It just never makes the news. No one talks about it."

Erin sighed. "You sound paranoid."

"I know," Logan said.

She looked at him, trying to gauge whether or not he was joking. It alarmed her to conclude he was not. "Look, seriously, you're more likely to die crossing the street. Like, right now." And Erin reiterated the point: "You're more likely to die *right now* than you are getting the Mark. You're more likely to die from food poisoning. Or cancer. Or, I don't know, lightning."

"I know," Logan said.

"So if you're gonna bother being nervous about the Pledge, you might as well just be nervous about every little thing you do in life."

"I am." Logan shrugged.

The indifference in his tone was suddenly infuriating. "You're not gonna die from getting the Mark!" Erin said forcefully. "Everyone got it when the program started. Millions of people in the A.U. Millions more in the E.U. They're all *fine*. And the kids who turn eligible each year are fine too. We've all heard the rumors about flunkees, but honestly, that's just ridiculous." She wasn't sure exactly what frustrated her so much about the turn in their conversation, but Erin found herself feeling increasingly defensive.

"Sorry. I know your dad works for DOME," Logan said.

And, in fact, that was it. That was what irked Erin so much about what Logan was saying. "Yeah, so what?" she said, admitting nothing. The last thing she wanted was to get into a conversation about her father. His secret was so fresh in her mind, she didn't trust herself not to slip up and reveal something about it, even to this stranger.

"Well, I'm not questioning it or anything. I mean, DOME's great and all. I'm just . . . I don't know. I just don't think it's unreasonable to be a little nervous about it."

Erin didn't blink. "It is unreasonable. No one actually dies from the Pledge, okay?"

Logan looked away. He shrugged and was quiet for a moment. "My sister did."

┐

The morning of Lily's thirteenth birthday, it was Logan's job to corral the guests and family. Being eight at the time, and the youngest of his relatives by several years, he'd been sent to bed long before the previous night's festivities had died down, and while Logan had managed to spend half the evening sitting with his ear to the floor, listening to the laughter and music and chatter leaking from every level of the house, by the time the sun rose, he was still easily the best rested and first one up. So Logan went floor by floor that morning, banging on doors, switching on lights, throwing open curtains, and jumping on beds until every last guest was wide-eyed and vertical.

"Get up, get up! It's Lily's birthday!" Logan said to his aunt Susan and uncle David. "It's Lily's birthday! She's thirteen!" he said to Grandma. "Today's the biggest day of her life!" he said to his cousins, Selma and Jake, without quite knowing how right he was.

So the family gathered around the kitchen table, groggy but excited for the day, and Lily's best friend Daniel even stopped by on his way to school. Mom was making pancakes and French toast, and everyone who wanted it was welcome to leftover cake.

Aunt Susan and Uncle David were the owners of a bakery over in New Chicago, and every year for Logan's and Lily's birthdays they would bake a particular treat. Usually they'd bake black forest cake, or cheesecake, or chocolate mousse cake, or angel food cake, but this year's was special. This year's, double layered and the size of four or five dinner plates, had been crafted precisely to look like an enormous . . . well . . . *hand*, palm up, with an elaborate, speckled pattern tattooed in frosting on its wrist. This had been the source of much merriment the night before, of course, for as unappetizing as the cake looked to Logan, not even he could deny the craftsmanship involved in designing a cake that looked so much like the hand of a Marked. Desserts like this were not unheard-of at a thirteenth birthday celebration, but they were something of a novelty otherwise, and since Lily was the first in Logan's family to turn in some time, its design was new to him—and revolting. So, as excited as he had been for his sister's big day, when his aunt gave him, as a treat, the entire pinkie the night before, Logan couldn't bring himself to eat a single bite.

This morning, Logan helped himself to a pancake and sat at the table, quietly enjoying his family's excitement. He dangled his feet off the chair as he carefully drowned each bite in a plate-sized lake of taste-enhanced nanosyrup, and he waited for Lily to join them.

"So, she have any plans for a job?" Aunt Susan was asking, between bites of cake thumb.

"Not yet," Dad said. "But she's looking. We don't want to rush her at all."

"I'm just glad she can run errands for us now," Mom joked, and everyone laughed.

"Yeah, I'm sure that's just what she wants to think about on her big day!" Uncle David said. "Chores! Real nice!"

Out of the laughter, Grandma spoke quietly, but her voice cut through the room and commanded attention. "Shame on you," she said. "All of you. How easily you've forgotten about life before the Unity. Before Lamson, and Cylis over in that awful E.U. It's not a joke!"

"We know, Grandma," cousin Jake butted in. "Paper money, citizenship from birth——"

"Walks to school in the snow——"

"Uphill!"

"Both ways!"

The family all chimed in, talking over one another and laughing. Grandma's reminder of the old ways was one they'd heard a hundred times. Even Logan knew it by heart.

"You laugh now," Grandma said. "If I could cut this Mark out right here, I would." She fingered a charm on her necklace as she spoke. Logan had seen it before, but he didn't know what it meant.

"That's enough." Mrs. Langly shook her head. "This is hardly an appropriate conversation to be having the morning of——"

"It's the *perfect* conversation to be having the morning of Lily's Pledge! While there's still time to walk away!"

"Mama, stop it! Today's about Unity, country, quality of life! The States War——we were falling apart!" Logan had never seen his mother so worked up, especially not at his grandma. "Who knows what would have happened without Lamson? Do you think we'd even be here? This town was *burning* when he turned the tide. Your home was *burning*."

"Oh please." Logan's grandmother clawed at her Mark until the skin around it was red and chafed. "You all think——"

"So why'd you get it, then?" Aunt Susan interrupted. "Why not just turn it down and live with the rest of the bums on Slog Row? Huh? Think we would have missed you too much?"

"Well, if I'd have known then what it was starting——"

"Mama, I cannot believe that you really t'
the best time——"

But then Lily entered the kitchen. "Let her finish,
"Grandma's right. It's important."

"I'm finished, sweetheart," Grandma said, and then she was
silent, and she stared again at her own Mark, remembering.

"It's all good review for the test, anyway, right?" Lily said,
lightening the mood. And everyone laughed nervously, and looked
at their own Marks, and ate.

And it was true what his mom had said, that in the years before
Logan's birth, before General Lamson came along, his family and
all the families in Spokie had suffered, had feared for their lives.
There wasn't a year in school Logan wasn't reminded of this, of
the war his generation was born into but just barely remembered,
when states still divided the continent and fought horribly among
themselves over things as simple as economics and religion and
basic human rights. Logan couldn't remember which state his
would have been. Wisconsin, maybe? Minnesota? They'd all been
called such strange things. Even the American Union had a weird
name——the United States——as if separate states could ever be
united.

But was it also true what his grandmother had said? Had always
said? About life being better before the Unity? It was hard to imagine. In school the lessons stopped short of any real exploration of
the topic. They simply didn't teach the time before the war, except
to say that everything about it had led to the fighting, to the chaos,
and was worth forgetting and never repeating. On the Internet,
Pedia articles that might have explained the era were perpetually
"Under Construction" or "Down for Maintenance," even when
the rest of the Web worked fine. And whenever Logan got up the

nerve to ask a parent or teacher about it outright, whenever he wondered—innocently, curiously—what possible advantages the old government might have had, or what details separated the myriad religions prior to the Inclusion, he would be told only, "Not to worry, not to worry," that it was best this way, no doubt about it.

"But can't you just give me a straight answer?" Logan would ask.

And the adults would grow nervous and say quietly, "You just never know, Logan. You just never know which walls have ears."

So in this way, over time, Logan was made to forget his lingering questions of long ago, and Grandma was the only person he'd ever known to say a single negative thing about it. At this point, of course, he and everyone else chalked up most of what she said to senility—"She's lost her marbles," Mom would tell Logan—but something about it was hard to ignore, even so.

"You don't wanna be late," Dad said to Lily, finally, once the mood was back to bright and the chatter around the table returned to its frenzied clip. "This is, indeed, the biggest day you'll have for some time. We gotta get you to the Center."

Lily's birthday was on a Tuesday that year, a school day ordinarily, but by law, students were exempt from school on their thirteenth birthday, so as to facilitate the Pledge. It wasn't compulsory, getting the Mark, but the idea of spending your thirteenth birthday doing anything else was unheard-of. In the ten years since it had been implemented, the Mark had quickly become the capstone of a childhood well spent, the crowning achievement in a young man's or woman's life, the opened door to adulthood and independence. Logan couldn't wait to see how it looked on Lily's wrist when she got back.

"Wish me luck," Lily said as she walked out the door.

"Good luck," Daniel said.

"Good luck," Grandma said.

"You don't need it," Dad said.

That was the last anyone ever saw of Logan's big sister, Lily.

日

Logan found himself telling this to Erin—all of it, all at once—
without thinking, during the rest of their walk home. He didn't
know why. Maybe it was because he finally had her attention, and
he didn't want her to look away. Maybe it was just on his mind
recently, and easier to talk about with a stranger. Or maybe,
deep down, Logan really did have a bone to pick with Erin and
her DOME bureaucrat father. Either way, he kept going, telling
everything he remembered, telling all the details, layers and layers
of them, beyond any he'd ever heard himself give before, even to
his closest friends. And his words surprised him.

By the time he was done, they'd made it all the way to Erin's
apartment building, and it was there that Erin surprised herself
too. She invited Logan in.

"So you've been paranoid ever since?" she asked.

"I don't think I'm paranoid," Logan said. "My mom does, as if
she's one to talk. And my dad, but he puts it in different terms."

"What's wrong with your mom?" Erin asked.

"I'm not sure. I think the day my sister didn't come back from
the Pledge, Mom just . . . checked out. Everything inside her just

left. Like poking a hole in an egg and sucking out the yolk . . .
Mom's all shell now."

The furniture in Erin's apartment was mostly still wrapped in
shipping tape, and the floors were littered with boxes, so Logan
made his way toward the kitchen table and sat in a folding chair
beside it.

"My dad won't be home 'til late. Last night he didn't make it
back until morning, I think. So we're on our own."

"Okay," Logan said, his voice cracking a little.

But he nearly fell to the floor when something darted up
the curtains beside him. To Logan it looked like a dragon, hanging by its claws, four feet long, scaly and wild. "Erin!" he yelled
helplessly.

"Oh." She laughed. "Except for my iguana."

"You have a pet iguana?" Logan looked at it stupidly. "Shouldn't
that be illegal or something?"

"It is," Erin said. "Funny thing about having a law enforcer for
a dad, though . . ."

Logan inched his chair away from the window. "What's its
name?"

"Iggy."

Logan stared at it. The lizard basked in the light of the window, tilting its head to peer at the two of them thoughtfully. "You
named your iguana 'Iggy'?"

Erin reached up and grabbed the animal, draping it gently
around her neck. It paced from shoulder to shoulder. "I guess."

"You gonna name your kids 'Kiddies'?"

"First of all," Erin said, walking to the cupboard, "I'm never
having kids. And second of all, it's an iguana. What's he gonna do
with a proper name? You think he's struggling with self-identity?"

She picked out an apple and began rubbing it on her shirt, right where the lizard's tail had been. "Snack?"

"I've heard those pets carry disease . . . ," Logan said tentatively.

"Yeah." Erin nodded. "Salmonella." She held the apple out to him and smiled.

"No, thanks," he said.

"So, your sister . . ." Erin sat next to Logan and pulled the iguana down to her lap, petting it in a way it didn't particularly seem to mind. She ate the apple as she spoke. "What happened when she didn't come back?"

Logan sighed, keeping an eye on the lizard but mostly looking down, one distant part of him ecstatic to have made friends with the new girl so quickly, but the other devastated to have done so in this way. He couldn't imagine his sister's story being the basis of any positive relationship. "You mean that night?" he finally said. Erin shrugged. "I was shielded from a lot of it. But of what I can remember, some DOME officer came to our house. Said something like, 'We regret to inform you your daughter won't be returning from her Pledge,' which my parents didn't understand. So he told them sometimes the Pledge process didn't agree with the Markee, that it was rare, but that on occasion, it happened. 'Procedural risk,' I guess he called it. And my parents asked, 'Dead? Is she dead?' And they started to cry, and the officer said we'd be compensated for our loss."

"Compensated?"

"Mom doesn't have to work anymore, if she doesn't want to. And her medical bills are covered by DOME. Prescriptions and such. Though the deal terminates on my thirteenth birthday, in November, if I don't Pledge. DOME's little form of persuasion, I guess."

"What about your dad?"

"Same offer, but he refused it."

"How come I've never heard of anything like this?"

Logan frowned. "It's probably not in DOME's interest to talk about it, even among themselves." He shrugged. "Anyway, things have been sort of rough for me ever since. I've spent a lot of time . . . scared."

"Of the Mark?"

"No. Of being watched. Soon after Lily didn't come back, I guess I started feeling . . . haunted. I'd hear footsteps in her room at night. I'd see faces in my window. Or thought I did. Things in my room seemed to move on their own while I was away. There were a few years where it had gotten better, even went away. But recently . . . it's come back big-time. These last few months, every-where I go, I feel like I'm being followed, or . . ." Logan stopped himself. "I know it sounds crazy."

Erin leaned down to put her iguana on the floor, and it dashed out of sight. "You don't actually think you're haunted, do you?" she asked.

Logan laughed. "Not by Lily. Not by ghosts," he said. "That'd be less scary, I think." He shook his head. "No. Someone really has his eye on me."

"Do you have proof?" Erin said.

"None. Nothing I can point to, anyway. That's why it all sounds so ridiculous. But I'm not crazy, Erin. I swear to you." He stared at her for a moment, and she stared back, curious, evaluat-ing, piecing him together like a puzzle. Inside her head, something uncanny rang out, some distant alarm about . . . *Peck?* . . . *the Markless threat in Spokie?* But none of that surfaced just yet. Instead it weighed on Erin, a pressure just under her skull, waiting to get out. It hummed like a teakettle in the silence of the room.

"Hey, you know . . . I should probably get going," Logan said. He looked at the time on his tablet and noticed his father's three missed calls. "It's getting dark. My parents are probably worried." He tried to look nonchalant about it when he tapped the tablet to call his dad back, but Erin noticed he made it a private call.

"Yes. Yes, I'm *so* sorry, Dad. Walked a friend home from school and just lost track of time—I'm on my way, I promise." Logan ended the call.

"I'll see you around," Erin said with a small wave.

"Tomorrow." Logan nodded.

Erin was slow about closing the door behind him.

ᑫ

As he exited the building, Logan tried to take in the possibilities of his new friendship. He knew he liked Erin—a lot. And here he was, leaving her apartment, to which he'd *actually* been invited. But his excitement quickly went dull against the grinding prospect of a long and terrifying walk home in the dark.

Logan didn't like evenings even when he was safe in his own home. A stroll by himself through dimly lit sidewalks on empty streets was enough to make his heart race.

You're stupid, Logan told himself. *There's no danger in this. It's just a stupid walk home.*

But he didn't believe it.

No one is after you. No one is watching you. It's just you and your stupid secret flashlight and the mile between here and your front door. No problem at all.

He refused to call home. He refused to call Erin. He would be fine.

But a trash can rang out in a nearby alley.

It's a cat, Logan thought. *Or a raccoon. Nothing with its eye on you.* But Logan picked up the pace even so.

He wasn't far now from Wright Street. Just another couple blocks, and he crossed each with increasing speed. Along the way he gazed up periodically into the yellow-lit windows of the houses along the street, looking at each for the warmth inside. This one belonged to the Coles, that one to the Conways. He ran through the list of names in his head, bringing each to the tip of his tongue, ready to shout them out at the slightest sign of trouble.

Carl, help! he thought. *Rachel, I'm being attacked! Yes, good, that would work. That would bring them out here.*

If he'd had the Mark, Logan would have hopped on an electro-bus. He would have at least stopped in a deli or a convenience store on the way home, just for the respite of a lit room with a cashier to watch over him for a minute. But he didn't have the Mark. And he had to get back.

Footsteps. I hear footsteps behind me! Logan spun around and took in the scene. Long shadows under a crimson, three-quarters moon; tall, thin buildings lining the streets; wind blowing trash and stray leaves from a nearby park. No one visible. But there were plenty of places to hide.

"Hello?" Logan called. No answer. Desperate, he took the flashlight from his backpack and swung it around in long, frantic arcs. Nothing. The shadows danced in its beam.

"I can see you!" Logan bluffed, speaking to no one, knowing no answer would come, sure that this was just another one of his own delusions, but indulging it even so.

For a split second he even contemplated walking *toward* the sounds in the alley, imagined confronting whatever it was that haunted him right here and now, to prove it to himself: that there was nothing there, that these fears were unfounded, that he was being ridiculous. But Logan knew that was a fantasy. He shuffled one step forward, and that was exactly as far as his nerve would take him.

"So you might as well just come on out," Logan said, startled at the sound of his own voice, the beam of his flashlight shaking wildly in the grip of his trembling hand. *Stop. Playing. Games.*

Then Logan heard a shuffle just past the garbage bags on his left, and thought, *Trash, leaves . . . that could have been anything. But it wasn't a person. It couldn't have been a person, because no one is following you.* And with all the willpower he could muster, Logan shut the flashlight off and forced himself to turn around, to finish this walk home like a grown-up. Like someone he could respect. Like someone not afraid of the dark.

But Logan heard another footstep now, close this time, and he couldn't help but indulge his fear once more.

Just one look, he thought. *That's it. That'll be all I allow myself.*

He would glance over his shoulder.

He would turn in place and face the moonlit alley . . .

And that's when Logan saw the boy. Real. Born not of imagination or paranoia or delusion but of blood and bones and skin and nerves. He was a teenager, unidentifiable in the shadows among the trash, but solid and actual and horrifying in a way entirely new from the abstract fears Logan had known until now.

Five years of bottled terror flowed through Logan all at once, paralyzing him, filling him with a grave sense of acceptance that if this boy were to charge or attack, right at this moment, Logan would simply let him. Logan would simply let it end.

But the boy didn't attack.

Instead the boy turned and ran fast down the blood-moon streets.

And Logan followed before any part of him could think better of it.

1☐

Back in her apartment and still a little spooked by what Logan had been saying, Erin checked the locks on her front door twice before crashing onto the bubble wrap of her living room couch. It squeaked and popped beneath her as she slumped down and pulled her knees up, tucking her chin into the collar of her shirt and resting a tablet computer against her legs. She unfolded it and stared at her reflection in its blank screen, noticing her hair sticking out in unkempt wisps, seeing the bags under her eyes, realizing that her brow and lips were curled down in an ugly grimace. Finally she turned the thing on, dragging some files aside and opening its message window. Then she stared at that too for more than a few minutes before she finally made the call.

"Mom," she said. "Hi." And a hologram of Dr. Arbitor's head popped up out of the screen.

"Erin! How have you been? I haven't heard anything, and I've been so curious—how's Spokie? How was the train ride? How's your new school?"

Erin immediately felt a flood of guilt for not calling her mom sooner. "It's . . . good." She swallowed.

"Yeah? What's it like out in the country?"

"Quiet," Erin said honestly. "But Iggy seems to be adjusting."

"That's good." Dr. Arbitor laughed, and Erin turned the tablet so her mom could see the lizard, perched under a reading lamp and absorbing its heat.

"How's Beacon?" Erin asked.

"The same. Lonelier now." Dr. Arbitor smiled, and it broke Erin's heart.

"I shouldn't be out here," she said. "You shouldn't have let Dad do this to us."

"I had nothing to do with it, sweetie."

"You should have let me stay with you. I wanted to stay with you!" Her sadness turned to anger now.

"That wouldn't have been possible, Erin. You know I'm in Europe half-time these days. There wasn't a choice in the matter."

"Wasn't a *choice*? At what point is one of you going to stand up and put this family first?"

Dr. Arbitor was quiet for a long time.

"Mom?" Erin said finally. She thought hard about which words to say next. "Are you and Dad . . . okay?"

Dr. Arbitor frowned over the connection. "Why . . ." She cleared her throat. "Why would you ask that?"

"He insists everything's fine. To hear him tell it, you're joining us out here any day now. But I know you're not going to, and I tell him so." She scanned the small, undecorated space of the room around her. "So then he changes his story, says it won't be long before *we* come home to *you*." Now Erin's eyes found the DOME box in the corner, holding the truth behind the scope of her father's assignment. "But I don't think that's true either. In fact, I'm starting to think the job he took here is supposed to last a good long while . . ."

Dr. Arbitor left the tablet's field of view. Through the

connection, Erin could see the living room of her apartment back in Beacon, and a new wave of awful homesickness swept over her. She could see her mom's hunched shadow in the reflection of a far window, and Erin thought with some alarm that her mother appeared to be wiping her eyes.

"Mom, when are we going to be a family again?"

"That's up to your father, dear."

"No! It isn't! It's up to both of you! You're in this marriage together!" And immediately, Erin was hysterical. "How could you let things come to this? Did you really think you could keep it from me? Who gave you two the right to destroy my life like this?" She went on and on, not listening to her mom's stuttered interjections and not wanting to.

"Erin, please!" Dr. Arbitor finally snapped, and Erin subsided. "There's no reason to get so worked up about—"

But Erin *was* worked up. And for no good reason she thought of bedtime reading and Shakespeare in pajamas, and then her heart broke in two and it sank and burned in little pieces in the acid of her stomach and suddenly she was *very* worked up and she said, "Are either of you even *trying* anymore?"

And Dr. Arbitor said, "Of course we are," but the words hit Erin like a punch in the gut. Because her mother's voice was hollow. It was broken. Her mother was lying.

"I love you, Mom," Erin said, ending the call so fast she wasn't even sure all the words made it out. She was not about to let her mother see her cry.

Dr. Arbitor called her back, of course, immediately and probably frantically and surely wanting at least to say, "I love you too." But Erin would not let her do that. She declined the call. And when she did, she saw her own reflection again in the glass of the tablet's screen, and this time it was red and blotchy and it disgusted her. So she threw the computer into the bubble wrap of the couch, and she insisted to herself that she was disappointed when the thing didn't break.

It's up to your father, dear.

It's up to your mother, dear.

It's up to the other to keep us together, dear.

Erin paced across the room, sobbing, mocking herself. *Dear. Sweetie. It's up to your—*

And she made her way to Iggy, whom she picked up and kissed on the head.

"I heard those pets carry disease," Logan had said.

And she hoped it would give her salmonella. She hoped to puke her guts out. She kissed the lizard again. She wanted to puke her brains out and die.

She cried and held Iggy in her lap for a long time. And it was in that odd moment that Erin found her resolve.

She would be the one to get herself back to Beacon.

She would be the one to pull her family back together.

And if that meant solving the mystery of Peck and the Markless threat in Spokie herself, then that's exactly what Erin intended to do.

11

At that moment, seventeen stories below, a boy named Blake ran over the shadowed sidewalks of Spokie, furious with himself and weighing the consequences of having been seen.

Not as bad as getting caught, he concluded, darting unpredictably through side alleys and streets. *Whatever they are, they're not as bad as getting caught would be.*

Behind him, he heard the heavy breathing of the boy he was supposed to be pursuing. But that was botched. This was backward.

What Blake had witnessed, just moments before in their showdown on Wright Street, was a new side of the boy he and the Dust had followed all these years. A latent spark in the eyes of a kid he'd always seen as broken. Perhaps it was this spark that Peck had seen all along. Perhaps that spark was the danger.

Half a block behind and running off pure, stupid adrenaline, Logan yelled between breaths, "Just tell me what you want from me! It's all over now! Just tell me what you want!"

But it wasn't over. And as houses turned to empty lots and streetlamps faded off into the far distance behind them, Logan began to lose his nerve. Slowly it dawned on him exactly where he was chasing this boy, exactly where he himself was headed, and the realization was far from welcome.

Slog Row. The most dangerous, sordid street in all of suburban New Chicago. The street crawling with Markless, with disease and crime.

He could not go there. Ever. To walk down Slog Row was to walk with death.

Whoever this boy was, he had as good as escaped. Logan's steps slowed to a stop, and he caught his breath with his hands resting on his bent knees. He could follow no farther. Before him now, beyond the several empty lots and across the crumbling, abandoned six-lane expressway of years ago, was the silent and decaying street of so many parental warnings. He could see its panorama all at once, and in the moonlight, it was seething, a corpse lined with maggots.

What was I thinking? Logan thought. *Following even this far?*

And yet something in Logan had come alive. Something in him had flirted with the danger he'd spent so long avoiding, and the danger flirted back.

But no. That's crazy. And your parents will be worried sick. So all at once Logan's nerves dropped out from under him like a trapdoor, and he turned to burst full-sprint down the quiet Spokie avenue from whence he came, not looking back, not catching his breath, not stopping for anything else until he'd reached the safety of his own front door.

FOUR

THE INVITATION

1

THE NEXT DAY AT SCHOOL, LOGAN WAS JUMPY, even for him.

"You always been this wired?" Dane asked as they filed out of computer science. "Looks like you had about four cups of nanotea this morning."

Logan spun around as if Dane had poked him with something burning. "Sleepless night," he said, without a trace of humor in his voice.

"Sorry to hear it." Dane frowned. "Hey, Tom!" he yelled. "Aren't you Pledging today?"

"Just finished," Tom said. He held his wrist up. Its nanoink was so fresh, it sparkled. "First thing this morning. I walked straight here from the Center. Couldn't wait any longer to show this bad boy off." He pointed smugly at the Mark.

"That's *awesome*," Dane said. "Hey, buy me a soda!"

"You bullying me for my lunch money, Harold?" Tom asked.

"Sure am!" Dane laughed, and he pounced on Tom's arm, wrestling the class president, grabbing at his wrist with fake effort to pull the guy's hand off. Tom, who had Dane by four inches and at least thirty pounds, stood and waited for the joke to be over while Logan tried not to laugh.

"Dane Harold, knock it off!" the school secretary said as she hurried past.

"Sorry, Ms. Carrol." Dane gave up the act and brushed his hair down.

Tom turned to Logan with fresh interest. "So, Logan, you coming to auditions after school?" Logan shrugged, the Spokie Middle drama club being the furthest thing from his mind. *"Mark of a Salesman*, remember? Be a great chance to meet people if you made the show. Make some friends."

"What's that supposed to mean?" Dane asked.

"Oh, I just thought . . ." Tom backpedaled. "I mean . . . you know . . ."

"I'm zonked, anyway," Logan said. "I think I'd better not."

"Well, suit yourself." Tom clapped him on the shoulder. "You coming to English, Dane?"

"Yeah," Dane said, and soon Logan was alone in the hallway.

He walked to history through the Prairie Wing, where in the virtual window a lion crouched low and followed him the whole way to class.

School that day was slow, but Logan's mind couldn't have stopped racing if he'd begged it to. All those years spent certain he was crazy, exasperating his parents, visiting doctors and refusing prescriptions, answering questions and absorbing doubts and suspicions that were anything but fair . . . *all* of that, overturned in an instant by one stalking silhouette. He'd been right. This whole time. And he didn't know what to do about it.

He hadn't told his parents. If they'd believed the story of his walk home, it would have been a miracle; more likely it only would have led to a disappointed look and perhaps another doctor's appointment.

He would not tell Erin either. Logan was already angry with himself for going on so long about his sister and his fears the night before. Next time he and Erin talked, Logan was determined it would be about how much homework they had, or how the teachers compared to those in Beacon, or where to find the best pizza in town, or which after-school activities they might be interested in joining together.

"So!" Logan said. "Got any big plans tonight?" By the time economics rolled around, he had practiced this opening line about a hundred times.

"Huh?" Erin asked. She looked at him as if from a far-off place.

"Uh . . ." Logan cleared his throat. "I said, 'Got any big plans tonight?'" He'd rehearsed the words so extensively in his head that when he said them a second time, they came out in exactly the same cadence.

"It's Tuesday," Erin said, brushing him off. "Why would I have plans?"

Logan was crushed. He couldn't have guessed that her response was coming from a place of paranoia and guilt.

Truthfully, Erin *did* have plans that night. And not only were they big; they were illegal. They would begin with the deliberate theft of classified information, and she couldn't imagine they'd get any rosier from there.

"I just . . . thought . . . maybe . . . I mean . . ." Logan struggled to form a complete sentence. He hadn't prepared for this particular contingency.

But Erin laughed in a way that was friendly and genuine, and Logan caught his breath and shut up.

He's not onto me, Erin thought. *He's just being dorky ol' Logan.*

"I'll prob'ly mostly be doing homework," Erin lied. "Don't wanna get behind already, being the new girl and all."

"That's smart," Logan said. "I'll probably be doing that too. Maybe study for the Pledge some." He felt himself calming down now. This had been the idea. This was exactly the conversation he'd had in mind.

"If I finish early, maybe I'll sneak a movie on my tablet," Erin continued. She'd heard once that the key to dishonesty was specificity. "Sounds boring, I know."

"That doesn't sound boring."

"Oh, it will be." Erin laughed. "It'd just be some romantic comedy."

"I like romantic comedies," Logan said.

Erin laughed again, more nervously now. "Yeah, but . . . like . . . this'll be a really awful one, though."

"How bad could it—"

"Bad," she insisted. There was much too much to be done before her father got off work tonight for Logan to get any ideas about following her home again.

But Logan wasn't inviting himself over. He was simply making the small talk he had been so determined to make. And throughout the lesson, each time he'd lean over to whisper a joke, or to pretend to need clarification on a point the teacher had made, Logan forgot a little more completely about the stress he was under and the danger he was in.

In all of it, Logan never once mentioned the stalker on his walk home from Erin's the night before.

And Erin never once mentioned her unfolding plans to moonlight as an unlicensed spy.

2

By the time Dane called that night, Logan had already finished four full sweeps of his house. He had already checked all the locks twice, he had already determined his bedroom unfit for sitting, and he was already sandwiched safely between his parents on the living room couch.

Providing the calm company Logan needed while he distracted himself with Pledge prep, Dad watched the television frame on low volume, and Mom sat upright, though she might have been asleep. Meanwhile Logan curled up nose-deep in his tablet computer, skimming Pedia articles on the Unity for the hundredth time and by now practically memorizing their words.

He'd just finished reading twice the five-part article about the history leading up to the Total War, and he could have recited by heart the precise ways that rising temperatures had led to extinctions, crop failure, famine . . . how hurricanes and earthquakes and floods had forced relocation, had strained infrastructure with refugees and changed ecosystems for good . . . how countrymen had fought over land and water. He could have explained the migration of mosquitoes and other pests to the northern regions, the specific path each disease took across continents. He could have listed by name the spokesmen and leaders in those first waves of unrest, quoted the speeches and rallies and television programs that had prompted men and women to violence. He could have spouted off without blinking an eye the specific body counts of various battles and epidemics, the total dead and missing persons adding up to a staggering amount.

For political history, he'd reviewed the ways in which the States War differed subtly from the European War, and he studied the ways in which the two fit together to become, simply, the Total War. He'd read about the meteoritic rise of Chancellor Cylis in Europe, and the successful military trajectory of General Lamson in America. He'd memorized the ways in which each leader co-operated increasingly over the years, how Lamson had come to implement Cylis's Mark program across the A.U., how both had brought about the worldwide religious Inclusion, all to ensure that nothing as cataclysmic as the Total War ever happened again.

The Inclusion was of particular interest to Logan, partly because it was so far-reaching, and partly because it was the least talked about of all the major historical events. Logan knew, from piecing together what he'd read, that there had been a time not long ago when people around the world practiced a variety of different religions, each with its own system of values and culture and beliefs. Christianity, Islam, Judaism, Hinduism, Buddhism . . . the idea of it fascinated Logan, even though he hadn't the slightest idea what those religions taught. After Lamson and Cylis instituted the Inclusion, everything that might once have been considered spiritual was just sort of lumped into a single, bland system that mostly preached patriotism and peace. Not bad ideas by any means, and yet Logan couldn't help but wonder if somehow, in all of it, something important was being lost.

In any case, this brought Logan to present-day news, to articles about the treaty and the speculation over the Global Union, along with editorials enthusiastically describing what a milestone it would be. Logan tried to imagine it as he continued to study.

Any question was fair game in the oral exam at the Pledge, and after the incalculable tragedy of his sister, Logan was simply doing everything he could to stack the deck in favor of him leaving that Center alive.

So by the time Dane called that night, facts upon facts upon facts all swam in Logan's head with such intensity that he began to lose track of where one ended and another began, and when his tablet buzzed with the incoming message, Logan accepted the distraction eagerly.

"You up for hanging out?" Dane asked. "I'm done with home-work, and we've got another hour of daylight."

"I need to study. I'm terrified of this Pledge," Logan admitted.

"Oh please. You're gonna ace that stupid thing. Besides, your birthday's not for months. And it's the first week of the school year. We're practically obligated to cause some trouble tonight."

Logan smiled. "That sounds good," he said. "I'll see what my parents think."

3

It had been several hours since Mr. Arbitor had messaged to say it'd be another late night, and presently Erin sat on the floor of her apartment among no fewer than five empty DOME boxes, three of which had come from the Spokie office just the night before, brought home by her father and hidden deep in his bedroom closet under the irresistible label "SUPPLY ROOM—113B."

Their contents were bizarre, but promising. A small roll of

clear tape, an ounce of chalk dust, gel, pellets, sticky beanlike things, a button . . . Erin stared at the pile with reverence, as she might a loaded gun or a rattlesnake. She knew what very little of the equipment was, and she knew even less about how to use any of it, but she was determined not to let that get in her way.

She'd already looked again through her father's confidential papers, and she'd caught plenty she missed the first time around about the particular "threat" Spokie faced, about who this "Peck" might be, about the spy games he employed, and about the crimes he'd committed in this quiet Corn Belt town over the last few years. She'd certainly caught enough to know that she needed a tactical advantage for her mission not to be suicide. The details of the case were horrifying, and it was little wonder that they'd brought in the big-gun Beacon talent to handle it.

Erin rolled up her sleeves. From his hiding spot under the couch, her iguana scampered over to see what all the intrigue was.

"You wanna help, little buddy?" She picked Iggy up, and he looked at her cockeyed, paddling his claws in the air like he was swimming. His tail swished back and forth, and he stuck his tongue out in a short, funny rhythm.

Erin laughed. She decided to take this as a yes.

4

There was a rule in the Langly household about throwing anything upstairs in the yard on their roof. The rule was: don't throw anything upstairs in the yard on the roof.

But Dane had brought over a hoverdisk, and he had long ago convinced Logan that actually, if the Langlys had thought about it,

the rule they'd really meant to lay down was "don't throw anything *off* the yard on the roof, and don't fall off yourself when
you're trying to catch it." So the two of them stood up there now,
watching the sun lower into the evening parts of the sky and toss-
ing the disk back and forth on its lowest "fake out" setting.

"You're likin' that new girl," Dane said after a bit of small talk.
His throw zigzagged back to Logan.

"What, uh, makes you say—" Logan lunged for the catch and
didn't finish his thought.

"You should introduce me sometime—she seems cool."

"Sure," Logan said, his voice cracking over the word. "How
was New Chicago, anyway?"

"Boring," Dane said, but he missed his catch, and the two of
them watched wide-eyed as the hoverdisk floated over the roof's
edge and out of sight.

"You broke our own rule!" Logan said.

Dane looked down over the railing and shook his head. "To
the letter of it, yes. But I'm pretty sure the *spirit* of that rule is
actually 'don't hit anybody on the street with anything you throw
over the side, and don't break any neighbors' windows.'" He
smiled. "We're blameless."

So the two of them set about retrieving Dane's hoverdisk from
the tree on the opposite sidewalk—guilt-free, but with every intention of finishing the job before Logan's mom or dad saw.

They were halfway down the outdoor spiraling staircase when
Dane stopped for a moment just outside Logan's room.

"Hey, I meant to ask you," Dane said. "What's this fishing line
for?"

Logan turned around, confused.

"I saw it on the way in but forgot to mention it." Dane reached out over the stairwell, on his toes with his arm fully extended, and plucked the twine like a guitar string. It made a low and eerie twang that rang all the way across the street.

"I've . . . never noticed it," Logan said. He stepped back to have a look.

The line was clear, and invisible unless the sun caught it just right. It was attached to the corner window of Logan's room (a window that didn't open) with a small dollop of clear superglue, and it extended, taut, into the distance, to some unidentifiable point. Beyond a few feet out, nothing could be seen of the thing, and it was unlikely anyone could spot it by looking through the bedroom window, or by using the stairs in any normal way.

"How'd you see it?"

Dane shrugged. "Just caught my eye on the way in. The light hit it funny. I figured it was some sort of experiment you had going or something. Like a . . . zip line for ants." Dane laughed at himself. "Is it a zip line for ants?"

"No . . . ," Logan said, hyperventilating a little.

"Weird." Dane shrugged. "Come on. Let's go get my hoverdisk. We'll rock-tablet-laser to see who has to climb that tree."

5

On weekends, growing up, Erin would spend Saturdays shadowing her mother in the offices on Barrier Street in Beacon. For a household run by two busy parents, it was either that or playdates, and as soon as she was old enough to say so, Erin admitted that she much preferred the office.

The trading floors, of course, were the most exciting thing

on Barrier Street. Long, cavernous rooms filled with thousands of tablet computers attached to women and men by brain-computer interfaces, or BCIs. With markets fluctuating as fast as they did, the time it took for keystrokes or hand gestures or words was unacceptable. These days, stocks rose and fell with brain waves.

But Erin never stayed long on the trading floor. Her mom was not a part of that particular frenzy.

Her mom was above it.

So Erin would spend her days in the corner of a small, windowless office, its wallscreens decorated with economic charts and program algorithms, and with the occasional electronic drawing made by Erin.

It wasn't long before Dr. Arbitor recognized that Erin needed stimulation, so she'd soon set her daughter up with a computer and her own BCI.

At first, Erin wasn't much interested in the tablet her mother had given her. Its preloaded games were too easy and bored her quickly, and its movies were bland. But a few weekends in, Erin's mother took a minute between E.U. calls to show her daughter that the tablet she'd been given was more than just a tool for consuming—it was a tool for creating. Under the surface, it was a blank slate, one that could be manipulated, programmed, hacked . . .

And a month later, when Dr. Arbitor noticed her daughter delving into source code on her own, she thought it might be time to send Erin to her friend Mac down the hall.

Mac was a computer wiz employed by DOME. Mac could sign on to the tablet at his desk in Beacon and orchestrate an electrobus jam five minutes later in Sierra. Mac could do anything.

And he soon took a liking to Erin. Erin was bright and curious . . . and more than a little mischievous. So Mac began teaching hacking tricks to Erin while her mom fooled herself into thinking she'd found a good babysitter for her daughter. Mac giggled endlessly the time he showed Erin how to make all the lights on the trading floor go out, and again the time he taught her how to tap into the building's security system and set off the fire alarms. One Valentine's Day a few years in, he even showed Erin how to stream "I Got You Babe" over the loudspeakers for a full minute and a half before the building's mainframe immune system kicked in and booted Erin's tablet from the network permanently.

Dr. Arbitor didn't let Erin see Mac after that. But it wasn't long before Erin figured out how to hack into Mac's operating space, and over the next few years he taught her the rest of what he could by IP chat and text message.

Now, in her lonely Spokie apartment, Erin sat with her computer and was finally putting these skills to good use. Through trial and error she'd hacked her tablet into communicating with the DOME technology spread across her apartment floor, and to her programmer's eye, the data it transmitted (in machine code and assembly language) painted a picture of how each object might be used.

The chalk dust, it turned out, wasn't chalk at all, but surveillance powder capable of absorbing sound and translating it to radio frequency, which the accompanying gel picked up live, like a one-way walkie-talkie. The tape worked similarly, but had proven more useful for recording than for live communication.

The sticky beans would short out when squeezed, turning into a strange, taserlike defense; the button was a tracker; and on and on, each item coming together to give its user a powerful set of advantages. Erin surveyed the inventory, no longer feeling like an amateur.

But suddenly a scream let out deep inside her ears, and Erin clutched at her head in shock and pain.

It was the gel. At the start of her experimentation she'd put the radio gel in her ears, along with a generous dose of surveillance powder on her iguana, and she'd set the lizard loose in her apartment building to see if the gel would pick up any outside conversations. Until now, she'd heard nothing, and truthfully, in her excitement over the rest of the equipment, she'd forgotten all about her little audio test.

But the screaming continued in her ears, hollow and tinny, a voice shouting, *"It's a monster, someone kill it!"* And while Erin was happy to know that the powder-gel combination she'd tested was working, she was now faced with the more urgent task of tracking down an illegal pet iguana that had clearly just escaped into the unforgiving streets of Spokie.

ㅂ

Across town, Logan and Dane's old friend Hailey Phoenix put dinner in front of her mother and sat down at the table to eat. Tonight they were having lentils and cabbage.

Hailey's mother, Mrs. Phoenix, worked long and grueling hours on the floor of the nanomaterials plant out of town. Her commute, by electrobus, was an hour and a half each way, so she would leave at four thirty each morning, and she would return home at six o'clock each night. This was her routine seven days a week, fifty-two weeks a year.

When she did come home, Mrs. Phoenix would invariably spend her first thirty minutes or so in the bathroom upstairs, coughing violently and murmuring things about "all that nano-dust," which usually gave Hailey enough time to prepare dinner, since their dinners were never elaborate.

It had not always been this way. Just three years ago, Mrs. Phoenix was still an Unmarked, stay-at-home mother, and Mr. Phoenix worked as head manager over at the plant. They'd never had much money, but they'd had enough, and they enjoyed the quiet life Hailey's father had always supported.

Then, in Hailey's sixth-grade year, Mr. Phoenix died of a heart attack, brought on, the doctors said, by the drinking habit he'd never quite been able to outsmart since his time serving in the States War. Ironically, his autopsy confirmed that it was in fact the nano-enhancements in his favorite drink—manufactured at the very same plant Mr. Phoenix managed—that finally did him in.

But neither Mrs. Phoenix nor Hailey ever saw the humor in this, and when they'd called in every last favor they could from friends across Spokie, when the food and everything else simply ran out, Mrs. Phoenix had no choice but to receive the Mark and beg her way into a pity hire at the lowest levels of work the nano-materials plant had to offer.

"How's school this year?" Hailey's mother asked.

"The same. We're doing holograms in art."

"That's great!" Mrs. Phoenix said. "You've gotta be the best in the class!"

Hailey smiled. "I am, I think."

Outside of schoolwork, Hailey had taken up two hobbies since her father passed away. The first was a habit of long, nighttime walks outside of town. Hailey liked the countryside feeling of the cornfields and sparse woods, and she often imagined herself living deep in the no-man's-land between the Union's great cities. Hailey had no idea how this would ever be possible—she hadn't even the means to travel to New Chicago, let alone the faraway flatlands, and anyway she had her mother to worry about—but she allowed herself the fantasy all the same.

The second thing Hailey had taken up was sculpture. Every chance her mother got, she would bring home machine scraps and discarded equipment from the plant, and Hailey would spend her free time turning it into art, which her mother kept around the house or displayed proudly on the front steps.

This odd hobby began after Mrs. Phoenix noticed what great things Hailey was making with all the garbage she'd found on the street (there was a lot of garbage on Hailey's street), and before long Hailey got the impression that her mother entertained wild dreams of Hailey Phoenix becoming the great modern artist of Spokie. This was even more ridiculous than her own plans to move out to the flatlands, Hailey thought, but at the same time she had to admit that it was kind of nice.

"Holograms," Mrs. Phoenix said. "Imagine that."

After she'd washed the dishes and bid her mother good night, Hailey slipped out of the house, as she almost always did, to take her nightly stroll.

The sun was sitting low in the sky at this point, and since Hailey's block was as close as any inhabited street got to Slog Row, there were more than a few Markless roaming the sidewalk. But Hailey didn't mind the Markless the way most people did, partly because her mother had been one until recently, and partly because, living where she did, Hailey just saw so many of them. Sure, her house was robbed—every couple of months, in fact— and yes, Hailey had been accosted while coming home late one night just a few weeks before. But since there wasn't any paper money left for anyone to steal, and since Hailey and her mother had so little besides lentils and garbage sculptures lying around the house, Hailey figured she just didn't have that much left to lose.

Even so, Hailey wasn't much interested tonight in crossing the expressway to explore Spokie's dark outskirts, and she soon found herself ambling the other direction, toward the fancy center square downtown, thinking happily that it would be a rather nice night for window-shopping.

She was almost there when Hailey ran into a fellow eighth-grade student looking lost and flustered and a little frightened just outside Spokie Central Park.

"You okay?" Hailey asked. "Need any help?"

"I lost my iguana," the girl said. "You're from Spokie Middle, right?"

Hailey said that she was.

"It's all right, though. He's wearing a tracker. I can follow him on my tablet, see?" The girl showed Hailey her tablet and pointed to a satellite picture with a little glowing dot moving around inside the park beside them.

"I'm Hailey."

"Oh. Erin. Hi." Erin began walking in the direction of the dot on her map.

"What are you doing with an iguana?" Hailey asked. "And why is it wearing a . . . tracker?"

"Not just a tracker," Erin said distractedly. "He's got some powder on him too—*wait!*" Erin cocked her head and listened for a moment. Hailey heard nothing. "He's by running water. Is there a fountain in this park?"

"You're new here, aren't you?" Hailey said.

"Yes. From Beacon."

"They let you take iguanas for walks in Beacon?"

"I didn't *take* him for a *walk*—he *escaped*! Or . . . well, I sorta let him out into the hallway, but I didn't think—look, it doesn't matter! And no, Beacon doesn't—oh, forget it," Erin said.

"Come on," Hailey told her, laughing a little. "I'll take you to the fountain."

⌐

Back on Logan's street, Logan and Dane were trying to beat the sunset and retrieve Dane's hoverdisk before it got too dark. But its perch in the tree was awfully high.

"I don't know why I'm the one up here," Logan said, as Dane laughed sympathetically from the sidewalk. "You're the one who missed the catch."

"Yeah, 'cause your throw was off!"

"It's a hoverdisk. It's *supposed* to veer off."

"It was on the lowest setting!"

"Whatever!" Logan said. He was standing on the highest branch that could possibly have supported him, ten or so feet off the ground, and straining to touch the sports disk just out of reach.

"And anyway, you lost rock-tablet-laser."

"I did *not*!" Logan said. "Who ever heard of a rock-tablet-laser match where you don't play best two out of three?" He wasn't actually angry, but the banter took his mind off his precarious foothold.

"Well, when you get back down here, we can have a rematch." Dane laughed.

"Great, thanks," Logan said, but his own laughter stopped short.

"What's up? You knock it loose?"

Logan hadn't knocked it loose. Logan hadn't touched the hoverdisk at all. Instead, in the fast-approaching darkness of night, he'd stumbled upon something else, high up in the tree.

A can. A tin can, like the kind you'd find tomato soup in, or beans. It was hanging off a twig above him. It was hanging from fishing line.

Logan unwrapped the line from the tree and pulled the can to his ear. The clear twine travelled off across the street toward Logan's house and pulled tight against him.

"Honey, do you know where the boys went?" said a distant voice in the tin can.

"They're on the roof."

"They aren't, though. Wait a second—I see Dane outside."

Logan looked on in horror as his dad stepped out onto the stairwell outside Logan's room.

"Dane!" he called from across the street. "Do you know where Logan went?"

Dane flashed a glance to Logan in the tree and immediately thought better of admitting it.

"We're, uh, racing, Mr. Langly. We took a lap around the block. He's still catching up."

"Well, you boys come in when you're done. Dinner soon. You're welcome to join if you'd like."

"Thanks, Mr. Langly," Dane yelled. "I'll think about it."

Mr. Langly stepped back inside Logan's room, and in the tin can he held to his ear, Logan could hear his father's voice say, *"Boy's growing up faster than I know what to do with him . . ."*

Logan's hands shook almost too much for him to hold on to the tree. In one clumsy motion he knocked the hoverdisk from its branch and tore the tin can from its fishing line.

"You got it!" Dane whispered, trying to be cautious after lying to Logan's dad. "Good job!"

Logan climbed to a safe height and jumped the rest of the way down the tree and onto the sidewalk.

"What've you got there?" Dane asked. Logan was holding the can. "You okay, dude? You look like you're gonna faint."

Logan felt that way too, weak in the knees. He had to sit down.

Dane put his hand on Logan's shoulder and said, "Look, it was a close call with your dad, but it wasn't *that* close. He's not even angry."

Logan was grateful for the alibi, as the last thing he wanted to do right now was explain to Dane what he'd just found. "You're right," he said. "I'm just being stupid."

At that moment, two girls appeared together down the sidewalk. When they came a little closer, Logan could see that they were, in fact, Hailey and Erin. Erin was holding her iguana tightly in both hands, and speaking loudly and excitedly to Hailey though she wasn't yet close enough for Logan to hear the words.

"Yo, girls!" Dane called out. "Hey, over here!"

Hailey turned and smiled upon seeing Dane and Logan. Erin smiled too.

"What's up?" Dane asked when they'd come a little closer.

"Just out for a stroll," Hailey said.

"I lost my iguana." Erin held him up.

Dane cleared his throat, and Logan snapped out of his daze.

"Oh! Dane! This is Erin," he said. "Erin, this is my friend Dane."

Dane nodded approvingly at Logan and waved to Erin.

"Hi," Erin said.

Logan managed a thin smile. "I didn't know you two knew each other."

"Just met," Hailey said.

Erin laughed. "Playing kick the can, I see?" She gestured with Iggy to the can Logan was holding.

"Yeah, what is that?" Dane asked Logan.

"It's nothing," Logan lied.

Dane pointed up. "You find it in the tree?"

"Uh . . ."

"Dude, it was prob'ly a bird's nest or something! And you stole it!"

"Shut up, Dane," Logan said, rolling his eyes. "It wasn't a bird's nest." He hesitated. "Actually . . . it was attached to that twine you found."

Dane frowned. "Why?"

"It was, uh . . . it was picking up the sounds in my room." Logan felt himself go white as he said it.

"So you *did* have an experiment going!" Dane said.

Logan laughed distantly. "Yeah . . ." He chuckled. "Works better than you'd think."

But right as he lied, Erin caught Logan's eye. She read the look on his face. And suddenly many pieces of some grand puzzle clicked into place.

Could it be? Could Logan really be Peck's next victim? Could this be what all the "haunting" stories had been about last night? Could that be the explanation behind this tin can too?

Erin's eyes went wide. Without thinking, she hoisted Iggy up onto her shoulder and steadied him with one hand. With her other, she took Logan's, her touch surging through him: "Listen," she said. "There's something I need to show you," and the two of them turned.

"Dude, where are you going?" Dane looked at Logan pleadingly, stealing a short glance at Hailey. "I thought we were gonna eat dinner or something."

"Dinner can wait," Erin said.

"No, it can't," Dane said. "Logan, not cool!" But Logan was already gone, dragging wildly behind Erin as she pulled him down the road.

"Peck," Erin whispered once they'd run some feet away.

"What are you talking about?" Logan said. "What's going on? Who's Peck?"

"I think you're lying about that tin can being yours. But I think everything else you've said to me has been the truth."

Logan was starting to breathe heavily. "You're right, but— Erin, what is this about? Who's Peck? Where have I heard that name before?"

Back by the tree, Dane looked at Hailey. She smiled apologetically.

"So," Dane said.

"Hi," Hailey said.

The two of them shrugged. And they made their way home.

目

Erin shuffled through boxes in her father's closet, fielding Logan's frantic questions.

"He *what?*"

"Killed someone. Guy named Jon Pulman. Jon was fifteen at the time."

"Why?" Logan felt a shudder run down his back.

"No one knows. Peck had a history with him; they'd been friends for years, apparently. Jon had the Mark; some speculate Peck couldn't tolerate it any longer——"

"Peck doesn't have the Mark?"

"That's right."

"And he killed his own friend because his friend did? That doesn't make any sense."

"No. But it's consistent, if you keep digging." Erin found the box labeled "DOME——CONFIDENTIAL," which she'd hidden before she left, and exhumed it once more. "Something about the Mark seems to rub Peck the wrong way. Big-time. Turns out he attacked another one of his oldest friends, Trenton, just six months later. Trenton is seventeen. He's been in a coma ever since." Now Erin corroborated her story with pages that she took out from her father's box one at a time.

"How long's that been now?"

"'Bout four months. Hasn't woken up."

Logan looked over the papers. "What'd Peck do to him?"

"Same thing he did to Jon. Blunt object to the back of the head."

"Over the Mark?"

Erin could tell Logan was skeptical. "You wouldn't think so, necessarily. Not just from those two instances alone. But the story continues."

Logan had to concentrate hard on his breathing to keep from hyperventilating. He could already see his peripheral vision fading.

Erin continued. "See, a DOME agent was at the scene the time Peck went after Trenton. Tried to stop Peck in the act. That's why Peck couldn't finish the job. But Peck didn't run. Not right away. Went after the DOME agent first. Hit him with a chair."

"You've gotta be kidding me."

"I'm not."

"No one attacks a DOME agent. You'd have to be . . ."

"That's right," Erin said. "You'd have to be crazy."

Logan sank to his knees beside Erin, not quite able to stand as the gravity of all this crept up on him. "But why would a DOME agent have even been there? Police, I'd understand—someone calls a disturbance, an officer shows up . . . but a DOME agent? DOME doesn't ever handle crimes not related to the Mark."

"*Exactly.*" Erin paused so the conclusions could sink in.

"But it still doesn't make sense. Why go after his own friends?"

"Who knows? The guy's Markless. He's a criminal."

Logan shook his head. "It isn't a crime to be Markless, no matter what age you are."

"It's not, no. Not in itself. But to survive like that . . . no way to eat . . . nowhere to stay . . . it'd make a criminal out of you pretty quick."

Logan thought of Slog Row. "I guess it would."

"But you're right," Erin admitted. "All this, by itself, is still weird. Why his own friends? Why a DOME agent?"

"Right."

She handed him another page. "Well, turns out the DOME

agent wasn't killed. Just banged up a bit. Couple months ago, he was able to testify."

"Okay."

"Apparently he'd had his eye on Peck for some time. They still don't know much about him, or his history, at least according to these papers. They don't even know his full name. But they know what he's been up to recently. And the incidents with Peck's friends? Those are the exceptions. Mostly, Peck doesn't kill, and mostly, Peck doesn't target those with the Mark."

Logan had a feeling he didn't want to hear the rest of this. But he couldn't help himself from asking, "Then what does he do . . . mostly?"

"Mostly, he targets kids."

Logan shuddered. "*Kids*? What for?"

"All DOME knows is, in the past three or four years, Peck's had a history of tracking kids while they prepped for their Pledge. Some of them, he tracks them—then he seems to let them go. Forgets about 'em. Lets them just get the Mark and live their lives. Many never even realize they've been watched."

"And the others?"

Erin looked Logan in the eyes. She put a hand on his shoulder. "The others disappear."

Logan couldn't believe what he was hearing. "What do you mean, they disappear?"

"'Bout two months ago Peck kidnapped a girl named Meg Steward. Meg was twelve at the time. Your age. Would have been thirteen by now, and Marked, of course, but . . . no sign of her."

"How do they know it was him?"

"He left a note—on paper—asking Meg to meet him at some playground. Apparently she followed the instructions."

"Why would she have done that?"

"Beats me. She took half the note with her, and the part that remained was charred, like it'd been burned up. DOME could only make out part of it, but the rest must have made a pretty compelling argument. Anyway, that was the last anyone saw of her."

"Did Peck kill her too?"

"Hard to say. They haven't found a body."

Logan cursed under his breath.

"According to these documents, DOME's pretty convinced Peck's done this a few times. They've found burned notes in the past, but this is the first with any traceable evidence on it. Coupled with the DOME agent's testimony, it's launched the full-scale investigation that brought my dad here."

Logan swallowed. "And you think I'm next?"

Erin frowned, scanning the papers she and Logan had strewn about the floor. "I dunno," she said. "Not if we find him first."

9

Before Logan could respond, his tablet rang and his dad appeared on the screen. "Dinner's cold, buddy. This is the second night in a row now. I look out and you and Dane are gone. You got an explanation?"

All at once Logan remembered he was still a twelve-year-old kid with twelve-year-old responsibilities, like letting his parents know where he was and being home in time for dinner. Problems very far from those he'd been worried about over the last hour.

Logan apologized, laying it on thick on account of this being strike two for him. He said he'd run into his new friend Erin on the sidewalk—which was, of course, true—and promised he'd be home in just a few minutes.

But when he ended the call, Logan was entirely back to business. "We need to go to your dad," he told Erin.

"And tell him what? You have no evidence."

"I have my testimony. It's consistent with what's known about Peck—"

"Logan, what's known about Peck is *confidential*. I could be *arrested* for showing these papers to you. I could be arrested just for having looked at them myself!"

"I would think they'd make an exception if it led to the capture of—"

"And how exactly would it do that, Logan? How exactly would it lead to anything other than two kids with wild imaginations and a treasonous curiosity? DOME doesn't mess around with this stuff. I'm not even allowed to know what my dad *does* every day."

"Yeah, but under the circumstances—"

"The circumstances are speculative. Do you know where Peck lives? Could you pick him out in a lineup? Do you have fingerprints? DNA evidence?"

"Well, no—"

"No, that's right. You have nothing. *We* have nothing. But that's going to change. We're going to make sure of it. And when it does, you have my word, we'll go to my dad."

"And I'll be safe again?"

Erin nodded. *And I'll be on my way back to Beacon.* "In the meantime, this is our secret. We tell no one, right? Not a soul."

"Okay," Logan said, a little uneasy about it.

"And if you notice anything—call me." She gave Logan her phone number, which he keyed into his tablet and stared at reverently. Too bad he couldn't tell Dane.

"Get out of here," Erin said. "And be careful."

She gave him a hug just before he left, and Logan tried to be casual about it.

It was the first time he'd ever been hugged by a girl.

10

Ten minutes later Logan ran up the spiraling staircase outside his house, not willing to wait for the elevator's street door to open. He raced up the first flight of it and pounded directly on the door to his kitchen. "Mom, Dad!" he called. "Let me in!"

Nothing had happened on the way home. The night was cool and peaceful. But Logan's heart had not slowed since he'd found the tin can.

"Hello, Logan," Mrs. Langly said.

In the five years since his sister's Marking accident, Logan had never once heard his mother raise her voice. She spoke exclusively in slow, breathy whispers, often with great pauses between them, which complemented the delicate pace of her steps. Each movement of an arm or hand was small and distracted, and she even blinked with a speed that suggested an infinite, drowsy calm. In the past few years she'd aged quickly, with deep wrinkles sketching the years on her face. She opened the door now as if in slow motion and said, "Your dinner is cold. I was worried sick."

"Hey, buddy!" Mr. Langly said, bounding over from the kitchen table with enough energy and volume for Mom and him both. "Logan Langly, big man on campus, can't keep the ladies off him! Come on over, tell us what's new!" His enthusiasm seemed forced, somehow, striking Logan as oddly overpowering. Was his father angry with him? Ashamed? As he spoke, Mr. Langly took his wife's arm and guided her gently back to her seat. For a moment, Logan stood, thinking he would confess the events of the last two nights, thinking he would explain what he'd learned about Peck. But Erin was right. This was their secret. So instead Logan followed, quiet, playing his part in the familiar scene.

After dinner, Logan excused himself and took the elevator to his room on the seventh floor, feeling guilty and scared, if glad, to be home.

He wanted nothing more than to crawl into bed and sleep for as long as he could.

But something wasn't right.

That smell—what was it? Smoke?

The elevator door opened to a horrifying scene.

There, on his desk in the darkness of his room, glowing orange and yellow and sporadic and awful, was a fire.

Logan ran to it swiftly. A paper note, burning. Logan read what remained of it through the smoke.

> Logan
> ... Spokie Playground ...
> ... Midnight ...
> ... Or Else ...

No sooner had he finished reading than the paper turned to ash, burning up completely before him on his desktop, which had been wetted carefully with a protective coating of water from Logan's nearby glass. The flame went out and fizzled in the puddle beneath it, and nothing remained of the note but a couple of charred, disintegrating tatters.

Logan was scared beyond the capacity to scream or run or defend himself or even breathe. And when finally his heart snapped back to life it pumped white-hot fear into his brain, and the only thing that registered with any sort of clarity was: *Right now, someone is here.*

Upon thinking this, Logan spun around. And the face in his window fled from view.

FIVE

SPY VS. SPY

1

BLAKE JUMPED FROM THE SPIRALING STAIR-
way, hitting the ground hard and looking for a place to hide.
The sidewalk in front of Logan's house was well lit, but he fell
in among what shadows he could find and ran through their
darkness.

At the speed he was running and at this time of night, it was
impossible to see, so Blake oriented himself by Logan's shouting
behind him. "I know you're there!" it went. "I know you're out
there!"

But Blake was long gone.

He strained to listen for footsteps or sirens behind him.
Nothing. Logan hadn't followed.

The settlement was across town, on the outskirts of Spokie, among
gutted apartments and abandoned buildings isolated from the
sparkle and disinfectant of the rest . . . the neighborhood on the

wrong side of the expressway, where Spokie residents knew never to go, where cops turned the other way, where the dust settled and was never stirred . . . on Slog Row, Blake's home among the Markless.

Still winded from his run, Blake stepped over shards of glass, between boards of wood nailed clumsily over the broken storefront window, and into the abandoned Fulmart that once anchored the neighborhood. There was a time when everything you could want rested inside these cavernous walls—clothes, hardware, food . . . but those days were long gone.

It started with the old firehouse, which had been abandoned for years, too far outside what had become central Spokie to be of any use. The Markless, unable to pay rent and quietly kicked out of their homes one by one, took refuge in that old building. At first, cops would make sweeps and clean the place up each night, since residents along the Row would complain. But with nowhere else to go, the Markless always returned, and as crime on the block steadily rose, residents saved up and moved out, one family at a time, to the better parts of town. In just this way, over the years, poverty on the long block spread all the way from the firehouse to the Fulmart at its other end nearly a quarter mile away, and Slog Row earned its name.

Blake didn't mind. The arrangement suited him. Because he was Markless. And because inside the Fulmart, second shelf up from the floor, was Blake's home on aisle 3.

He walked there now, stumbling a little in the darkness broken only by shafts of moonlight filtering through the boarded storefront windows, and was pleased to find the other Dust waiting up for him.

Tyler and Eddie sat on the floor, playing cards by candlelight. "Wanna join?" Tyler asked.

"What's the game?"

"King's Punch-Out."

"Never heard of it."

"That's 'cause we just made it up."

Blake sat between them. "How do you play?"

"You split the deck among the players." Tyler handed him roughly a third of the deck, and he and Eddie began playing as he explained. "Each round, you flip a card over."

Blake followed along.

"The player with the lowest card gets punched in the face."

Blake looked at the cards. Tyler's was the jack of clubs. Eddie's, the nine of hearts. Blake saw he was holding a three of spades, and suddenly his nose was bleeding. "Very funny, guys," he said, and Tyler and Eddie laughed and laughed.

"So what's the news?" Eddie asked, as the three of them turned another set of cards.

"I let him know," Blake said. Then they all flipped cards and he and Eddie punched Tyler in the face.

"You got my eye, ya stingy piker!" Tyler said, and he held his face but still managed to squint with his good eye, undistracted, at Blake. "Think he'll come?"

"'Course he'll come, tightwad," Eddie said, and after they turned over the next round of cards, he punched Tyler again. "If Peck says it's time, then it's time."

They went through half the deck this way, hitting each other and spewing at one another the worst possible slurs that had cropped up over the years to demean the Markless—*piker*, *tightwad*, *stingy*, *miser*—words that had taken on new and awful meaning since the Mark program began; words that disparaged and mocked the Dust's own helplessness and lowliness. The boys didn't care. It was all part of the game.

Blake snatched up the cards and threw them down the aisle and out of sight.

"Hey—"

"That's enough! Listen. There's more to it."

Eddie stared at him for a moment. "What do you mean? More to what?"

"He's onto me."

Eddie shrugged. "So what else is new? He's suspected you for months."

"Yeah, but last night he *saw* me. And today he found the tin can I'd set up."

"I told you that wasn't gonna work," Eddie said.

"Eddie. Listen to me. It gets worse. He made a new friend yesterday."

Tyler stuck a finger in his mouth. "Good for him," he said. "I think you knocked my tooth loose."

"Whaddaya know about him?" Eddie asked.

"It's not a him; it's a her."

"Nice! A lady friend!" Tyler said, lisping over his finger.

"Shut up." Blake turned to Eddie. "Only what I could pick up through the girl's apartment wall."

"And?"

"It's bad, Eddie. She knows about us. Definitively. Well, not us—Peck."

"*What?* How?"

"Not sure."

"Well, how much does she know? How much did she tell him?"

"It was hard to hear anything from the hallway."

"Great. Real good detective work there, Sherlock. What else couldn't you hear?" Tyler spit into his hand and checked it for blood, and Blake already wished he hadn't thrown the cards, so he'd have an excuse to punch him again.

But instead he just said, "Look, if all goes well, none of it matters after tonight, anyway."

Eddie frowned. "Sounds like this directly affects whether tonight goes well or not."

"It won't," Blake said. "He'll show. And if not . . ."

Tyler stretched his jaw in a circle, rubbing it, assessing the pain but still undistracted by it. "You spent all night listening and didn't pick up a single other thing, did you?"

"Hey, lay off, skinflint!"

"Make me!"

"Stop it." Silence. "Does he know?"

Blake, Tyler, and Eddie froze. Blake spun around, still sitting cross-legged. The other two inched back, trying to look nonchalant about it. Joanne towered above them all. "Hey, Jo," Blake said, hoping not to escalate anything too quickly. "Where's Meg?"

"Tied up. I stuck her on a shelf in the sports section. The racks go higher there."

"Think she'll get down?"

"Nah. She struggles too much, she'll fall. It'd be a long drop with her hands tied behind her back."

Blake listened to the store for a moment. "You gag her too? I don't hear anything."

"Didn't need to. Girl's practically a mute." Jo sighed and clucked her tongue.

"What'd she do this time?" Blake asked.

"Tried to burn the place down," Eddie said.

Blake shook his head. "That little miser."

"I don't know why we picked her up," Tyler said. "I say we leave her up there for the night so she can think about what she's done."

Jo looked at him. "Forget it, Tyler. She's coming along." She turned to Blake. "Anyway. Peck know about the girlfriend or not?"

"Not," Blake said. "I haven't seen him. He here tonight or what?"

"Warehouse. He's preparing. Like you beggars are supposed to be."

Blake got up and stood face-to-face with Joanne for some time. She was taller than he was. Probably weighed more too. He hugged her. "It's good to see you again. I didn't think you'd be coming by."

"Wasn't planning on it," Jo said. "He asked me to. Wanted to get the final update before tonight."

"Well, you heard it," Blake said. "We're good except for the girl. Kid read the note. Saw me too, again, but . . . that shouldn't matter at this point."

"Yeah," Eddie said. "'Cause he's not coming."

"He *is* coming, ya little skimp—forget the girl."

"What makes you so sure?"

"'Cause I'm the one been watchin' him the past six months!" Blake paused, shook his head.

"Good work," Jo said sincerely. "Now come on. Midnight approaches. There's work to be done."

Blake, Joanne, Tyler, Eddie—they were a family. Not a real one, of course, but without a doubt the closest thing any of them had to it. Blake was fourteen, a runaway who'd left home nearly two years ago. Joanne was fifteen and had been on her own twice that long. Tyler and Eddie were thirteen, new to the life in the Dust. Then there was Meg . . . the newest addition to their group. All of them misfits, all of them Markless . . . all of them brought together by Peck.

"So what's your take on the kid?" Jo asked, meaning Logan. She led the three boys through the darkened Fulmart aisles as they talked.

"You really want it?" Blake asked.

"Yeah. I know what Peck thinks. But you're the one who's been watching him, so what's the verdict?"

Blake sighed. "He's a good kid. I wish we didn't have to do this to him."

"Oh, come on!" Eddie chimed in. "It'll be fun!"

"Yeah," Tyler said. "We got some *games* for him."

Blake tried to ignore them. "Anyway, Peck's right. He does need to go."

"And now's the best time. You're sure?" Jo asked.

Blake shrugged. "That's been the plan. Peck's plan, anyway."

"But you agree?"

"This new friend of his could be an issue. But yes. I think we need to pounce."

Tyler started punching him on the arm. "You gonna screw it up, like you did with Trenton? Huh? Huh? You gonna botch it? You gonna drop the ball?"

Blake grabbed Tyler's collar and threw him against the shelves so hard a couple of jars rolled off and crashed onto the floor. "You will *never* say anything about Trenton to me again! Do you hear me, Tyler, you crummy little beggar? As long as we're in this thing together, you will *never*—"

Jo put her hand on Blake's shoulder, calmly. "Enough. Save it for midnight."

Eddie waited until they started walking again to say, "Tyler's right, though. What if tonight doesn't work out? What if this girl put enough ideas into Logan's head that he doesn't show?"

"It's a miracle they ever show," Jo said.

"It's not a miracle." Blake shook his head. "Peck just knows how to pick 'em. And when to move in. If it fails, I'm telling you right now—it'll be the girl's fault."

"Whatever," Jo said. "I suppose if it comes to that, we could just bag 'im, take him here by force."

The boys all laughed. "You crazy?" Blake said. "It'd never work. He's too suspicious now. We can't get close to him if he doesn't want us to. It wouldn't be like it was with Meg."

Jo shrugged. "Logan's always been suspicious. Been jumpy for years, right?"

"He's had reason to be," Blake said. "We've made sure of that."

Jo nodded. "I haven't eyed him in months, since you took over. Maybe more." She paused. "Think he has any actual sense of how much danger he's in?"

"Jo. Come on. Do they ever?" Blake nodded in Meg's general direction, over in the sports racks. The four of them stood now by the Fulmart's back door, about to exit into the moonlit alleyway.

Jo laughed. "Not so far."

"No," Blake said. "Not so far."

And Tyler laughed too, and Eddie, but Blake didn't crack a smile. He just stared at the three of them, very grim, until the whole Fulmart behind them was silent. "Guys." Blake shook his head, and then the slightest, bemused smile did cross his face. "He has no idea."

2

"Starting fires—!"

"*What* were you thinking?"

"It wasn't me—!"

"Who *was* it, then?"

Once the smoke alarms had gone off, the scene in Logan's room turned quickly from one of solitary, quiet horror into a frenzied chaos of anger and panic. Mom and Dad loomed over Logan, arms crossed and catapulting accusations, while he sat on the bed and tried repeatedly to explain in the calmest possible tones that there'd been an intruder, that he'd left a note, and that it was burning by the time Logan found it.

"This has gone too far, buddy," Mr. Langly said. "These delusions are dangerous."

It occurred to Logan to tell them everything. About Peck, about the murders and kidnappings, about DOME's involvement . . . but he'd made a promise. And anyway, he had no evidence of any of it. He'd had enough trouble believing Erin's conclusions while she held the case files right in front of him. If his parents didn't believe his story now, they certainly wouldn't believe him once he turned it into a full-fledged conspiracy. So Logan was stuck. He'd cried wolf one too many times, and now, with one right at his door, his parents couldn't bring themselves to help.

By the end of it, Logan got off with what amounted to a

warning. "But no more acting out," his dad said. And he lumped Logan's "after-school romp" in with the rest of it.

It wasn't two minutes after they left that Logan was on the phone with Erin.

"What's up?" she asked, looking excited over the connection. "Any more clues?"

Logan didn't say a word. Instead he pointed his tablet toward the desk, toward the ashes and the puddle of water.

"Is that—" she started to say.

"A note," Logan told her. "Burning at the time I found it. And someone in the window, watching me read. Now can we go to your dad, please?"

Erin looked disappointed in him. "And tell him what? That you started a fire on your desk?"

"I didn't start a fire on my desk! Someone left a burning note!"

"Well, *you* know that. And *I* know that . . . I guess. But it wouldn't hold up. The kid covered his tracks. There's no trace of him other than a couple of ashes you could have easily made yourself. Is there anything left of the message? Any words or handwriting?"

"No. Nothing." Logan's heart sank.

"Unless it said something so completely incriminating that . . . I mean, were you even able to read it?"

"It said to meet at the Spokie playground at midnight. Or else."

Erin was still for a moment over the connection.

"Or else what?"

"I don't know. Most of the message had burned away."

"But you're sure about all this?"

Logan nodded.

"If you're messing with me . . ."

But the look on Logan's face left no room for doubt. "Logan," Erin finally said. "Do you realize what this means?"

Suddenly Logan felt angry and righteous. "Yes! I know exactly what it means! It means they're trying to kidnap me—*tonight!*"

"Can you get out of the house? Right now?"

"No way," Logan said. "The whole walk home I'm sure I was followed. No way I'm going back outside."

"So you're just gonna sit there and wait for Peck to come get you?"

"He's not coming here. He's going to the playground."

"Yeah, and what do you think will happen when you don't show up?"

Logan knew she was right. "Look," he said, even more nervous now. "My parents are totally freaked out. They wouldn't let me go anywhere right now if I begged."

"Well, can you sneak out?"

"Are you kidding?" Logan asked. "Are you nuts? Of course I can't sneak out!"

"I can," Erin said. And she ended the call.

∃

She was at his window five minutes later. Logan jumped when he saw her, but he opened his stairway door.

"If my parents find you here—"

Erin put her finger to his lips. "They won't," she whispered. "We're leaving."

Logan shrugged impatiently. *And how do you propose we do that?* he seemed to ask.

"Tell them you've had a long day. You're going to bed." And before Logan could object, Erin was pressing the intercom on his wall.

"Yes?" his dad answered through the speaker.

Erin looked at Logan and nodded toward the microphone.

"It's . . . been a long day," Logan said reluctantly. "Think I'm gonna go to bed."

"That's a good idea," his dad said. "I'll be right up."

The intercom cut out, and Erin looked at Logan with a sudden, confused fear. "What does he mean, he'll be right up?"

For a moment Logan was too embarrassed to say it. When he finally did, he said it to the floor. "To tuck me in."

Erin rolled her eyes but spared him outright mockery. Sounds indicated the elevator's approach, and without another word, she dove into Logan's closet and shut the door.

Improvising, Logan stripped down to his underwear and leaped into bed, wondering how his life could have spiraled this far out of control so quickly.

"Think you can sleep through the night?" Mr. Langly asked, the elevator doors sliding open before him.

"I'll be fine," Logan said.

"You want your night-light tonight?"

Logan glanced toward the closet and felt his face grow hot and flushed. "No, Dad. I . . . of course I don't."

"Just asking. Listen, about everything that happened today—"

Logan interrupted him. "Dad." Mr. Langly stopped, and sat, and waited for his son to continue. But Logan didn't. Instead there was silence as something inside him came to an unexpected, rolling boil. "Look, you can't keep babying me all the time, okay? I can take care of myself. I don't need you to tuck me in anymore. I don't need a stupid night-light. I'm almost Marked now. I don't need you to treat me—I need you to treat me like a . . ." With the top blown off, Logan's boil cooled to a simmer, and then to nothing at all. His words fizzled out, and he shook his head, tired and ashamed.

Mr. Langly nodded, understanding, frowning a little. He leaned over and kissed Logan on the forehead with horrible finality. Then he sat still for a couple of breaths. "You got it, bud," he said. And Mr. Langly got up, turned out the light, and let the elevator carry him away.

Logan sprang out of bed and dressed as quickly as he could. "Not a word," he whispered furiously when Erin emerged from the closet. She cooperated graciously. "Now why are you here and what in the world are you planning?"

"My dad's still at work," Erin said. "Thought you might wanna pay him a little visit."

4

The breakout was easy once Erin had finished decoying Logan's bed with pillows. The two of them snuck down the outside steps and made it to the street corner without another word uttered between them.

Erin ran to the streetlamp at the sidewalk's edge and began untying something. Logan strained to make it out under the artificial light of the diodes.

"Is that . . ."

"Yeah," Erin said. "It's mine. In Beacon, everyone has 'em."

A rollerstick. Logan had never ridden one before.

"So that's how you got here so fast," he said.

"Of course. It's the only way to travel."

The rollerstick rested upright, perfectly balanced, above a single metal ball coated in perforated rubber, about the size of a cantaloupe. An electromagnet held the stick in place a few centimeters above the ball. At the top of the stick was a rubber grip, and at the bottom was a small platform for a person's feet. Controlling it was supposed to be easy—just lean any way you want and you'll roll in that direction—but with their quick acceleration and top speeds at over thirty miles an hour, the thought of them had always made Logan nervous.

Erin swiped her Mark over the stick's end and stepped onto its platform. It tilted and rolled, adjusting itself under her weight. "Hop on," she said, and she rolled her eyes when he didn't. "It's fine, Logan. You can hold on to my waist."

Logan felt his palms begin to sweat, but he did as he was told. The ball rolled erratically beneath them and the stick swayed at their feet, but its top stayed steady, like a pendulum, agitated and finding its stasis. Once it did, they stood perfectly balanced, motionless.

"They're not really built for two," Erin admitted, strapping padding to her elbows and knees, "but I can make it work. Just don't shift your weight too suddenly or we're both likely to get ourselves killed." Erin handed him her helmet as she said this, then leaned forward, and, just like that, they were off.

The pair rode along the nighttime sidewalks at a blinding speed, their rollerstick angled so severely that Logan had to crane his head back just to see in front of them—to look forward would have been to look straight at the ground. Erin grasped the stick tightly with both hands, her arms bent but rigid, and the wind blew her hair wildly into Logan's face.

"You say these things are pretty common in Beacon, huh?" Logan yelled over the rush of wind.

"Everyone has one," Erin said. "It's the only way to get around."

Logan tried to imagine it. "Anyone ever get hurt?"

Erin laughed. "All the time. Think I was kidding about getting ourselves killed?"

She shifted her weight slightly, and the two of them turned sharply to the right, down a side road. Logan kept very still after that.

Finally, from behind closed eyes, Logan felt the welcome sensation of slowing down. Erin pulled back into an upright position, and as she did, the stick glided gently to a stop.

Erin turned her head back toward Logan. "You can hop off now," she said. "We're here."

Logan looked up. In front of him was the Center for the Department of Marked Emergencies—two monstrously wide skyscrapers that filled the block from one end to the other, and a spire between them about ten feet in diameter at its base. The spire stretched high into the air, just an elevator shaft and a stairway that spiraled maybe fifty times around it on the outside. At the spire's top was a wide, Frisbee-shaped disk, with several smaller domes above it, making the whole structure look like an odd umbrella, which was in fact how the building was known. Logan had seen the Umbrella many times, but he had never dreamed of going inside.

"This is the DOME headquarters for all of New Chicago," Logan told Erin.

"I know."

"I thought we were visiting your dad's office."

"We are." She headed straight for the spire.

Logan didn't understand. "But DOME's standard offices are way downtown. These Center buildings are for the highest ranks. The Umbrella's for the top of the top——"

"You're right," Erin said. "It is." She raised an eyebrow playfully, and Logan began to understand the extent of what her father's "government work" really meant.

Erin swiped her hand under a Markscan at the spire's base, and the elevator door opened.

"Am I allowed up there with you?" Logan asked.

Erin stepped inside. "Almost certainly not," she said, looking at Logan as though he were the stupidest boy in the world. "So hurry up before someone stops you!"

Logan darted into the elevator.

"You need to learn," she said, "that it's usually easier to ask for forgiveness than permission."

Logan smiled. "And I suppose this is one of those times?"

"You bet," Erin said as the elevator closed and lurched into motion. "I have clearance 'cause I'm family. Though I'm only supposed to use it in an emergency."

"Is that what this is?" Logan whispered.

She glanced at him uneasily, and Logan guessed the answer.

"Just do as I say and keep quiet."

"We're going straight to your dad, right? To tell him what happened?"

Erin looked at the elevator doors. "Just do as I say."

Logan nodded, bewildered by the speed at which he seemed to be breaking rules all of a sudden. "No buttons in this elevator," he noticed idly.

"That how you keep quiet?"

Logan took the hint.

5

When the elevator doors opened, it was to the disk on top of the Umbrella. Logan followed Erin out and he immediately felt a horrifying sense of vertigo. The disk was as big as his school's cafeteria, and the entire enclosing structure was made of glass. Logan looked at his feet and saw nothing below him but the sidewalk, fifty stories below.

"It's tinted so you can't see from the outside," Erin whispered. "But the whole floor's made of glass. Don't be alarmed."

Thanks for warning me, Logan thought. To him, it felt like standing on a cloud, and about as safe. He tried to steady his balance as Erin led him through the space.

Even at this hour of the night, the room buzzed with the frenzied energy of a newsroom or a trading floor. DOME agents worked on long tables that wrapped around the space in concentric circles, the highest ranks at the outer rings along the Umbrella's glass edge. The tables themselves were computers, their surfaces creating one large composite touchscreen over which each agent huddled, shuffling virtual documents with flailing arms and typing or writing with a stylus directly onto the interface. Everyone was busy. When Erin and Logan walked in, not a single head looked up.

"Quickly," Erin whispered. "Very quickly, now." And she ducked back toward the shaft in the room's center, into a manual door resting exactly opposite from where they came in. Logan followed, wondering how they were ever going to find Erin's father.

"I thought we were looking for your dad," he whispered, entering the more private space of the stairwell inside the spire.

"I told you on the phone. We don't have evidence yet. The only way he'd believe us now is if we admitted we'd read his documents."

"So what!"

"So my dad doesn't play around, Logan. It'd take him all of *one second* to throw you in jail for treason. And even if he didn't—even if you wanted to take that risk—without physical evidence he'd just think we read the brief and then let our stupid imaginations run wild." Erin turned and began walking up the metal staircase. "We go to him—first thing—when we have evidence that stands on its own. Not a minute sooner."

"But Peck's gonna *kill* me by then!"

"Oh, give me a break. He's not trying to kill you," Erin said dismissively. "He's probably just trying to kidnap you."

They'd walked one floor up to a smaller enclosed dome above the main disk of the Umbrella. In here, everything was still and quiet, a narrow hallway spiraling out from the spire and lined with unlabeled doors.

"My dad showed me around on Sunday," Erin said. "The Umbrella and the Center, both. Thought it'd cheer me up about the move if I saw how cool his new office was."

"Did it?" Logan asked.

"It has now." The hallway became straighter as they spiraled farther away from the center spire. "We've gotta be sneaky," Erin said. "We're looking for room 113B. Most of these rooms are offices, but 113B is for supplies. At least . . . according to the boxes in my apartment."

"How sneaky can we possibly be?" Logan asked. "I would think there'd be cameras everywhere in here."

"There are," Erin said, looking around and trying to spot one. "But they know I've scanned in, and I'm green in their system. Just walk with purpose, and with any luck they won't second-guess us 'til we're gone."

Logan bit at a hangnail on his thumb. "Are you at least going to tell me what it is we're doing here?"

"If I did, you'd chicken out."

Erin slinked off to the right, opening a door and slipping into Room 113B. Logan scrambled behind her.

It wasn't much bigger than a closet, but the sight of the space stopped Logan cold.

Erin smiled with relief. "Bingo."

"Erin, what *exactly* are you planning?"

"If we're gonna do this," Erin said, "we need to stock up on the right equipment." She had depleted the stash she'd had in her apartment that afternoon just by learning how to use it.

"Do what?" Logan asked, refusing to grasp the insanity of Erin's unfolding plan. "Erin. Seriously, do *what*, exactly?"

Erin grabbed indiscriminately at the shelves and drawers, filling her backpack and lining her pockets with what she now knew as bug tape, surveillance powder, flash pellets, taser beans, smoke bombs, pepper spray, chloroform . . . all the stuff she'd experimented with earlier, and more. She threw a handful of para-phernalia at him and smiled a wicked, knowing, beautiful smile. "Catch Peck tonight," she said. "What else?"

"Erin!" Logan shot a harsh whisper her way. "Are you nuts? This is totally illegal! We're *not* vigilantes. We're *certainly* not DOME agents. Put all this stuff back, and let's get out of here before we get caught!"

"Not a chance," Erin said.

"Erin, I'm just a kid. And so are you. We're not spies."

Erin zipped her backpack and threw it hurriedly over her shoulder. She shrugged. "We are now."

ᄂ

The elevator ride out of the building was tense, and Logan could feel himself sweating the whole way, but they made it. Soon Logan and Erin were speeding down the sidewalks of Spokie with a priceless amount of tactical espionage equipment in their pockets.

"You don't seem to understand," Erin said once they were far enough away from the Umbrella. "This is a war. DOME's the biggest thing Lamson and Cylis have going, and any threat to it is a direct attack against them. Do you want another Total War?"

"Of course not," Logan said, exasperated.

"I know you didn't ask to be on the front lines of this thing, Logan, but you *are*. They didn't send my dad and me across the country for a field trip. Whatever Peck is doing, it's serious. Attacking Pledges is serious. Killing the Marked—and attacking a DOME agent—is serious!"

"I know that," Logan said. "Can you slow down, please?" Logan held Erin tight but felt increasingly unsteady as the roller-stick zipped along the Spokie side streets.

Erin pulled back imperceptibly. "Like it or not, you're part of something big tonight, Logan."

"Then why didn't we just go straight to your father! How is stealing DOME equipment less serious than having looked at a couple of documents?"

"He won't know about the stealing," Erin said. "Besides, this is bigger than that now. You and I, we need to beat this little piker at his own game. Find out what he's up to, find out who he's working with, and turn the whole lot of misers in."

The Markless slurs grated against Logan's ears; he couldn't understand why Erin hated them so much. In Spokie, anyone without the Mark was largely ignored, and Logan had never heard anyone talk like that about them. Like they were less than trash. He didn't quite know what to say. "That's your dad's job, Erin."

"But my dad has to follow the rules. Due process—laws— jurisdictions," she snapped.

"And we don't?" Logan asked, incredulously.

"That's right. We don't." Erin pulled up on the rollerstick and took out her tablet to look at the time. "In forty-five minutes, we're gonna know everything we need to know about this guy. All at once, just like that. No warrants. No bureaucracy."

"And then what?"

"And then I hack into DOME, plant the evidence, and make it look like my dad did all this. DOME moves in, they catch Peck, you get the best night of sleep you've ever had, and I'm on my way back to Beacon in the morning. Piece of cake."

"W-wait," Logan stuttered. "You're going back to Beacon?"

"If we catch Peck, sure. That skinflint's the only reason I'm here."

Logan hadn't understood until now Erin's motivations in all this. Ridiculously, he'd allowed himself to believe it had something to do with him. But of course that was a fantasy. And suddenly he felt himself sour on the whole thing.

"Erin, just stop. This—this is crazy. *You're* gonna hack into DOME. You—a thirteen-year-old! This plan's already so full of holes I don't know where to begin. And you're just getting started."

"That's exactly right," Erin said. "I'm just getting started." The look on her face stopped Logan's protests cold. "Now point me to Spokie's playground."

7

The jungle gym in Spokie Central Park was made almost entirely of wood. *Nothing* in Spokie was made of wood anymore, but the jungle gym was. It had been a decision made at the town hall some years back that the park's playground was tradition. It had been an attraction for generations, residents said, just exactly as it was, and the last thing it needed was plastic and fiberglass and diodes and wires and computer processors and television screens hooked up to the Internet.

Consequently, Spokie's playground was a relic from bygone days. Nothing on it lit up. Nothing on it made noise. Nothing on it moved by itself or performed calculations or computations of any sort. The playground was for climbing on, and that was about it. There had been just enough renovations over the past few years to keep the jungle gym from rotting and falling apart, but not a single thing in or around the area had been replaced or tampered with in any way since the park's unveiling long before the States War.

Blake was aware of all of this. When the sun went down, the playground was the darkest, quietest, most private place in Spokie.

It was also great for playing on. But Blake was not playing on it tonight.

He climbed alone to the top of the old slide, where the view of the park was best. The metal sucked the heat from him, and he shivered a little in the late-summer breeze, scanning the scene for signs that Logan had already arrived, or that anyone unexpected was on their way. *They don't make slides like this anymore*, Blake thought. So high up off the ground, straight and built for speed, hard metal and nothing covering it. *The way a slide should be. A perfect lookout with a fast escape.*

Below him, the scene should have been still. They were all set up for Logan now, and Tyler should have stood, waiting silently in the wooden underbelly of the playground castle's main turret. Meg should have swung gently on the swing, bound to its chains by her hands (but not noticeably), the lone, visible, unintimidating guest of the park, kicking innocently at the ground. And Eddie should have been lying in the sandbox, ten feet away, keeping an eye on her for sudden movements or signs of trouble.

Instead the scene looked remarkably like a jungle gym filled with children at play, which Blake supposed is what it was.

"Guys!" he shout-whispered. "Back to your positions!" He looked at his watch and figured they had about twenty minutes before Logan arrived, if they were lucky.

Jo was far off, hidden, poised to protect Peck and to ensure his escape to safety should anything go wrong. The last thing Blake wanted was for her to have to risk that just to help him calm down the rest of the Dust. That was supposed to be Blake's job.

"I'm serious!" he whispered. "*This second!*"

Eddie grabbed the lower rungs of the slide's ladder and called up to Blake. "Having some trouble with Meg over here. Could probably use your help."

"I can see that," Blake said. "She's not on the swing. What's the matter?"

"She's playing with a mouse she found in the cedar chips. Says she'll only cooperate if we let her keep it for a pet."

"So then we keep it. Big deal."

"But it's dead!"

Blake shook his head and went down the slide, landing on the ground and walking swiftly into the wooden castle. "What is the *matter* with her?"

Eddie shrugged.

"Well, tie 'er up or something! We can't have her acting out on us. Last thing we need is to chase the little beggar down while we're prepping an ambush—"

An explosion behind him cut Blake off midsentence.

"Tyler, knock it off!" he hissed.

"Make me, tightwad," said a voice from somewhere behind the wooden wall.

"I will, ya little cheapskate! Just see what happens if you make me come over there—"

But Tyler already wasn't listening. He yelled over to Meg, who must have been with him, "Okay, okay. New game! Get this—"

"No bottle rocket games!" Blake said at the top of his whisper. "We're here to rendezvous with the target. You can play your stupid miser rocket games another time."

"You just know you're gonna lose."

"Whatever, Tyler."

"You know it's true."

Blake emerged from the castle and strode over to where Tyler was leaning down to the ground, readying another rocket. And that's when he saw motion at the edge of the park.

"Shut up! Get down! I see someone." The playfulness across the park left like air sucked from a balloon. It was suddenly dead silent, each member of the Dust perfectly coordinated. In the corner of his eye, Blake even saw Meg freeze and kneel to the ground, cooperating entirely, aside from the dead mouse she held in her hand.

Blake realized they didn't have the luxury of returning to their assigned places. Slowly, he led the four of them out of the playground area and into the shadow of a nearby cluster of trees.

"That's him," Blake whispered. "He took the bait."

Eddie squinted into the distance. "Wait a second," he said. "Something's not right."

"What's not right? That's definitely him."

"Yeah. Fine," Eddie said. "But he isn't alone."

Blake focused on the shadows and cursed under his breath.

Eddie was right. Logan wasn't alone. He'd brought the girl with him.

目

"Keep your voice down," Erin said, as though she knew what she was doing. "They could be here any minute."

"Erin, we should *not* be here. Please, let's go home before it's too late."

"Not a chance." Erin frowned. "We have one shot at this." Logan shook his head desperately while Erin said, "Let me ask you something. Peck's not a dumb guy. Why do you think he would have left you that note tonight?"

"What kind of question is that? You know as well as I do."

"No, I don't."

"Because he's a sociopath, that's why. He kidnaps kids."

"That's not my question. The guy broke into your room after sundown and left a burning note on your desk. A self-destructing message for your eyes only. What could have *possibly* led him to believe you were going to do anything it said?"

"Was he wrong? I'm here, aren't I?"

"Yeah, but you're here 'cause of me. That couldn't have been his plan. His request wasn't exactly trivial. Why do you think he made it with any confidence?"

Logan thought about it. "I guess . . . I guess he just knew me well enough to know."

"Know what?"

"That I'd be fed up enough to show. That I was tired of the games. That I'd come just to end it, no matter what, I guess. And he was right. Even without you . . . I think I would've."

"That's a pretty specific assumption to make about a person's reasoning in a rather unusual situation, don't you think?"

Logan frowned, saddened at how easily he was being manipulated. "He's been watching me a long time. I guess he has my number."

The two of them arrived at the castle, and Erin set her backpack on the ground. She began rummaging through its contents.

"What now?" Logan asked.

"Now we prepare."

⌐

"What is she doing?" Eddie whispered.

"How should I know?" Blake said.

"Looks like she's throwing powder everywhere."

"Why would she do that?"

"She's pretty," Tyler said.

"Shut up."

Among the chatter, Meg sat silently, petting her mouse, which was still dead. Blake was glad she had something to distract her—his one stroke of luck the whole evening. The four of them sat perched, totally invisible, in the shadows, fifty feet from the castle where Logan and his friend stood.

"We wait to see what she's up to," Blake said. "No one moves until we're sure."

10

"This is surveillance powder," Erin said. "Powerful stuff." She sent it around the play structure in chalky billows, which hung in the breeze before settling invisibly to the surfaces and ground. "It's made of nanomics, essentially. They're sensitive." She took out a small tube that looked like it might have held hair gel and squeezed a pea-sized glob onto Logan's finger, as well as her own. "Now rub this into your ear canals."

"I'm not gonna—"

"Just do it." Erin put her finger in her ears, and Logan followed suit. "Really get it in there."

It felt cool in Logan's ears, and he could feel it dry and cake onto his skin.

"Now walk ten feet that way."

"Great idea, Erin. Separate us in the darkened playground where we know *for certain* a convicted killer is waiting to abduct me. How 'bout a round of hide-and-seek while we're at it?"

Erin rolled her eyes. "Fine. Take this if it'll make you feel better." She handed him one end of a clear piece of twine. "It's a weapon. You'd use it to choke a person. But we'll just use it to keep tethered to one another. Now walk."

Logan looked at the twine and hoped with all his heart that he would never have to choke anyone, ever. But he held the twine tightly and walked away from Erin, all the same. Once he'd gone a ways out, Erin cupped her hand over her mouth and spoke quietly near the area where she'd dispersed the chalk. "Can you hear me?"

It was as if she'd whispered it right into Logan's ear. "Loud and clear," Logan whispered back. But Erin shook her head. He returned to her side.

"It's not for communication; it's for surveillance. The gel in our ears is tuned to the powder. Anything anyone says around this play structure, we'll be able to hear. Even a whisper. Even a breath. You could walk five miles and still hear what was happening in this castle. Hold on to that twine, by the way. You might need it."

"How much does this powder cost?" Logan asked.

"It's not for sale. As far as anyone outside DOME knows, it doesn't, strictly speaking, exist."

"Well, that's just great," Logan said sarcastically. "And here we are with a bucketful."

"Yes, Logan, for *security*, so we know who's around." She rolled her eyes. "Wind should carry it out to a pretty far perimeter."

"Fine," Logan said. "So now what do we do?"

Erin was glad he asked. "To catch Peck, we need tangible, recorded evidence. That means laying a wire." She pulled something else from her backpack. It looked like a roll of Scotch tape. "This stuff does the trick." She began lining the upper corners of the castle with it, standing on tiptoes to reach. "Everything this tape picks up is sent directly to DOME headquarters. They have a system recording day and night. At least that's how it seemed when I hacked into their system this afternoon."

"You *what?*"

Erin ripped a piece off and smoothed it out with her fingers. When she'd finished, the tape was invisible, and you could run your hand directly over it without feeling it was there. "I bet you'd be amazed, the places you'd find this stuff," Erin said, shaking her head.

"I thought your dad never told you DOME secrets."

"He doesn't. I'd be amazed too. Anyway, after tonight, I'll be able to quarantine the data from whatever's recorded here in the DOME system, so I can control who sees it and where it goes."

"This is through your magical second hacking session later on?"

"Not magical. I learned from the best." Erin thought of Mac and smiled, thinking how proud he would be.

"Clearly," Logan said.

"I'll be watching closely," Erin told him. "And I have the surveillance gel, so I'll be able to hear anything that goes on as soon as it—"

"Wait, where are you—"

"He'll never show if I'm here with you," Erin said, as if Logan should have realized this. "But I won't be far."

"Erin, you can't leave me here."

"Oh, don't be a baby," she said. "You're almost Marked, remember? Don't even need a night-light."

Logan gritted his teeth.

"So your job," Erin said, as if uninterrupted, "will be to get Peck to say something we can use against him. We already know he's guilty, so the point's not to entrap anyone—we just need clues. Where Peck's been hiding, where he's trying to take you, what he's done with Meg . . ." Erin's face grew a little dimmer. "On the other hand, if events do start to deviate from what we might call . . . our ideal scenario . . ." She paused for a second. "I guess . . . just try to make sure they deviate with this in your pocket." She handed him a small button. Logan knew what it was.

It was a tracker.

11

"I don't like this," Blake said, still in the shadows. "She's planning something."

Eddie squinted. "What is all that stuff she has?"

"No idea. It's high-tech. But it's clear she's laying a trap."

"That meddling little—"

"Tyler, I need you to find Jo. Tell her to relay to Peck—we're packing up. I'm calling it off."

"I told you you'd blow it," Tyler said, grinning.

"When we get back to Fulmart, I'm gonna strangle you in your sleep."

"Too bad I'll be sleeping on a shelf too high for your fat hands to reach." Tyler disappeared into the shadows, giggling as he went.

"He's right," Eddie said. "You blew it. We should've pounced before school started back up."

Blake didn't say anything for a minute. Then he just said, "You're right, Eddie. I blew it."

12

Logan looked at his tablet: 3:00 a.m.

"I don't get it," Logan said into nothing, knowing Erin could hear him. "Where is he?"

A minute later Erin appeared from the shadows. "You made it up, didn't you?"

"What are you talking about?"

"You set your own fire."

"I saw a *face* in my *window*—"

"An easy lie. You met a pretty girl and got her attention, and you thought you'd take advantage of it. You win, Logan." She sighed.

"I didn't *lie* about anything! And this wasn't my idea—it was *yours*! I have no idea why Peck didn't show! Maybe he saw you *bugging* the place and decided—"

"Right, Logan, of course it's my fault. That's convenient."

"Whatever," Logan said. "This could have gone a lot worse. 'Least you didn't get me killed tonight."

"Yeah, there's that," Erin said without sincerity. She had her fingers in her ears and scraped violently at the gel inside, tearing it out in flakes that she flicked impatiently to the ground. "Stupid echo," she said. "Can we at least move to where there isn't so much powder? Everything I say shouts back at me inside my head."

"I've got a better idea," Logan said. "Let's go home."

"Fine." Erin went to her rollerstick and grabbed its top, dragging it behind her with visible frustration as she walked away from the playground.

"We're not gonna walk—"

"Yes, we are," Erin said.

"It's over a mile back. It's three in the morning—"

"Too bad."

"But what about your roller—"

"It wasn't built for two."

121

The walk back to Wright Street from the park seemed longer to Logan than it ever had, and it was silent except at the end, when he spoke.

"What do you suppose he wanted?" he asked. "If we hadn't scared him off, I mean . . . what do you think he really wanted from me?"

"He was never coming," Erin said. "Admit it."

"You not believing it won't change the truth, Erin."

She looked at him and frowned. "I'm not going home anytime soon, am I?"

"That I don't know. I have a feeling we came close to something tonight, though. Closer than it seemed."

"Maybe." Erin shrugged. "Or maybe you're just stringing the new girl along."

"Right," Logan said sarcastically. "Anything for a second date with 'the new girl.' Since tonight was so dreamy and all." He paused and kicked a rock, sending it skipping down the sidewalk. "I'm not, though."

"I can't believe we took all this stuff," Erin said, changing the subject. She bounced the backpack on her shoulders, glad it was too dark for Logan to see the blush she felt in her cheeks. "Maybe I can return it."

"Or maybe it'll come in handy yet."

Erin shrugged. "Either way."

They turned onto Wright, and Logan could see his house ahead.

"Don't get caught on your way back in," Erin said.

When Logan snuck back into his own bed, in his own room, he was more tired than he'd ever been.

How long had he been asleep when Logan woke to the whisper in the dark, its faint vibrations directly in his ear?

"Surveillance powder. Very clever." There was a pause in the words, and the stillness of Logan's room rang in their place. *"Well, Logan, if that's how you want it . . . we can play this little game."* And then a rushing sound filled Logan's ears, like water crashing inside them, and his line to the chalk went dead.

Logan lay under the covers with his eyes wide and horrified. He didn't sleep again after that.

SIX

REGROUP

1

LOGAN STOOD IN THE SAHARA WING AT Spokie Middle, just staring out the fake window into the virtual dunes beyond. The sand was red and untouched, isolated from everything and everyone. It was all Logan wanted, to be there, to forget about this week and the world of trouble he was in.

"You okay, Logan? You look like you've seen a ghost." Logan jumped; Hailey had come up behind him and spoken before he knew she was there.

"Something like that." He laughed and turned around. After everything else that had happened, his memory of seeing Hailey last night on the sidewalk felt like it was from years ago.

"It was nice bumping into you yesterday, briefly." Hailey stared intently at her hands, which she was wringing. If there was anyone in Spokie more nervous-looking than Logan, it was usually Hailey.

"Yeah." Logan chuckled. "Sorry about that . . . whole . . . running off thing. What can you do, right?"

"Right." Now Hailey looked out at the desert too.

"I'd rather be there," Logan said, without turning to Hailey. "Of all the hallways in this school, if you could, which one would you go to?"

"The moon," Hailey said.

Logan laughed. "Probably the one place farther from people than I chose."

"Do you like the new girl, Logan?" Hailey asked. The quiver in her voice was gone. She asked it with purpose.

Logan didn't know what to say. "We get along all right," he finally admitted. "It's not romantic, if that's what you—"

Hailey made the smallest sigh, barely perceptible, but Logan heard it. "You always say we should hang out more. But we never do." Hailey was paying close attention to the wind on the dunes.

Girl trouble? Now Logan was having girl trouble? Is that really what this was, on top of everything else? How much crazier was eighth grade going to get? He thought back to last year, when his biggest concern was algebra, and whether or not he'd get the last throw in during his food fights with Dane and Tom at lunch.

"Well, let's hang out," Logan said, heading this complication off at the pass. "Seriously. I mean it. I think that'd be great."

"Okay," Hailey said, brightening up immediately.

"Sometime next week?"

"Good," Hailey said.

Logan smiled inwardly. His sudden excitement surprised him, and yet it was sincere. A date next week with Hailey—that'd be all right.

But this was silly. It was hardly a date. It was hardly anything at all.

And if it was, how would Erin feel?

Fine, Logan. Erin would feel fine. Don't kid yourself. Erin wouldn't bat an eye. After last night, she doesn't even like you as a friend right now.

And in any case, the way things were going, Erin would probably be on her way back to Beacon by next week.

Or Logan would probably be dead.

"What should we do?" Logan asked. "We don't have Marks. We can't even get ice cream."

"We'll take a walk." Hailey smiled. "Walking's still free."

Now Logan smiled too. "Cool. All right," he said. "Well . . . see ya."

Logan sighed and turned to make his way to English. What he didn't see was Dane, waiting at the end of the hall.

He didn't see Dane's clenched fists.

And he didn't see the look on Dane's face.

2

At lunch, Logan found Erin sitting by herself on the lawn above school in the one patch of sunlight between the shadows of the surrounding buildings.

"You hear it last night?" Logan asked.

"Hear what?"

"I don't know what time it was. A voice. In the gel. It was faint, but the powder picked it up."

"I don't know what you're talking about," Erin said.

"Erin, you *must* have heard it."

Erin chewed her soy cheese sandwich and looked toward the sun, closing her eyes and letting it warm her face. "I didn't hear anything."

That's when Logan remembered Erin getting fed up on the playground. She'd picked the gel right out of her ears before they'd even left the scene. *Great*, he thought, *she won't believe this either.*

"Well, it happened. It must have been Peck. He showed last night, I'm sure of it. After we'd left."

Erin laughed. "That's a likely story. Did he come with a unicorn?"

"Look!" Logan was quickly losing his temper. "I'm sorry last night didn't go perfectly according to your crackpot plan—which was no less dangerous just because we weren't kidnapped, by the way—but I have no reason to make up any of this stuff. You're the one who wants it to be true so bad. I'd much rather see it all go away."

Erin stuffed the rest of her lunch into her backpack. Logan noticed the equipment still inside.

"But if you can get over your self-pity for two seconds, I got to thinking last night."

Erin looked at him, eyebrows raised. *Impress me*, they seemed to say.

Logan could not believe what he was about to propose. Just two days ago, it had seemed insane to him, impossible. But the game was different now. "I don't know how it is in Beacon, what you do with your Markless—"

"In Beacon they sleep on street corners," Erin said. "Filthy, begging, crazy, dangerous. They're a menace. They're useless. They're picked up by the street cleaners with the trash and the spit."

"—but in Spokie the Markless mostly stay in an area called Slog Row. They stay away from us, and we let them be."

"That's very civilized of you."

"Well, it's that or—forget it, I don't need to defend Spokie to you. That's not the point."

Erin squinted at him in the sun. "What is your point, Logan?"

"My point is that whether or not you've given up on this thing already, it seems to me that we . . . or *I*, if that's how it's gonna be . . . that we might be able to find some dirt on Peck if we . . ." He sighed, his heart pounding just at the thought of it. "If we took a little detour through Slog Row one of these days."

Erin shook her head. "If you were right about that, DOME would have been all over it already."

"I'm sure they have tried. I'm sure they'd love to be. But the Markless won't *talk* to DOME," Logan reasoned. "DOME's the enemy."

"They have ways," Erin said.

"Oh yeah? And what would those ways be? DOME can't send a mole in 'cause all their men are Marked. Anyone on Slog Row would spot it a mile away. I suppose they could bug the place with some of that nano-equipment you stole . . ."

Erin picked at the plasti-grass. "Unlikely, actually, without a warrant. Laws still protect the Markless unless you can catch them for a crime. And DOME's a huge bureaucracy. Unless they have proof Peck's staying there—and I'm sure he's not—they wouldn't risk botching his trial."

"So there you have it. Slog's not an avenue for DOME. The two groups cannot work together. People on that street have nothing to lose. They'd sooner die than help an agent. I'm sure some have." Logan shook his head. "It's a closed door to DOME." He looked at his empty wrist. "But it's not to me."

Erin considered this. "Let me get this straight. You wanna visit Slog Row . . . ourselves?"

"Yeah."

"To find a trail that leads to Peck."

"It's not as elegant as your bug tape, I admit."

"Forget elegant—it sounds deadly. That whole street must be seething with degenerates and crackpots."

"The people there are desperate, yes. You'd have to be crazy to visit."

But at the sound of the unfolding plan, Erin got a look in her eyes that was precisely that.

"What are you doing after school today?" Logan asked.

"I dunno." Erin shrugged, but she couldn't help smiling just a little, playfully. "I could be free."

彐

At the Fulmart, Blake sat with Tyler and Eddie while they opened condensed soup from the store shelves and drank straight from the cans.

"Good thing this stuff doesn't go bad," Tyler said. It looked about ten years out of date, which is precisely what it was.

The three of them couldn't talk about the night before. Only the Dust actually slept in Fulmart, but at mealtimes, Markless from all over Slog Row came to scrounge for food.

The store was maintained by an elderly couple known as Mama and Papa Hayes, who took it upon themselves to watch over the place when it went belly up, seeing it for the lifeline to the Row that it really was.

It was all sorts of illegal, of course, for a Markless couple to appoint themselves "managers" of a bankrupt store and continue running it as a black market for other Markless. But it wasn't *more* illegal, necessarily, than many of the other things happening on Slog Row, and, as with the rest of it, the Spokie authorities recognized the value of an insular system that kept the bums away from the rest of town.

So this afternoon, as with every afternoon, families rummaged the shelves, taking what they needed under the watchful eyes of the Hayeses, but never taking more than enough. Mama and Papa made sure everyone knew the limits of the supply, and the punishment for greed was banishment, with the help of a seriously illegal shotgun.

Today, a small boy covered in dirt and tattered clothes sat silently next to Blake and Tyler and Eddie as they ate their lunch. He might have been five or six years old, and he visited them often during mealtimes, eating some small portion of something and listening to the boys' banter. He seemed to enjoy their company, though he'd never once uttered a sound. Blake had long since given up on learning the boy's name, so he and the others just called the kid Rusty. Under the filth, Rusty had bright, messy red hair. Blake guessed that if he hadn't been so dirty, he might have had freckles too.

Today the boy ate a bag of chips. He licked his fingers for the salt.

"Any good?" Eddie asked.

Rusty nodded. Tyler and Eddie stayed on better behavior when he was around. Maybe they liked the company too.

"I like that flavor," Tyler joked. "Don't eat all of it, okay?"

Rusty smiled and guarded the bag closely.

"Do you have a mom or a dad?" Eddie asked for what was probably the fifteenth time since they'd met the boy. "Anyone who takes care of you?"

Rusty didn't nod or shake his head. Blake wasn't sure the kid fully understood the question. "Let it go," Blake said. "It doesn't matter."

Around them, couples strolled the aisles, pretending for a few minutes out of the day to live normal lives. They read the labels on packages, compared ingredient lists and nutritional information. Blake knew it was a pretense. The only food left in the store was junk. And everyone holding the boxes was frail and starving.

"Afternoon, Mama Hayes," Blake said. "Papa Hayes." A little less than a year ago, Mama and Papa Hayes started finding the kids of the Dust hiding out in their store during the Hayeses' nightly sweep of the place. The first dozen times, of course, they kicked the group out without discussion. But somewhere along the line, the old couple realized these kids weren't looking to take anything or cause any trouble. They were just looking for a place to sleep that wasn't quite as cold as the hard winter ground. So the Hayeses made them a deal—if the Dust would watch the store at night and make sure no one came around after hours looking for more than their share, then Blake and his friends could stay.

"How are you boys this afternoon?" Mama Hayes asked.

"Just fine, ma'am," Eddie said. "A little tired, is all."

Mama Hayes nodded. "Us too, boys. Us too."

After lunch, Blake and the others headed to the "outdoor adventure" section of the store. Between tents set up for display and various skiing and hiking equipment, there was some space for games. Eddie had a soccer ball from the sports section, and the three of them kicked it around while they talked more privately.

Meg sat in the corner, tied to a pipe, not moving or blinking. It wasn't long before Joanne joined them.

"Hey, Jo," Blake said, kicking the ball to her. "What's the good word?"

"Today we regroup," Joanne said. "When you're ready, Peck wants to speak to you."

Blake suddenly became very nervous. "He here now?"

"No. Can't risk it after last night. You hear he went back after we'd all come home?"

"Why'd he do that?"

"Wanted to scope it out. See what Logan and that chick left behind."

"Sounds risky," Blake said. "He shouldn't be out on his own right now with things as they are."

"He knows that, but he had to see what we were up against. 'Laying a trap' wasn't specific enough for him, I guess. Anyway, I gather you haven't heard what he found when he went back."

"You're the only one who could have told me."

"Surveillance powder."

Blake frowned. "Never heard of it."

"He says DOME's been using it to follow him for a few months now. It's this new stuff—nanotech—like microphone dust, apparently. DOME fills a place with it and then they can listen to you as long as they want. You can't stumble across it, you can't find it."

"How'd he figure that out?"

"Peck's an observant guy. Anyway, water cleans it right up if you know where to look for it. He thinks he got it all, but he's not sure. So stay away from the playground from now on."

"Well, that sucks," Tyler said.

"Deal with it."

"Wait a second." Blake was beginning to understand the breadth of their new problem. "What you're saying is that Logan's new girlfriend has access to DOME-grade equipment."

"Not just DOME-*grade*. It's the real stuff. Straight from DOME."

"She's a kid. That's not possible. They have kid agents now?"

"Who knows how she got it. Or who she is." Jo clucked her tongue. "But we got a new player in town."

"Well, what do we do now? Give up?"

"We can't. Before yesterday, Logan was a problem. But we had the advantage. Last night the tables turned."

Eddie chimed in. "So I say we forget about the little miser. Let him go—he won. He's not worth getting caught over. Let's just move on to another kid already."

"That's not the point, Eddie." Jo kicked the soccer ball to him. "The point is, Logan's gone from being a problem to being a threat. He's tipped off to us now, and instead of falling into our little setup, he went straight to DOME."

"How'd he know to do that? *How'd* he do that?"

"Doesn't matter. What matters is that we stop him before he stops us. The stakes just changed. The game just changed."

"So what's the plan?" Blake asked.

"We redouble our efforts."

"But, Jo, he saw me. He saw my face. I need to lie low."

"I know that."

"Then what now? What do we do?"

"Peck's at the warehouse until tomorrow, collecting his thoughts. He's asked you to visit him tonight." She sighed. "And that's precisely what he wants to talk about."

4

"Hey, Dane!" Logan called out in the Arctic Wing at the end of the day.

Dane looked at him. He didn't say anything back to Logan.

"I still wanna see you ride that rollerstick! Think your dad'll start it up for us?"

"Not for you," Dane said. He shook his head, as if Logan had said the least considerate thing in the world.

Logan frowned. What was this about? Was Dane mad at him? "Hey, man, everything okay?"

"Whatever." Dane shrugged.

"Wait, what'd I do?"

Dane stared at Logan a moment before letting out two years' worth of pent-up jealousy all at once. "It's not enough to have all the attention of the new girl, huh? You gotta claim Hailey too?"

"What?" Logan asked, genuinely confused.

"I saw you set up your little date with her today," Dane said. "Real smooth."

Logan couldn't believe what he was hearing. "Dane, look, first of all, whatever that thing is with Hailey, it's not a date. And second of all, Erin's only even interested in me because . . . well, listen, it has nothing to do with her liking me, all right? Also, why do you even care?"

Dane shook his head. "You honestly never figured it out, did you?"

"Whoa, dude, back up." But upon hearing this, Logan immediately realized how much sense it made. Dane liked Hailey. How had Logan never realized it before?

"Just stay away from her, okay?" Dane said. "I'm serious."

"All right," Logan said. "Fine."

Dane nodded. "Fine."

But before Logan could say anything else, Dane turned, abruptly changing character. "Hey, Hailey—where're you going? Stop being so weird!" and he ran down the snowy tundra hall.

Logan still felt rotten when he made it up to street level, and when he approached Erin on the sports lawn, she only made matters worse. "Hey!" Logan called, but when she saw him, Erin swerved quickly to walk down the street without him.

"Erin, wait up!" Logan yelled, and to his frustration she walked even faster. *Great*, Logan thought, *so everyone's mad at me.* It was a full block before she made eye contact with him, and then when Erin did, she crossed the street away from Logan, to walk on the other side.

"What's the deal?" Logan yelled.

"Do I know you?" Erin said, and then she turned a corner down a side street and out of sight. Logan broke into a full sprint after her.

"Erin, what in the world is this all about?" he demanded once he'd caught up to her.

"We can't be seen together," Erin said dramatically.

"Why?" Logan asked. "Because of Dane?"

Erin laughed. "Huh? Of course not. Why would you even—"

"Never mind," Logan said quickly, and Erin narrowed her eyes.

"Listen, if you're right about what you heard last night," she said, "and I'm not saying you are. But *if* you're right about any of it, we need to start being more careful about how we act."

"Oh," Logan said. "Right."

"I mean, either you're lying to me about that whole playground ambush, or you screwed things up so the deal didn't go down, and whichever one it was, it got me no closer back to Beacon."

"Yeah, okay," Logan said, his voice dripping with sarcasm. "Totally—your getting back to Beacon City is so much more important than me not getting kidnapped and killed. Sorry. For a minute there, I forgot why I was doing all this."

"Oh, give me a break," Erin said lightly, hitting Logan's shoulder. "You're all right."

Logan looked at her, and Erin's bright smile immediately cleared the dark clouds around him. He knew she hadn't quite forgiven him for things going wrong last night. But she hadn't given up on him either.

They walked without speaking for a few blocks.

"Hey, what's so great about Beacon, anyway?" Logan asked after a while. He genuinely wanted to know.

"It's not about the city, Logan. It's about my family." Erin frowned. "You wouldn't understand."

Logan shrugged and said, "Still, the city must be cool. My dad calls it the greatest architectural achievement in history."

"Of course it is," Erin said. "That goes without saying. It's the center of the Western world."

"We're not so far from New Chicago, you know. If you want to see a city—"

"New Chicago's *rural* next to Beacon," Erin said.

"Oh."

"Beacon . . . ," Erin began. "First thing you need to know about Beacon—it's right on the water."

"Okay."

"Like, the waves literally come right up to it—come between some of the buildings, even, lower down on the hill."

Logan had seen videos online but tried to imagine it now through Erin's eyes.

"And City Center's way high up, right? So first of all, anywhere you are, you get this beautiful view of the ocean, day and night."

Logan had heard of this too. The Rupturing of the Dam was a pivotal moment in the States War, and every student in the A.U. knew the story. At the time, the East Belt Dike protected the old capital and all its surrounding land from the Atlantic Ocean that had long since risen above it. But a few years into the fighting, one of the states, led by General Lamson, decided to blow the thing up, and most of the coastal states were destroyed in the ensuing flood. So Lamson had a huge hill constructed over the ruins of the old capital, rising half a mile high and with a ten-mile plateau on top. Lamson named it Beacon and finished leading the war effort from there as a new metropolis began to grow rapidly around him. After the Unity, Lamson chose Beacon City for the new A.U. capital, as a reminder of how the war had been won and how peace had been achieved. These days, City Center filled the entirety of the hill's plateau, and expansion had continued quite a ways down the sides, right to the water's edge. This was fine for the first few years, but nobody expected the water to keep rising. When it did, Beacon's outer boroughs flooded. It happened slowly, though, so rather than relocate, the outer-borough skyscrapers were simply reinforced, and east of City Center, people just got used to getting around on boats and bridges.

"But that's not all," Erin said. "Six layers of roads and sidewalks connect City Center—one on the ground, and *five* suspended in grids above it."

"Why do you need that?" Logan asked.

"Are you kidding? You'd never fit all the people and roller-sticks and trams and electrobus traffic on one layer. Besides, it'd be way too annoying to have to enter every building from ground floor all the time."

"How high do the buildings go?"

"From bottom?" she said. "You can't see the top."

Logan tried to imagine it, and could, but barely. The whole city sounded like a fantasy.

"And there're lights and screens and speakers the whole way up, on every one. People are *alive* there, Logan—24-7. Spokie is dead by comparison. It's rotting in the ground."

"Thanks."

"You'll see, someday," Erin said.

"I doubt I'll ever make it out there."

"Well, that'd be a shame." Erin frowned.

"I guess," Logan said. "I'm still hoping I make it through the week."

5

Slog Row was a couple miles from Spokie Middle, and the walk there seemed endless. The last stretch was barren, a no-man's-land, where the buildings went from run-down, to abandoned, to condemned, to crumbling, to nothing at all—just empty lots filled with trash and hazardous waste. And then, on the horizon across the silent, old expressway, it stood: the haven for the Markless. Logan could not believe what he was about to do.

"We'll start with the firehouse," he said. "A lot of people probably stay there."

"Outlaws, Logan—psychopaths. Stop calling them people."

Logan looked at her. "Maybe it'd be best if you waited outside."

"Fine with me," Erin said, and she slipped her hands into the pockets of her shorts. "But if you're in there longer than ten minutes, I'm calling DOME."

Logan shrugged. "I wanted you to call them last night."

He looked up. Outside, the firehouse looked like it might fall down any day now. The roof sagged, the walls were torn apart with large pieces missing altogether, the windows were broken or missing entirely. The stoop leading to the front door (which rested, unattached to any hinges, against the wall) was covered with trash, stains, and graffiti.

Inside, the firehouse was much worse. The stench was awful. People sat, slumped in the corners and along the edges of the room, and mice scurried between them, often right up to their legs. Logan had never felt so out of place. But he didn't feel scared. For as long as he could remember, he'd always been warned to stay far away from the Row, far away from these dirty, sordid people with their unpredictable behavior and their desperate acts. But standing here now didn't match up with those stories of danger and risk. The scene in this firehouse wasn't frightening. It was tragic.

Logan held his hand up so that anyone who cared could see his empty wrist. Only one man, reclining on the crumbling steps that led to the second floor, seemed lucid enough to notice. Logan walked over to him tentatively, his heart pounding out of his chest.

"Hi," Logan said. "I have food."

At this, several others looked up and eyed Logan with cautious hope. He put his backpack on the floor and unzipped it, suddenly very glad that he hadn't had the appetite to finish his lunch. "It's not enough," he apologized. "I'm sorry." Somehow it never occurred to him how much his leftovers might matter to people living so close to his own front door. They were just a couple miles away . . . and yet they lived in a different world entirely.

But the man on the steps didn't seem to mind. He smiled a great, big, toothless smile.

"Aw, eh, yer gottem food, ah?"

Logan struggled a little to understand him, but at the words, he extended his half sandwich to the man, who took it. Logan saw that where the man's hands touched the white bread, they left dark, filthy smudges.

"What's your name?" Logan asked.

"Oh, eh, Wallace, um?" It was almost another language.

"It's nice to meet you, Wallace. You eat that, now. It's good, and . . . and I just made it this morning."

But Wallace had already finished the sandwich. He burped, and a couple wet crumbs tumbled down his chin.

Wallace couldn't have been more than thirty-five, Logan guessed. Certain signs of youth were unmistakable. And yet Wallace was, in so many ways, an old man. His missing teeth were just the beginning. Those that remained were yellow and stray and broken. His eyes were yellow too, and his hair, while long and drawn back in a brown ponytail that reached past his shoulder blades, was unduly thin and fragile. The man's skin was leathery and covered in liver spots. His clean-shaven face made matters only sadder, since it suggested that this was a man who cared about his appearance . . . who was doing everything he could for it.

Others had gathered now, men and women of all walks of life, some very old, some younger, all close to death. Logan divided his leftover carrots and celery and apple slices among them.

He guessed he'd been in here nearing on ten minutes now.

Almost time to go. Logan made idle chatter with the group around him, asking about their afternoon, how it was going, and mentioning the sunny weather. The group smiled, laughing softly, perhaps not quite understanding his words either but nodding even so, touching his shoulders, hugging him, shaking his hands, thanking him . . .

Logan wondered if these people had ever had a visitor, had ever been given a sandwich made that day, or an apple, or carrots and celery that still crunched. Somehow, he couldn't bring himself to ask about any of that.

He didn't ask about Peck either.

ㅂ

"How was it?" Erin asked. "Was it awful? Are you all right? You look dirty. You smell terrible."

Logan didn't answer right away. He came off the stoop and walked immediately down the block, toward the houses a few lots over. Erin rushed to follow him.

"It was fine," Logan said finally.

"Hear anything about Peck?"

"No. Not in there."

"Was it scary? Are you okay? Did they hurt you?"

Logan shook his head but didn't speak, and Erin didn't ask him anything else about the firehouse.

"We need to find some younger Markless. They must be around." Logan wasn't sure if he'd suggested it as a strategy, or simply because he needed to see someone with some life left in him. Either way, up ahead was a stretch of houses with younger people, late teens and early twenties, sitting and shouting to one another on stoops. Logan and Erin approached.

"You're lost, kiddies. This ain't Old District," one girl yelled. Erin seemed to shrink into herself, but Logan fired back.

"Good thing," he said. "I wouldn't take those hoarders' money if *they* begged *me*."

The girl on the stoop narrowed her eyes. Logan held his hands so his wrists were showing, though he didn't make a big deal of it.

"What's the pretty doing with you?" the girl asked, nodding at Erin.

"She's thinking of losing the Mark," Logan said. Erin glanced at him sideways, frightened. Last night, she was in her element. Today, Erin very much was not.

"You can't lose it, sweetheart," a guy said from another stoop. "You can't ever lose it."

"Can if you cut your arm off," Logan said. Erin let out a stifled yelp, but no one besides Logan seemed to hear.

The people on the stoops lifted their eyebrows, intrigued. Logan made his move.

"We're looking for a man named Peck," Logan said. "I'm wondering if any o' you fine folks had some ideas."

Immediately, laughter erupted from the stoops of houses all the way to several lots over.

"Nice try, DOME. Move along, now, move along." They weren't intimidated. They weren't shy about it. They just laughed and shook their heads as Logan and Erin passed, ashamed.

"Cavalier *and* ineffective. Very impressive, Logan. You play it that cool in the firehouse too?"

"It was worth a shot," Logan said. "We still managed to learn something."

"Which is?"

"They know the guy. They know he's wanted. They're on his side."

"Correct me if I'm wrong, Logan . . . that all seems like *bad news for us.*"

"It is," Logan agreed. "But at least now we know it."

⌐

Back in Old District, Dane Harold spun in circles on his dad's rollerstick while Hailey watched. "It's really not so tough!" he said, though he swung wildly and fell off to the ground as he did. "Wanna give it a try?"

"No," Hailey muttered, her arms crossed.

Dane shrugged, feigning total apathy. "Fine. I gotta practice the mitts anyway. Did I tell you the Boxing Gloves are playing a concert at the end of the month?"

"Yeah."

"It's a battle of the bands."

"Mm-hm."

Dane had hoped for a more enthusiastic response. "Well. I'll see you around, then."

"Can I try your mitts?" Hailey asked.

"Um . . . sure," Dane said. "Yeah, cool. Of course." *It really must be a whole new school year*, he thought. Hailey hadn't given him the time of day since the summer after fifth grade. She lived just past Old District, so yes, she often walked home along the same streets as Dane. And sure, quite regularly, she'd stand, arms folded, insulting him for a few minutes before she'd continue on and go home. But she'd never asked him to let her come in. And he wasn't about to waste the chance to spend more time with her.

Dane's house was one of the few remaining pre-Unity homes in Spokie. Old District was the wealthiest district in town, and among the wealthiest in all of suburban New Chicago. The streets here were wider and lined with enormous trees. Most of the greenery in Spokie was made of bushes and saplings, five years old at best before they shriveled and died. But in Old District, the trees were taller than the buildings, with great big trunks so wide that if Dane and Hailey had stood around one, they couldn't have touched hands. Presently, the two of them walked under the green shade of an oak much different from the skyscraper shade on the rest of Spokie's streets. Warmer. Brighter, somehow.

The homes in Old District were only two or three stories tall, but they were huge. Each sat on nearly an acre of property, and they stretched out over a good bit of that land with many adjacent rooms and hallways and wide-open space inside them. Dane's house was built in what was called the Tudor style, which Dane didn't much like talking about. In fact, Dane didn't much like talking about Old District at all, and Hailey guessed that his flashy jeans and high-tech black t-shirts, whether Dane realized it or not, were a certain kind of disguise. But not even cyberpunk clothing could hide the fact that Dane came from money.

Inside, the place was even showier than Hailey had remembered from her visits as a kid. Dane led her quickly through the bigger rooms of the house, with their sculptures in the corners and paintings on the walls, and he didn't seem at ease with himself until they'd reached a small den in a far corner where he kept his music gear. Posters hung sloppily on the walls, and food wrappers cluttered the corners.

Dane reached down and picked up his new pair of wailing mitts. They were a sleek red that sparkled a little in the light, each one of them a hemisphere, like a high-tech turtle shell, with a strap on the bottom for a wailer to put his hands through. Dane handed the pair to Hailey, and she tried them on. The straps closed tightly on her palms, and her fingers and thumbs slipped into ten rings on the underside of the shells.

"You turn them on here," Dane said, and he flipped separate switches on each. Immediately they hummed a musical drone. "Now, um . . ." Dane seemed a little nervous. He moved her hands so that they were held out horizontally from her body, his palms a little sweaty on hers. "This is standard position. Hear the sound it makes?"

Hailey nodded.

"Now, if you move your hands up or down, notice what happens." The drone raised in pitch as she moved her hands up and lowered as she moved them down. "If you tilt your hands, that affects the timbre." Hailey tilted her hands out so that her palms faced up, and the drone became distorted and much harsher. She tilted them back and it went gentle again. "The farther you hold your hands out to your sides, the louder the mitts'll get. Those rings on the inside, they'll play your notes for you. There's a lot of different combinations, so the mitts have a pretty wide range, once you get the hang of it."

Hailey pulled her fingers against a few of the rings, and notes rang out like a cross between an electric guitar and a keyboard synthesizer.

"That's pretty much it," Dane said.

"You try." Hailey handed the mitts over to him.

"Well, I'm still learning," Dane said sheepishly. But as soon as he'd strapped on the mitts, Dane was moving, watching for

Hailey's reaction. His arcs were jerky at first, stilted and nervous, but as Dane played, he seemed to forget she was there. He closed his eyes. His movement smoothed. It became dance-like and intricate—real music, and beautiful. Dane was a natural. When the song ended, he looked at her.

Hailey nodded curtly. "You don't suck," she said.

"Whatever, weirdo." It was the happiest Dane had been in as long as he could remember.

曰

"It's getting dark, Logan. Can we admit this was a failure yet?"

Logan and Erin had walked most of the way down the Row at this point, and everyone they met was either too decrepit or too defensive to know or say a single thing about Peck. But even Erin had to admit—everyone recognized the name . . . in some cases, seemed to revere it.

"I wanna try one more place," Logan said. He stared at the Fulmart ahead. "Just one more, and we'll go home."

"I'm holding you to that."

Logan shrugged. "Either way, we've reached the end of the Row." Beyond the Fulmart, the road ended, and a hill with young, thin trees led off to nothing. Logan's tablet rang. He looked at it and saw it was his dad calling. Logan declined the call.

He and Erin stepped between boards covering the front window of the big-box store. The only light inside was natural, coming from windows and holes in the ceilings. Nothing inside the store seemed to work anymore—none of the lights, vents, or security cameras, or the displays that, years ago, must have lit up and made noise and moved around for attention. But the store wasn't empty. Packaged food still sat here and there on the shelves, and remnants of toys, hardware, furniture, house supplies, and outdoor equipment still dotted the shelves in a couple of places.

"Hello?" Logan called. "Is anyone in here?" With all the aisles, it would have been easy to hide.

"Nobody here but us chickens!" someone called out, and suddenly Logan was being pelted from several directions with Nerf darts and tennis balls.

Two boys popped out from their hiding spots, laughing hysterically, but when they laid eyes on Logan and Erin, they froze so suddenly that it seemed all the life in them had just spontaneously dropped out from a trapdoor under their feet. The room was silent and tense.

"Who's the visitor?" a girl called from a few aisles over. "What's going on?" And then she, too, stepped out into the greeting area where Logan and Erin stood, and went silent and white.

"Can we help you?" the girl asked. She was bigger than either Logan or Erin by thirty pounds, pretty, not dirty or famished like the other Markless on the Row, and with a deathly cold stare.

Logan cleared his throat, uneasy. It was the first time that afternoon he'd truly felt scared. "We're looking for someone," he said. "Just want to talk to him, and we thought someone on this block might know where he was." Logan held his arms up.

"Put 'em down," the girl said. "I know you're not Marked." She looked at Erin, who held her hands in her pockets. "And I know she is."

Logan looked from boy, to boy, to girl. "Anyway," he said finally. "The name of the guy we're looking for . . . is Peck."

The girl before him didn't blink or flinch or move in any way. "Sorry," she said. "I don't know anyone by that name."

"Pack? Did you say Pack? Maybe he said Pack," one of the boys said to the other.

"We don't know any Pack," the second boy said.

"Okay." Logan nodded. "Okay. Sorry to bother you, then. We'll be going now. You have a good night." And he and Erin backed away slowly until their heels pressed up against the storefront doors. They stepped outside and ran quickly across the parking lot toward home. The girl watched them through the window the whole way.

ᑫ

"They're the ones," Erin said. "They know everything about him."

"Them?" Logan said. "They were scary, but . . . just 'cause they threw a couple tennis balls at us doesn't mean—"

"I could care less about that," Erin said. "I'm talking about Peck."

"What about him? They didn't even know the guy's name. Of everyone we talked to today, *those* are the kids you single out?"

"They're the only ones who had something to hide."

"I don't know," Logan said. "We were trespassing. That could have been all it was."

"I don't think so." Erin shook her head. "They're trespassing too. They don't own that store. They don't own anything. They're Markless."

"You don't think . . ." Logan thought of something new. "You don't think Peck could be . . . *working* with anyone, do you?" He had never considered that the boy he'd chased to Slog Row might have been anyone else. If that was true . . . he and Erin were even further from cracking this case than they thought.

"That's exactly what I'm thinking," Erin said. The sun was

setting. They were almost running now, back to the main part of town. "I think he's working with them."

"It's a stretch," Logan remarked, but he didn't dismiss the idea.

"Maybe it is, and maybe it isn't." Erin shrugged. "Either way . . . I know how to find out."

"I don't think I wanna hear it," Logan said.

"You don't," Erin agreed. "I'll tell you when I'm done."

10

"Well, that didn't go well," Tyler said.

"Could've gone better." Jo sat, expressionless, on a lawn chair near the beach section of the store.

"You think they saw us last night?" Eddie asked.

"It's possible," Jo said. "But I don't think so. They didn't seem to know who we were. At least not when they walked in."

"But now . . . ?" Tyler said.

Nobody answered him.

"He's smarter than we gave him credit for," Eddie said to Jo.

She sighed. "What he is—is fearless."

"And the girl?"

"She knows way too much."

"So what now?"

"Blake's left for the warehouse to discuss plans. We'll see what he comes back with." Still reclining, Jo kicked a beach ball into a shelf of Tupperware and knocked a half dozen plastic containers to the ground. A couple of them hit Meg, who growled.

"Stop it!" Eddie grabbed Jo in her chair and shook her. "You don't do that in here! This is our home!"

"Not anymore it's not," Jo said. And she shattered a sand castle display with a volleyball. "Pack your stuff. We're moving on."

11

It was nighttime when Blake arrived at the warehouse, and even the moon had sunk far below the horizon, so Blake moved carefully under pinpricks of starlight in the blackened sky.

By necessity, Peck had become more than a little reclusive in recent months. In the early days, he'd been the linchpin of the Dust. He'd shepherd them, rile them up, calm them down, teach them games, make them feel at home—wherever that home happened to be. He'd feed them and clothe them, he'd moderate disagreements, he'd make them think and teach them tricks about life without the Mark. . . . To the boys especially, he was more than just the leader of the Dust. He was the father.

And now he was a ghost. Only Jo saw Peck with any regularity ever since Meg's abduction prompted the DOME investigation. Tyler and Eddie hadn't seen him at all, and even Blake, Peck's right-hand man, had met with him just twice—first to receive his new set of responsibilities while Peck was away (watch over the boys, make sure Meg doesn't escape or kill anyone, and spearhead the intelligence effort on Logan while Joanne tended to other things), and second to discuss the plan of attack against Logan that was supposed to have played out last night. That attack having failed spectacularly, tonight would mark Blake's third visit to the warehouse, and for the first time, he wasn't looking forward to it. Twice along the way, he even turned around to head back, unsure if he could handle Peck's disappointment—but Blake pressed forward. The Dust was all he had.

The warehouse was well outside even the outskirts of Slog Row, in a sort of no-man's-land far beyond Spokie but just before the next town over. It was an old building, back from pre-Unity days, Blake guessed, judging by its bizarre architecture, with once marble-white stone walls and an ash-colored roof. Now graffiti and a thick layer of dirt made it seem dull and gray. The facade sloped up to a high point in its middle, with spires at each corner and a tall steeple to the side. The walls around the building were filled with colored windows that had pictures in them—of people and shining stars and scenes as if out of a story—at least the ones that weren't broken. The large double doors should have led, welcoming, into what must have once been a pleasant space inside, but instead they stood shackled, boarded shut and padlocked, the building around them closed and forgotten.

But not to Blake.

On the side of the big building was a bush, behind which was a small grate that led into a crawl space under the floorboards of the building's basement. Blake entered it, thanking the darkness for shielding him from seeing the spiders and rats and the confines of the claustrophobic space. He inched across the dirt until he came to a trapdoor outlined in pale light from above.

When he emerged, Blake stood inside a cavernous space, filled floor to ceiling with crates and boxes and the glowing of distant lights through those colored windows, and from candles at the room's end.

"Peck," he whispered, though he could see no one there. "It's Blake. Jo sent me."

"Come in, my friend, come in." The voice echoed across the space, bouncing off the high ceilings and through the maze of crates stacked fifteen feet high in haphazard rows.

"It's hard to see," Blake said, and as soon as he had, Peck appeared from between the boxes, holding a candlestick in one hand and a book in the other.

"You'll get used to it," Peck said, and he tucked the book under his arm to shake Blake's filthy hand. "You look hungry. Let's eat."

At the edge of the room was a podium on a raised stage, and beside it was a row of chairs. Blake sat in one, brushing the dirt off his clothes and skin, and Peck brought him a loaf of bread, which they split.

"Jo brings me plenty of food," Peck said. "From all over town. So eat as much as you'd like." The way Peck said it made Blake glance down at himself and wonder how much weight he'd lost since they last met.

"The new girl—" Blake began.

"I know," Peck said.

"I heard her conversation with Logan last night—well, part of it. Before everything went down. They just met, Peck, but she's dangerous."

"We'll keep an eye on her too," Peck said.

Blake took a deep breath. "That's the thing, Peck. I'm not so sure—"

Peck stopped him right there. "Eat first," he said. "We have all night to talk." And Peck opened the book to a page his thumb had held and read while Blake ate.

"Where'd you get that?" Blake asked, chewing the bread. You couldn't buy printed books anymore in Spokie, and everyone just read on tablets and screens, if they read at all.

"From here," Peck said. "These crates are filled with them. All pre-Unity, from what I can tell."

"This is a warehouse for . . . books?"

"Yes. Banned, I gather . . . I've yet to recognize any."

"Why?" Blake asked, his mouth full. "What's in 'em?"

"Lots of things." Peck sighed. "But it's hard to tell which really happened and which were made up."

"Listen. About last night," Blake said, unable to let go of the guilty feeling that was nagging him. "I know I should have pounced earlier . . . I know I shouldn't have waited for school to start. I tried to do it the weekend before . . . like we planned . . . I just . . . he was doing that sweep thing he does around the house, and I . . . I chickened out. I failed. I'm . . . I'm sorry . . ."

Peck was quiet for a moment. His expression was calm. "Back up," he said patiently. "Tell me everything you've learned since we last met."

"Not much," Blake said, shamefaced.

"What about the girl?" Peck pressed. "All I know of her is what I found left behind on the playground early this morning. Though that told me quite a bit."

"She's from Beacon," Blake said. "She just moved here."

Peck frowned at the thought. "What's a Beacon girl doing in Spokie?" he asked.

"I overheard something she said about her father being trans-ferred. She doesn't wanna be here."

"What's her father do?" Peck asked.

"I don't know."

"It's my assumption that he works for DOME. Is that plau-sible, from what you heard?"

"I dunno. I guess. It was hard to hear; I was using a cup against a wall."

"Okay," Peck said. "But I'm thinking her dad may have been transferred here because of me. Jon? Trenton? The investigation? We knew they had their knives out. But is DOME really so worried they'd send a Beacon man after me? I want to know what you think."

"Maybe," Blake said. "That would make sense."

"The girl knew too much about last night going into it . . . came too prepared. The only way to explain that is if she knew about Meg's case. I don't think any of those details've been released outside of DOME. So that means this girl must have a connection to the Department."

"Like I said, her dad being an agent would make sense."

Peck nodded.

"So what now? What do we do about Logan? He's a threat."

"Yes. He's a threat. But he's not unstoppable. We have to regroup. Keep on him—"

"That's the thing, Peck. I . . . I don't think I'm your guy."

"You're wrong," Peck said. "You are. You brought us Meg, right?"

"Yeah, but—" Blake protested.

"You warned me about Trenton, didn't you?"

"Yeah, but, Peck—"

"You're good at this, Blake. I can't have you getting cold feet."

"What about Jo?"

"What about her? She's busy with her own tasks."

Blake thought for a moment. "Look, I'm not getting cold feet. I can trail this new girl maybe a little bit, but—"

"Don't lose sight of the goal. I don't care about *her*," Peck said. "I care about her as she pertains to *Logan*. I care about *everyone* as they pertain to Logan. He's our biggest concern right now; he was even before all this happened—"

"And I can't keep spying on him, Peck, I'm sorry, but I can't. He's seen me. Twice. I've been careless."

"Stop apologizing."

"It's not just the risk of eyeing his house anymore—that kid sees me *anywhere* and he's calling the cops. Then they get to me, and they use me to get to you, and it's all over. Right?"

"That's right," Peck said. "You're right. That's all I needed to hear. Our next steps, then, have been decided for us."

"Eddie? Tyler?"

"No. I don't trust them," Peck said. "Not for something like this."

"But the goal is still—"

"Yes. The goal is the same."

"I don't know what to tell you, Peck. He's too suspicious now. And with that girl by his side, he's too aggressive. We needed a precise amount of fear for him to do as we said. Like Meg. We had it with Logan. I really think we did. But it's gone now."

"You're exactly right, Blake. It's gone." Peck put his hand on Blake's shoulder. "You've done great," he said. "I want you to lie low for a while. Keep an eye on Meg. I hear she's . . . restless."

"Okay," Blake said. "But what about Logan? The clock's ticking. Soon as November comes around—"

"Oh, I know," Peck said. He took the plate from Blake's lap and rested it on the podium behind him. "So we move to Plan B. Logan is simply too important to let go. Jo made a new contact for me last year, to help keep tabs on our other target."

"*Another* target? Who?"

Peck hesitated, weighing whether or not to tell him. Finally he decided. "It's a boy named Dane. He's what you might call . . . a cyberpunk. Has a rock band. He's a rebel."

"You think we need to pounce on him too?"

"I do. Yes."

"He seem worried yet?"

"No," Peck said, rubbing his eyes. "But he should be."

"Well, who's the contact?"

"Don't worry yourself with that," Peck said. "The important thing is Logan. It appears, now, that our contact will need to track him too. Which is fine," he added before Blake could apologize again. "I can arrange that. And anyway, this person, while not as experienced as you, does have a distinct . . . *advantage* . . . in our particular situation."

"What's that?" Blake asked.

"Logan's trust."

Blake frowned. "I don't follow."

"Fear is a powerful manipulator. It's been our strategy all along. But when you can get it . . . *if* you can get it . . . trust works even better. Best, in fact." Peck paused, thinking. "Our contact is a student at Spokie Middle, even shares a few classes with Logan. Has for years."

"And you got this person working for us?"

"That's right," Peck said.

"Logan's own classmate, spying on him at school? Leading him right into our hands? Without him even *knowing* it?"

"Now that we need this person to, yes." Peck shrugged. "Plan B."

Blake smiled.

And Peck returned to reading his book.

SEVEN

DUST ON THE LAM

1

I GOT IT WORKING. WE'RE IN BUSINESS," Erin practically shouted over the tablet connection.

Logan had been asleep, but the excitement woke him quickly. "Got what? What are you up to?" Logan asked it with a sigh, knowing he wouldn't like the answer. He was more than exhausted—he was ashamed and reeling. For him, the night had ended in a huge fight with his dad—the biggest they'd ever had. Late for dinner for the third night in a row, and deliberately dodging his dad's call this time, Logan had come home to find that he was standing on very thin ice. He'd always had a strong relationship with his dad, but in the last few days, he felt like he'd destroyed it almost completely. His dad seemed to be chalking his behavior up to teenage hormones, and Logan didn't know which was worse—that his dad thought he was turning into a moody, lying teenager, or that his dad had no idea just how much danger Logan was really in.

"The Fulmart. Where those kids were this afternoon."

"What about it?"

"I hacked into the Spokie power grid—"

"Erin!"

"Let me finish. I hacked into the Spokie power grid and fronted some juice to the Fulmart's old security system. Remember all those cameras on the ceiling?"

"Nope."

"Well, there were cameras on the ceiling; they just weren't on. So I got them going again. *And* I tapped into the data stream. I can see everything happening in there, right from my tablet."

"Well . . . that doesn't sound any *more* illegal, necessarily, than everything else you've been up to the last couple of nights."

"It isn't," Erin assured him.

Logan sighed and shook his head for her to see over the shaky video connection of his tablet.

"Well, don't you want to know what I've seen on this thing?"

"Yes, absolutely," Logan said.

"They're packing up. They're packing up shop!"

"What are you talking about?"

"They're leaving! The kids are gathering their stuff. They're moving on!"

"Isn't that bad news? They're fleeing. If they ever did represent a trail for us, it's about to disappear."

"True." Erin frowned. "But it as good as proves they're in cahoots with Peck."

"You think?"

"Are you *kidding*? Two strangers mention *a name* to them and a couple hours later these misers are leaving their *home*? Yeah, Logan. I'd say that's a pretty sure sign of a guilty conscience. Sprinkled with plenty of paranoia. We have them running scared!"

"This is all moving too fast," Logan said. "I think you were right today about us needing to be a little more careful."

"What? No! We can't slow down now. The tables have turned! Logan, wherever these pikers are going, it's gonna lead us straight to Peck!"

"But they're leaving right now. We're gonna lose them."

"*I'm* not," Erin said. She pointed the camera of her tablet away from her face, revealing her rollerstick and a blur of Spokie streets rushing past. "*I'm* almost there."

2

Erin raced through the town at a blinding speed. There hadn't been time to go to Logan's and convince him to come along. He just would have argued—and slowed her down.

Grab this thing by the horns. Get it done. Pull your family back together. Make it back to Beacon.

Of course, for all its people and flashing lights and noise and busy streets, Beacon never actually had this much excitement.

Now that she thought about it, Beacon didn't exactly have Logan either.

Whatever. He's just a boy. And he's mostly not even that good-looking. Or funny. Or cool. And he definitely doesn't like you much. Doesn't like you at all, Erin. He's made that pretty clear.

He's just a stupid boy, and Beacon is home. Focus on the mission.

And with that, Erin pushed all thoughts of Logan away.

She arrived at the Fulmart parking lot several minutes later and ducked into the shadows to watch the video feed on her tablet. The night was dark. Perfect for a stakeout.

The scene in Fulmart was unfolding quickly. Below the camera and amid the static of the weak connection, Erin could see the three kids running frantically, stuffing store items into bags, which they'd also taken from off the shelves. They were stocking up. They weren't coming back.

A fourth kid entered the scene too. A second girl, it seemed, different from the others. Every once in a while she'd hit one of them, not playfully—hard—and at one point she seemed to try climbing up to the ceiling to get out of the other three's reach. Finally the larger girl put an end to it with a swift knock to her head.

Throughout the chaos, the two boys of the group continued to roughhouse. They'd chase one another around the aisles, throw things, wrestle. Something about these kids was deranged. It was clearly a group that stuck together, but everything about its members seemed just a little . . . off.

A good crowd for Peck to hang around with, Erin decided.

She watched the scene inside for a good fifteen minutes before her concentration received a startling interruption.

"This was not the plan. This was *not* the plan!"

"*Man*, Logan, you just about scared me to death!"

Logan was out of breath and wheezing. "Good! How could you be so careless? Do you have any idea where you are right now? This is Slog Row at *midnight*, Erin! What are you *thinking*?"

Erin was dismissive. "Relax. I wouldn't have come if this wasn't important."

"Important to who?"

"Important to *you*! I'm trying to help you, you idiot!"

"Important to *me*? *You're* important to me, Erin. Don't you get that?"

Erin looked quickly down at her tablet, pretending to watch the security video feed. She didn't know what to say.

"And don't act like you're doing this for me. We both know you're just trying to get back to Beacon."

Erin cleared her throat. "Anyway, now that you're here, you can be of some use. By the looks of it, the beggars are fleeing out back. Smart choice, not to expose themselves in the parking lot."

Logan sighed. "And what exactly are we planning once they exit?"

"We're going to follow them. I think we should approach from different angles. If they split up, so do we. I don't think we can take the rollerstick. It's quiet, but not as quiet as we'll need to be. Anyway, by the looks of them, they won't be travelling too fast. Do you see how squirrelly these two boys are? And they've bound one of the girls. She didn't seem to wanna work with *any* of 'em."

"Some group of criminals."

"You said it. I think they're in over their heads."

"They have Peck on their side, don't forget that."

"Yeah. But no wonder he steers clear of them."

"Not clear enough, we're hoping."

Erin smiled. "Not clear enough. That's exactly right."

ヨ

"Okay, skinflints, knock it off!" Jo shouted across the Fulmart. It quieted momentarily. "We're out of here in five minutes, you understand me? Say your last good-byes."

"Good-bye!" Tyler shouted.

"Good-bye!" Eddie yelled.

"I never liked your layout!"

"Your sports section is weak!"

"And your shelves make terrible beds!"

"Yeah, peace out, Fulmart!"

"We're outta here!"

Meg hissed from Jo's shoulder.

Suddenly the back door opened. Everyone froze, including Joanne.

"Hello?" Jo said. "Hello?"

"What's going on in here? What's with all the shouting? You guys gone crazy?"

It was Blake. Blake was back from Peck's.

"Blake!" Jo dropped Meg on the floor with a *thud*. She flung her arms around him. "I'm glad you're back. We're leaving."

"*What?* Why?"

"Logan and the girl. They came by today, after you left."

"They came *here*?"

"That's right."

"How'd they find us?"

"We don't know. We're not sure it wasn't an accident. They were looking for—" She lowered her voice to a whisper and covered her mouth. "They were looking for Peck."

"Then it's worse than we thought."

"That's right. They're out for blood."

Blake shook his head. He whispered too. "Then we'll give them blood."

"But it's not safe here anymore. Not with that girl's tricks. If she doesn't have the place bugged by tomorrow, I'd be shocked. We're leaving tonight. Right now, now that you're back."

Blake nodded. "Where we goin'?"

Jo looked at him. Then she made a quick look around the store. "I'd rather not say."

Blake understood. He gathered a backpack's worth of stuff for himself, and the five of them prepared to leave.

"Think we'll ever be back?" Eddie asked.

"I don't know, Ed," Jo said. There was sadness in her voice.

"Bit off more than we could chew with this one, didn't we?" Tyler poked. "This Logan's a real tightwad."

"He's a challenge," Blake said. Then he whispered, "But Peck thinks he's worth it."

Eddie shook his head. "Then Peck's gone mad."

And Jo hit him so hard he'd never say so again.

4

"They're moving out." Erin folded up her tablet and stashed it in her pocket. No need for the video feed anymore. "We follow them all the way, but we never reveal ourselves. You got me? They need to think they're getting away. They need to think they're safe."

Erin's blood pumped furiously, her brain at full alert, her eyes locked on the cluster of skinflints ahead of her. But with Logan to her left, crouching invisibly in the shadows, she couldn't help but let her mind wander a little.

He came for me, she thought. *He was worried.* She hadn't expected that when she'd snuck out tonight. But she didn't follow the train of thought to its conclusion. She didn't allow it to reach the part where Logan had said, *"You're important to me."* Because that wasn't possible. He couldn't have meant it. Could he?

Logan, meanwhile, had one eye on the kids and one on the

darkness, right where he knew Erin was hiding beside him. Why had she come out tonight? Risking everything on her own in the worst part of town? What was in it for her?

Only home, Logan decided. *Bringing her family back together . . . moving back to Beacon. That's the tie that binds us. I'm just her ticket home.*

5

Dane Harold didn't much like spending evenings anywhere but in his den. He hated his bedroom. With its wide spaces and bare walls and impeccable neatness, it didn't even feel like his. Dirty clothes or stray wrappers from a previous night were always gone by the time he came home from school, and he'd long since realized that even his attempts to spoil the place were futile. Once he'd taken a pocketknife to his desk during a particularly frustrating homework session, cutting profanities into its surface with a wicked delight. The next day Dane had a new desk. To him, the message was crystal clear: these are not your things, and this is not your room to ruin.

The living room was worse. It had a ceiling that stretched nearly thirty feet high. Its polished wood floors and priceless art made Dane feel like a visitor in a museum, not a kid in his own house. And it made him feel ashamed. No one outside the few blocks surrounding his had homes like this or wealth like this, and the other kids in Old District who did were brats. So where did that leave Dane?

But the den was his. No one went in there but him—not his mother, not his father, not even the family's not-strictly-legal live-in Markless housekeeper, George.

Dane sat there now, noodling on his wailing mitts with the volume just a little too loud. He knew it, but he didn't care. Dane *never* had friends over at his house these days. And he had not been ignorant to the look in Hailey's eyes as she passed through the rooms on her way to the den, taking everything in. Did she see him as one of *them*, just another jerk from Old District, sitting on his acre of land? He cared about what she thought, Dane realized in his most honest moments. He cared a lot.

Maybe he'd sleep in here tonight, right in his cyberpunk clothes, curled up on his beanbag chair in the corner. Better than the king-size bed waiting for him upstairs, with its bleached white sheets. Better than the mound of pillows that suffocated him in his dreams.

"Master Dane?" George called gently from behind the closed door. He made no attempt to open it. "Do you think maybe it might be time for bed? Your parents have been asleep for some time now, and the noise cancellation in their walls can only go to such lengths . . ."

"George."

"Yes, Master Dane?"

"Open the door. Speak to my face. Don't call me *master*."

George opened the door a crack and poked his head around it apologetically.

"Oh, just come in already, will you?"

George did.

"Just . . . don't clean anything, okay?"

George stood at attention in the door frame.

"Close the door. Sit down. Just treat me like a kid, will you? Stop looking at me like that."

George found a stool by Dane's electric drum set and sat on it awkwardly.

"Something wrong this evening . . . Dane?"

"Do you hate it here, George?"

George looked at him, perplexed. He didn't answer.

"I won't tell my parents. I'm on your side, if you do."

"I don't," George said. "I don't hate it here."

"But haven't you ever thought about . . . just getting the stupid Mark, already? I mean, seriously, you wouldn't . . . you don't *have* to live this way."

"I know that, Dane."

"Then what in the world are you thinking? Why won't you just do it, already? Get out of here? Let my parents *pay* for a maid. Or take care of themselves, for Cylis's sake."

George smiled. "I told you, Dane. I like it here."

"You like living in a room to the side of a house that's not yours? You like calling my two rotten parents 'master'? Calling *me* 'master'? Being compensated in table scraps?"

George sighed. "There are things more important than material wealth, Master Dane." And very quickly, he flashed to Dane a charm, which dangled from a necklace he'd kept hidden under his suit. What was it? A symbol? Of what? Dane had never seen it before, but it seemed somehow rebellious to him . . . dangerous.

"What is that, George?"

George winked. "A reminder, Dane. Just a reminder."

George had left Dane after that, closing the door behind him, leaving Dane to play his mitts as long as he wanted, increasing the noise cancellation in the walls as he exited.

It wasn't until very late that Dane shot up and realized he'd fallen asleep with his mitts still on. He threw them to the beanbag. What was that noise?

A crack. A snap. Motion outside the den's window. Dane dashed to it and cupped his hands around his face, peering outside. Who was there?

Dane bolted through his house and out the front door, onto the lawn. The night was cool and damp. "Hello?" Dane called. "Show yourself, ya stingy miser."

There was no response. Just the stillness of night. The oak tree whistled in the wind.

Dane crept to the window outside his den, looking for signs of trespassing . . . or trespass*ers*.

No one was there. But in the flowers below the den's window, Dane saw three chrysanthemums bent and broken, lying in the dirt, trampled.

"I heard you!" Dane shouted into the black of his empty cul-de-sac. "I'm calling the cops!"

And when Dane went back inside, that's exactly what he did.

"I'd like to report a disturbance," Dane said over the video connection of the tablet. "Trespassing. The perpetrator got away."

"Noted," the woman said, unimpressed, on the other end of the line. She frowned. "Can you show me your Mark, sir? Just holding it up to the camera is fine."

"I'm not Marked," Dane said. "I'm underage."

A wave of interest suddenly flashed over the woman's face. "I see," she said. "Another one."

"What do you mean, another one?" Dane asked. "What is that supposed to mean?"

"It's probably nothing," the woman said. "But if you see or hear anything else out of the ordinary—*anything at all*—I want you to call this number." Then she flashed the digits on the screen.

Dane recognized the extension number. It was famous, drilled into children's heads right along with the codes for fires and police and medical emergencies. But the number was different from those. It was unique. The number was for DOME.

ᗡ

The Dust travelled silently through browned cornfields, already an hour's walk out of town. Tyler didn't devise a game. Meg rested limp and dull on Jo's shoulder. This was not a happy field trip, and everyone knew it.

But Blake knew something else too. *You can force us from our home, Logan. You can keep us on the run as long as you want. But we're not your big concern anymore. And Peck has a trick or two left up his sleeve.*

So you wanna play a game with us, Logan? Sure, we'll play a game with you. We'll go a round. We'll even go all in. Take a chance, Logan. Call our bluff. See what it brings you.

He couldn't hold his excitement any longer. There was hope, and he had to let someone else know it. "Logan's gonna have some fun at school from now on," Blake whispered to Joanne.

Jo nodded. She smiled too. Jo knew exactly what that meant.

"Boo!" someone whispered behind the two of them, and Meg stifled a yelp on Jo's shoulder.

Blake turned abruptly. "Don't *do* that, you little skimp!"

It was Eddie. Blake had sent him off earlier to do a sweep of their trail and make sure no one was following.

"See anything useful?" Blake asked. "Or were you just hanging back there long enough to scare us?"

Eddie leaned in, serious but perfectly relaxed about it. "A little of both," he said. "But, yes, we're being followed."

⌐

"They're walking in circles."

"What are you talking about?"

"We've been through this cornfield before. Half an hour ago. They're walking in circles." Logan looked at Erin in the dark and shrugged.

"Do you think they're lost?"

"Not sure," Logan said. He squinted across the field, over the husks. "But I only count four kids up ahead. Maybe one's lost and they're looking for—"

But a powerful knock to the back of Logan's head proved him wrong.

Erin screamed, swinging around to see a short girl planted behind her with a rock in her hands. The girl's eyes looked violent and unsympathetic under her thick set of bangs. Without hesitating, she hurled the rock at Erin, who barely deflected it off her arm. Immediately, Erin's hand went numb, and her elbow swelled in a way that made it hard to bend. Logan shuffled on the ground, trying to regain a sense of his surroundings.

Now three boys and a second girl encircled them in the clearing between rows of corn.

"You got 'em, Meg!" one of the boys said, jumping up and down. "Two points! Two points!"

"Shut *up* with the names!" the oldest boy whispered harshly.

"Why does it matter? They're not going anywhere."

"What do we do with them now?" another boy asked.

They weren't expecting retaliation. With her good arm, Erin flung a taser bean at the oldest boy's face. It stuck to his forehead and glowed lightning blue as it crackled and hissed. He fell to the ground with a dull thud.

"She killed Blake!" the smallest boy yelled, as if it was a game to him. "She killed Blake with her magic beans!"

"Shut up with the *names*!" the older girl said, and she smacked the boy hard before kneeling down to tend to Blake, who had started convulsing. Both smaller boys jumped on Logan now, pinning him to the dirt. He flailed, looking for anything to grab, tugging at their clothes and raking his fingers through the dirt.

Behind him, Logan heard another electric crackle as Erin flicked a second bean toward the girl named Meg. This one stuck to Meg's hand and glowed blue, her arm in spasm while she looked on in horrified fascination.

It was enough to get the two smaller boys' attention. They lessened their weight on Logan, and this gave Erin the chance to shove them off balance and pull Logan to his feet.

Together they sprinted into the shelter of the corn.

目

"They tricked us," Erin breathed when they were safely hidden in a nearby patch of trees. "The little cheapskates tricked us!"

"It's not the first time," Logan said, touching the back of his head gingerly.

"Well, excuse me for not being a pro at this," Erin said. "First week on the job, and all."

"But it wasn't a failure," Logan said. He winced at the sharp pain in his head.

"In what way?" Erin asked. "We showed ourselves and got nothing for it. Now they'll *always* be watching for us, *and* we don't know where they're going."

"Well, you're half right." Logan smiled. "They'll be watching. And yet . . ."

Erin laughed. "Oh, what, you have some magical clue as to where they're headed? I got news for you, Logan—they could have left that field in a million different directions. At this rate, DOME will find them before we will."

Logan looked puzzled. "Would that be a bad thing? Isn't your goal just to finish this case and go home?"

Erin shrugged. She honestly didn't know anymore.

"Anyway," Logan said, "I *do* happen to have a clue as to where they're headed. But it isn't any more magical than those taser beans." He leaned over and pointed to Erin's tablet. She pulled it out and he took it, calling up the map application. "Last night at the playground, you gave me a tracker—"

"You didn't . . . ," Erin said, realizing.

Logan nodded. "During the scuffle. I stuck it to the smallest boy's jeans."

Erin saw the glowing dot moving across the map, and her face grew bright and happy. "Oh, Logan, you're a genius!" she said, and she threw her arms around his neck in a big hug.

Logan didn't mind that the jolt sent his head injury into excruciating throbs. A hug from Erin was worth it.

"Look," Erin said after several minutes. "They stopped."

Logan studied the map. "The old stadium," he said, almost admiringly. "Clever . . ."

"What do you mean?" Erin whispered.

"They went to the old baseball stadium. Spokie's team moved to a new one a few years back, but the old structure's still standing. No one uses it anymore." Logan smiled. "Until now, that is."

"You think they're gonna camp out in a baseball stadium?"

"By the looks of it . . . yes."

"But that's so exposed."

"Not if no one ever goes there. The place was gutted years ago. It's not even a destination for sightseers."

Erin groaned as she thought it through. "And it's impossible to bug."

"Too big," Logan agreed. "Your powder can't fill a stadium, and there probably isn't enough tape in all of DOME. No security cameras either, I bet. All that's left are the stands . . . and the diamond."

"Smart little misers," Erin said.

"I wish you wouldn't call them that."

"Fine. Stingy skinflints." Erin smiled. "You like that better?"

"They're people, Erin. They're kids, actually. Like us."

Erin looked at him like his brain had dropped out and hung from his nose. "Are you kidding? They blindsided us with a rock an hour ago—"

"We were following them—"

"They had us surrounded!"

"They attacked in defense. And so did we."

"They're out to kidnap you, Logan. They're killers. And they're Markless. They're lower than dirt."

"No—they're not. They're people just like us."

"That girl must've clocked you pretty hard in the head," Erin said. "You're talking nonsense."

Logan sighed. He knew he wasn't going to win this one, so he changed the subject. "We need a new plan."

"You think Peck's in there?"

"I doubt it. It's a good hideout for the rest, but Peck wouldn't risk it. He's got to be somewhere . . . deeper."

Erin cursed. "They didn't lead us to him after all, did they?"

"Not yet. That's my guess, anyway."

"They will, though."

"They could. At the very least, we've bought ourselves some time. No way they make a move on me in the next few days. Not in this scenario."

Erin shrugged. "Let's go home. We know where they'll be. We can figure out a plan tomorrow."

"At school," Logan said. "Never thought I'd look forward to it so much."

"Our last safe haven," Erin agreed.

The two of them made their way back to Erin's rollerstick.

Logan was grateful for the ride home that night.

9

Hailey had just returned from one of her late walks through Spokie, and she wasn't surprised to find her mother asleep. But she needed someone to talk to. So Hailey knocked gently on the door of her mother's room, waiting for the rustle of covers, already sorry for waking her up, but not knowing what else to do.

"That you, Hailey?" Mrs. Phoenix said, before breaking into a spasm of coughs.

"It's me, Mom," Hailey whispered, her cheek to the door. "I'm sorry to bother you."

"Come in," her mother said kindly.

Hailey opened the door a crack and poked her head around it. "Pretty bad tonight, huh?"

"Just need a new pair of lungs is all." Mrs. Phoenix smiled and sat up under the covers.

"I just wanted to show you . . . I guess I couldn't wait 'til morning. You remember those bottles you brought me?" Hailey pushed the door open with her foot and carried something into the room proudly. "I finished."

Mrs. Phoenix rubbed her eyes and squinted through the dark room. What she saw delighted her, and immediately she waved Hailey in as she covered her mouth and worked her way through another coughing spell. "Hailey," she managed to say. "It's beautiful!"

What Hailey brought into the room was an intricate sculpture about twelve inches tall. She set it on the table by her mother's bed for them both to admire.

"It's a plant!" Mrs. Phoenix said, and Hailey smiled.

"They freshen the air."

"How perfect!" Her mother laughed, and she coughed a little as she did. "I feel better already."

"Careful with the petals, though," Hailey warned. "I sanded them down as much as I could, but a few are still pretty sharp." Out of a twisting tangle of springs and fabric, shards of bottle glass glistened on the ends of metal twigs.

"We'll put it in the kitchen. It'll get the most sunlight there,"

Mrs. Phoenix joked. They laughed, and then both were still for a moment. "But that's not why you came in here, is it?"

Hailey frowned. "What do you mean?"

"You're upset. I can tell."

"I am not!" Hailey protested.

"Suit yourself," her mother said, leaning back. "It's a great sculpture. And you're right—I'm sure it couldn't have waited until morning." Mrs. Phoenix winked at her daughter.

Hailey sighed. "All right," she said, finally. "You win. That's not why I came in here . . . I am upset."

Mrs. Phoenix smiled patiently. Hailey rolled her eyes.

"It's Logan and this new girl, Erin. She's messing everything up."

"What about Dane?" Mrs. Phoenix asked. Hailey and her mom had grown pretty close since Hailey's father had passed away; there wasn't anything in Hailey's life that Mrs. Phoenix didn't learn about during their nightly chats at dinner.

"We had fun this afternoon, playing those wailing mitts after school. And it was good to see his house. But I just . . . I'm afraid he's gonna end up . . . getting hurt."

"Because of everything between you and Logan."

"Yeah, sure, I guess. Me and Logan, me and Dane, Logan and the new girl . . . it's all getting complicated pretty fast."

Mrs. Phoenix nodded. "Have you tried being up-front with Logan? Up-front with Dane? About what's really going on?"

"How can I be?" Hailey shrugged. "If I tell Logan, he'll tell Erin, and then she'll come after me . . . if I tell Dane, he'll tell Logan, and then Logan'll tell Erin, and then—"

"I get it." Mrs. Phoenix smiled.

"But Logan has a good sense of things, I think. Today he even agreed to . . . well . . . sort of take me on a date."

"That's great!" Mrs. Phoenix said.

"Yeah. If Erin doesn't ruin everything first. And if everything doesn't get too awful with Dane."

Mrs. Phoenix smiled encouragingly. "I'm sure it'll all work out."

"How do you know?" Hailey said.

"Because you're better at this than you think."

Hailey smiled and kissed her mom on the forehead. "Take care of that cough," she said.

"Leave the plant."

"It won't actually freshen the air."

"Leave it anyway."

So Hailey did, and she left her mom's room feeling much better, as always, than she had going in.

But this relief lasted just long enough for Hailey to walk from her mother's bedroom down to the kitchen. It lasted no longer than that.

Because when Hailey entered the kitchen, she saw it glow with more than the starlight that shone through its grimy windows.

She saw it glow with fire.

A note was burning in the sink.

10

Despite his headache, Logan felt good when he got home that night. He wasn't crazy or paranoid. He'd been right all along. Someone *was* watching him, following him. His worst fears had come true, and finally, he was facing them. He and Erin had Peck in hiding, Peck's gang was running scared . . . and better still, he had a partner in all of it.

Not just any partner, either. Erin. Erin was smart. She was funny. She was brave—much more so than Logan, in fact. She was better than he was at so many things. He could see it. Clearly. For his sake, he hoped it wasn't quite so obvious to her.

It was with these happy thoughts that Logan snuck up the stairs outside his house to the seventh floor. He turned the key and opened the door and switched on the light. He was on top of the world.

And it was then that Logan saw—on his bed, hands folded neatly and eyes trained straight ahead—his father. No smile. No scowl. No expression at all.

"Hi there," Mr. Langly said, totally flat. "How ya been, Logan?"

EIGHT

LOGAN'S MANY FRIENDS

1

GROUNDED. ONE HUNDRED PERCENT, COMPLETELY, utterly grounded. Not just a little bit. Not just "no parties." Not just "no television on weekends." Not just "home by dinner." Logan was allowed to go to school. His father would escort him. And Logan was allowed to come home. His father would be waiting when the final bell rang.

He could forget about spending time with Erin. He could forget about going on the date he'd arranged with Hailey. He could forget about everything.

"Bummer," Erin said. "Guess we'll be doing all our planning at lunch. And in class." Logan frowned, but Erin quickly shrugged it off. "Maybe it's for the best. School's probably safer than my apartment would have been, anyway. Peck's friends don't exactly seem like the learning type, and Peck wouldn't come anywhere near such a public place."

Logan nodded. Erin had a point. This wasn't a total dead end.

The rest of the month slowed down, but not by much. Classes were spent sending messages back and forth on tablets, pretending to take notes on lectures. Hallway walks were spent scheming. Lunches on the lawn were for filling Logan in on Erin's adventuring the night before. "They're still at the stadium," she'd reported over a series of days. "They call themselves 'the Dust.' The boys are getting restless, and they're planning something big. Don't worry, though, Logan"—she winked when she told him this part—"you're still at the center of it."

Every night Erin would sneak out to spy on the Dust in person, since as far as she could figure, it was the only way to listen in. She was always careful, she said, but still it made Logan nervous. "The alternative is that we lose track of their plans," she'd tell Logan in response. "And then we're back to square one, and you've disappeared within the week."

This reasoning didn't make Logan any less nervous. But it did twist his arm into accepting the risks Erin was taking.

"What about your dad?" Logan asked at the end of the week. "Can't we go to him yet? We must have enough information at this point."

"What exactly do we have, Logan? That a group of kids is hanging out in an old stadium. Not exactly a crime, and certainly not one that leads us to Peck. It's circumstantial."

"I don't care. We need the support," Logan said. "I mean, what's your dad even been *doing* all month? We're breathing down Peck's neck, and, what? He's twiddling his thumbs up in the Umbrella? If he's so great an agent, you'd think he'd have caught the kid by now."

"I don't know," Erin said. "And I can't ask him. All I know is, no matter how late I come home at night, he comes home later. He's staying out of my hair, and he isn't asking questions. That's enough for now."

2

At that very moment, fifty floors up in the glass of the Department of Marked Emergencies' Umbrella, Mr. Arbitor looked over his intelligence on the tablescreen before him. A ring of agents encircled him, hanging on his every word.

"We have a rogue agent on our hands, boys and girls. A kink in the plan."

"Police, you think?"

"Not by a long shot. We had a security breach this month. Any o' you suckers hear about that?"

"No, sir," they chimed. "No."

"I didn't think so. But two days after I got here, we started picking up a sound feed from the Spokie playground in Central Park. Anyone wanna take credit for that? Anyone even *notice* it?"

Silence.

"Not one of you noticed the twenty-four-hour feed we've been getting of little kids in diapers running in circles around a wooden castle? No? None o' you?"

"We've been busy, sir."

"Busy doing what? Hm? You clearly haven't been listening to the tape stream. You clearly haven't been out bugging places—"

"What makes you say that?"

"Because not *one* of you has brought to my attention the fact that earlier this month, approximately *your salary's* worth of sup-plies *was stolen from right under our noses!*"

The agents murmured nervously at the news.

"When I heard the playground stream, I figured one of you clowns must've had a good idea. Last known whereabouts of Megan Steward . . . and a prime location for a private meeting . . . the perfect spot for a little strip of bug tape. So I checked the log-book. Figured a pat on the back must have been in order—for one of you fools, at least—for a little outside-the-box detective work. And yet, there's no record of tape being placed in the park. In fact, there's no record of tape being taken from storage whatsoever. So which one of you forgot to make a note of that, huh? Whose little oversight was that, hm?"

Nervous glances. No one answered.

"Come on, fess up."

Still nothing.

"None of you. That's what I thought. Because you know what else I found when I went up there to figure out *what in Cylis's name* was going on around here?"

Blank stares.

"*Pounds* of surveillance powder . . ." Mr. Arbitor snapped his fingers. "Gone. Two whole rolls of bug tape . . ." He snapped again. "Vanished. Flash pellets, smoke bombs, pepper spray, chlo-roform . . ." He snapped a third time, a fourth, a fifth. "Without a trace." Mr. Arbitor looked every one of his subordinate agents in the eyes. "That's not the work of a police officer. And if it also isn't the work of my own men and women . . . then I'm afraid Spokie's found itself a vigilante." Mr. Arbitor shrugged theatrically. "But I checked the security logs. No signs of a break-in. None whatsoever. Every single instance of that elevator door opening and closing in as far back as that security record shows—is green." Mr. Arbitor threw his hands up. "So I'm sorry to say, folks, that I've followed this path as far as it'll take me. I don't think I'm looking at a traitor among us. I might be looking at a bunch of idiots . . . but I don't believe I'm working with traitors. So that makes me just about stumped, people. Now, the intelligence gathered so far is in our favor, so there's reason to think whoever's using our stuff is doing so with our interests in mind. There's reason to think this little sleuth's on our side. But I don't like surprises. And I'm not one to eat a pie if I don't know who's cookin'. Do you catch my drift, agents?"

There was a general nodding of assent.

"I wanna know what this person is up to. Now, I *think* they're up to tracking Peck. Just like us. And maybe they're even a couple steps ahead. *Maybe* they want the little miser just as badly as we do. So more important than *what*, the thing I wanna know is—*why*." He looked at every one of his DOME agents again, and now he was seeing some excitement among them, an eagerness to please. "*Why* is this little go-getter on our side, risking life and limb for a cause that's not, as far as the public is concerned, anyone's but ours? After all, as far as I've been briefed, we've done a pretty good job o' keepin' Peck's crimes a secret. Don't want to alarm the Marked, after all . . . and don't wanna give any of the more . . . *impressionable* types any bright ideas. So how could anyone out there even know to *look* for this little piker? I'd love some answers to these questions, folks. The *whats*, the *hows*, and the *whys*—those sure would be nice. I sure would love to have 'em." The agents looked just about ready to bound out the door by this point. "But most of all," Mr. Arbitor said, grinning, proud of his speech, proud of the results he knew it would yield, "what I want to know, boys and girls—is *who*."

It wasn't until the next day that Erin came back with the news. She'd visited the stadium the night before, like every night, exactly according to plan, but in the morning, her look across the hallway was different. She didn't say hi to Logan, and she didn't say a thing about how the night had gone. Then at lunch, in the open space of the lawn, she called him over, and when he arrived by her side, she gave him a great big hug, rocking back and forth and not letting him go. It was the most affection- ate Logan had ever seen her act, anywhere. And everyone was watching.

"What are you doing?" Logan asked.

Erin nuzzled her face against Logan's cheek, her mouth to his ear. Murmurs and laughter spread across the field, but Erin didn't care. With Logan grounded and things as they were, she couldn't figure out any other way to do it. So Erin smiled wide for the whole lawn to see, and then she whispered horribly through clenched teeth, "Act happy. Don't look alarmed. There's a spy in the school. They're watching us."

Logan tried to pull away, confused and overwhelmed, but Erin wouldn't let him.

"We've been careless. Acting too suspiciously. Revealed too much. Time to make everyone think there's been nothing between us but romance. No more talking business at Spokie Middle. Nothing more in writing. I don't know who they are . . . but they see our every move . . . and they're bringing you to Peck."

Logan desperately wanted to hear more of what Erin had found out the night before. But he couldn't ask about any of that, because already Erin was reaching out to hold his hand. She forced her smile tight and said excitedly, in the best acting voice she could muster, "Now, isn't that *great!*"

In science & tech lab that afternoon, Ms. Dirkin was teaching about nanotechnology. Logan and his current lab partner, Tom, had been given vials of nanosyrup, nanosleep, nanosolvent, nano-gas, and nanoink, and it was their job to isolate and determine the effects of the technology in each. The nanosyrup was easy— it'd been engineered to taste sweet electronically, without the need for calories or chemicals. The nanosleep was a little more complex, seeming to attack first the cerebral cortex, then the hippocampus, and then the cerebellum: judgment, memory, and motor skills, in that order. But beyond identifying the glowing green sections of the brain scan, Logan was having trouble deci-phering what exactly the stuff was *doing* to the rats they'd been given to try it on, and testing the nanosleep on themselves had been strictly forbidden.

"This is stupid," Tom said. "Do you hate lab as much as I do? Because I really hate lab."

"Yeah, I kinda hate it." Logan smiled. "But the stuff is interest-ing once you figure it out."

Tom shrugged. "So . . . things seem to be heating up between you and Erin."

"We've hit it off," Logan admitted, trying to stay casual.

"You guys dating?" Tom asked, raising his eyebrows.

"Hold this vial for me," Logan said, refusing to answer the question.

"I hear you two've been spending all of your time together."
Tom smiled, nodding a little in encouragement. "Good job! She's
pretty."

Normally, Logan would be embarrassed by this kind of teasing, but today it only served to make him nervous and edgy. The
spy in Spokie Middle could be anyone. Including Tom Dratch.

"We gotta finish this," Logan said. "We still have the solvent,
the gas, and the ink to go."

Tom scoffed. "Here, look. Solvent—cleans better, no residue.
Gas—higher combustion temperatures, more efficient burn rate.
Ink—aw, who knows what the nanoink is for anyway? They use it
in Marks. Case closed." Tom scribbled on his tablet as he spoke and
turned it off when he finished. "Now stop being such a wuss, and
tell me about Erin! What's the deal?"

Suddenly Logan became very uneasy. He narrowed his eyes
at Tom.

"Come on, man—I saw you two at lunch. What's she like?"

It was as if Logan didn't even know who he was talking to
anymore. Everyone was suspect. "Wouldn't you like to know," he
said coolly.

After that, Logan worked by himself until the bell rang.

"People gossiped about me and my boyfriend at my old school too,"
Erin said loudly, laughing casually. "I wouldn't give it too much
thought!"

"Erin, this is serious. I'm not your—"

"Stop talking to me, dimwit," she whispered suddenly, trying not to move her lips. "Everything you say is a risk." Then she giggled and grabbed Logan's hand, twining her fingers in his.

Logan felt himself begin to blush. "Right," he said. "Ha-ha."

It turned out science & tech was just the beginning. Logan simply did not know who to trust. In gym, Hailey's friend Veronica picked Logan first for her team in hover-dodge. Veronica *never* picked Logan first for hover-dodge. He tried to be nonchalant about it as he ran around the hardwood floor, but he couldn't help bringing it up as he tossed the hoverdisk over the line.

"Feeling generous today?" Logan said.

Veronica kept her eyes on the disk, which zigzagged unpredictably through the air. "What are you talking about?"

"When's the last time you picked me for your team, huh? I honestly can't remember."

"You're good at this game," Veronica said. "You used to play in the Spokie league."

"Yeah, in fifth grade," Logan said dismissively. He dodged the disk but only barely.

"Fine. Whatever. Chalk it up to random luck. Didn't you wanna be on the winning team?"

"I dunno," Logan snapped. "Depends how badly you wanted the chance to talk to me. 'How's Erin, Logan? What are you doing with *Erin*?'"

Veronica gave Logan a disgusted look as the hoverdisk smacked their teammates and sent several players to the sidelines. "Get over yourself," she said. "Your new girlfriend doesn't impress me. Now pay attention to the game."

In the locker room afterward, Logan bent down to tie his shoelace and jumped violently when Tom approached him again, tapping his shoulder from behind. "Whoa, you okay, man? Listen, not here to bother you about Erin—I just wanted to say, the drama club still doesn't have a full cast for *Mark of a Salesman*, and I really do think you'd be perfect for the—"

"Tom, I'm not trying out for that stupid play and I never will, ever! Why do you want me to meet new people so bad, huh? I spend a little bit of time with the new girl and all of a sudden—"

"Why wouldn't I, Logan? We're friends."

It was fear boiling up inside of Logan, immense, implacable fear, but when it came out, it came out as red-hot anger. "What is your problem, Tom? Can't you take a hint? I'm *avoiding* you! I'm avoiding everyone in this lousy school, so just get lost!"

Tom looked like he didn't know what hit him. "Sorry, man. We'll find someone else. I'm sorry."

And Logan tied his other shoe alone.

Pretty soon, the whole school was abuzz with excitement and speculation over the budding relationship between Logan and Erin. Everyone had witnessed Erin's scene at lunch. The season of new-girl gossip wouldn't have been over even under normal circumstances, but added to the prospect of new romance, the rumors had reached a fever pitch. What was a pretty, Marked girl from Beacon doing with a quiet, underage boy from Spokie? It wasn't long before the hallway taunts began, followed by the prank tablet messages, the probing questions, the sideways glances, the curious invitations to parties and get-togethers . . . to Logan, everything was suspicious.

"You're on edge," Hailey said, catching him on the escalator as Logan rode up to meet his dad.

"You think? Everyone in school wants a piece of me." But of course he didn't mention the extent of his situation, and just how threatening that sudden popularity actually was.

"Well, you and Erin seem to be . . . heating up." Hailey stared intently at the railing of the escalator. She noticed it move just ever so slightly slower than the stairs and watched her hand begin to trail the rest of her. "We never did get that chance to hang out," she said. "If you wanna just call it off, I'd understand."

Logan immediately thought of his promise to Dane, and yet still he heard himself say, "No!" before he could stop it. Until that moment Logan hadn't realized just how much he'd been looking forward to seeing Hailey. How much it was anchoring him in the turbulence of everything else. "No, I don't want that at all. It's just . . . sorta on hold until I'm not grounded . . . and . . . other things . . ."

"Oh, I know," Hailey said. "Even so. We can just forget about it if you want." Hailey shrugged. "Like I said. I'd understand."

"Don't forget about it!" Logan called.

But she walked on up the escalator without looking back.

"Good one," Dane said behind him, with a venom that struck Logan blind and seeped right under his skin. "Thanks for keeping your promise."

"Dane," Logan said, horrified by his luck. "Look, honestly, it's not what you think." They'd emerged from the school's underground hallways and reached ground level at this point. Mr. Langly was at the edge of the sports field, waiting for his son.

"How would you have any idea what I think?" Dane asked. "You don't even talk to me anymore."

"Dude, please. We're friends—"

"You don't have any friends, Logan. Everyone here hates you. And the ones who didn't . . ." Logan couldn't help thinking Dane was talking about the two of them now. "Good job pushing them away." Then he left Logan in the field, letting his shoulder shove Logan's hard as he passed by and continued down the block.

Logan's head was down and heavy when he said, "Hi, Dad. Let's go home."

After a while Logan almost got used to spending his days in terror at school, in solitary confinement at home, outsmarted, cornered, beaten. There was nothing left.

By the end of the month, he was practically counting the hours until a faceless stranger named Peck, who had already ruined so much of Logan's life, just whisked him away and stamped the rest of it out for good.

4

Things were looking no better on Erin's front against the Dust.

Another night, another rollerstick trip to the stadium. She hoped they weren't expecting her. She hoped they were still there.

She hoped for anything that wasn't the situation she'd found herself in the last few weeks.

Home was a distant memory now. Her family reunion was a fantasy.

Erin was fighting for survival.

She rolled up to the stadium and stopped the stick far enough out to maintain her silence upon approach. It was dark everywhere under the towering bleachers and across the empty field. Erin stood still and listened for a voice.

"Clock's ticking," one finally said, the words echoing in the darkness. "We move in this weekend." Erin recognized it as coming from the girl she now knew as Joanne.

"What makes you so sure we'll have any more luck with this guy than we did with Logan?" a boy asked. Erin recognized him as the one named Blake. "This guy doesn't trust us and he's not afraid of us. What influence will we have?"

"None," Jo said. "We're gonna have to bag 'im."

"You're being reckless," Blake said. "Prompt a struggle? In *that* house? No way. We won't make it off the *yard* before police have the place surrounded."

"We won't bag him at home," Jo said. "An opportunity . . . has presented itself."

"Oh yeah?"

"Our contact says he's playing a concert tonight in a battle of the bands at the Spokie community center. Dark lights, loud music, big crowd. He can put up any fight he wants. No one will notice. He'll be gone before the evening's through."

"It's hasty," Blake said. "It's desperate."

"We *are* desperate," Jo said. "Hiding in bleachers, farming our spy games out to a middle schooler. Time's up, Blake. We need to finish dusting this town and move on. Logan's been a distraction for too long—"

"For good reason—"

"And we'll return to him. He's still Peck's top priority. But this is more urgent. This kid Pledges next week. We take him out now or never."

"Fine," Blake said. "Peck approves?"

"He insists."

There was a sigh of assent.

"Hey, boys!" Blake said. "We got a new game for you!"

Erin heard shuffling as the two younger boys ran across the bleachers above her.

Blake laughed. "And you're gonna love this one." He paused. "It's called 'Kidnap Dane Harold.'"

5

"That does it," Logan said. "Enough's enough."

Erin peered at him through the tablet connection. She'd only just begun explaining the most recent turn of events. "You're walking. Why are you walking? I can tell that you're walking." Logan had been sitting on his bed when she called.

"That's right," Logan said. And he went to his stairwell door. "With all due respect to my folks, they don't know what they're dealing with here. And you need my help."

"Logan, you're grounded. Like, *way* grounded. If your parents find you gone, they're gonna kill you."

"They won't," Logan said. "They'll be angry. But they aren't going to kill me." Suddenly he looked grim over the connection. "Peck will."

Erin realized he was right, or close enough to it.

"I need to get back in the game, Erin. Meet me at Center Square. You can explain the rest along the way."

And Logan slid out his stairwell door and off into the night.

"Why Dane, do you think? There must be a pattern here." Erin shook her head, frustrated. "But what? That's what I still can't figure out."

Logan thought about it. He had his arms around Erin's waist now, and they sped through the Spokie streets on her rollerstick like it was nothing at all.

"You said they mentioned 'dusting the town.' They're clearly targeting Pledges. You think they're trying to terrorize Spokie into going Markless?"

"That's impossible . . . ," Erin said.

"With DOME *this* worked up? I'm not so sure."

"It's simpler than that. At least so far. They aren't targeting *all* Pledges. They seem to have their hearts set on just a few."

"Lucky me," Logan said.

"So then what is it about you?" Erin asked. "What is it about Dane? What was it about Meg?"

"I have no idea," Logan said. "But I know it started after my sister Pledged. When she disappeared . . . that's when it all began."

"I can't understand it."

"Well, what about the assaults? Trenton and the agent, not to mention Jon."

"What about them?" Erin asked. "They *had* the Mark. It doesn't fit."

"It has to. They were friends, weren't they?"

"Yeah. Ever since Peck went Markless, they were his support—food, clothes, information . . . shelter, sometimes . . ."

"So he turns around to kill one and attack the other?"

"According to the report."

"It doesn't add up," Logan said.

"How are we going to warn Dane if we don't even have our story straight?"

"It's not *our* story, Erin. It's the *truth*."

They'd arrived at Old District. Erin slowed and Logan jumped off the stick.

"I'd come with you—"

"It'd only complicate things. He and I are friends . . . *were* friends, at least. Anyway, we've the best shot of him believing all this if it comes from me."

"He won't like missing his concert." Erin smiled.

Logan shrugged. "Life's not fair."

ᗷ

Fifty feet away, behind a noise-cancelling wall and several dozen posters, Dane stood at a microphone, shaking his wailing mitts to loosen up and talking to his band. "That sucked," he said. His drummer shrugged. His bassist plucked an idle note. "We have thirty minutes before we need to head out, and then we get one chance to win this thing. Now let's take it from the top." So the Boxing Gloves made their way through Dane's newest song, "Comet," and imagined the glory of winning Spokie's annual battle of the bands. None of them heard the chimes when the doorbell rang.

"Master Dane?" George asked over the intercom into the den. "Master Dane, a guest is here to see you."

"Dude, George, we're practicing in here!" Dane tried to keep his frustration as polite as possible, but it was hard.

"He says it's urgent."

"Who is it?"

"Your friend. Logan Langly."

"Tell him to go away," Dane said. And he counted his band back into the song.

"Master Dane, he's on his way to the den right now," George said on the intercom, over the music.

Dane stopped the song again. Even the drummer was beginning to look irritated now. Dane stormed out of the den without another word.

"You've got a lot of nerve coming here," Dane said, meeting Logan in the lavishness of the living room. "I should punch you with one of these." He held his wailing mitts up like cyborg fists.

"Like real boxing gloves, right?" Logan joked. Dane didn't laugh. "Can I talk to you for a minute?"

"No. For a dozen reasons, no."

"Dane, you need to get over this grudge—"

"Oh really?" Dane said caustically. "I need to?" He sneered at Logan.

"There's nothing between me and Hailey," Logan said, as calmly as possible. "There's nothing between me and Erin either."

Though on some level . . . he knew that might have been a lie. Logan wasn't quite sure what there was or wasn't between him and anyone anymore. "I'm not even here to talk about that," Logan added, with increasing frustration.

"You're not here to talk about anything. You're leaving. I'm practicing with my band. The battle starts in under an hour. What is this, sabotage?"

"Oh please. I don't care about your battle of the bands and you know it," Logan said. He paused. "But I *am* here to tell you that you can't go on."

"Get out," Dane said.

"It's too dangerous."

Now Dane laughed. "Is that a threat?"

"Yes. But not from me. Dane, have you heard of a guy named Peck?"

Dane gave him a look so frustrated and distracted, it proved he had not.

"There's a group of Markless," Logan continued. "They call themselves the Dust. They're led by a boy named Peck. He's wanted for murder, two counts of assault, and the kidnapping of a girl named Meg. And there's reason to think her kidnapping was just one of many."

"So what?"

"So, Dane . . . you and I . . . we're next on Peck's list."

"That's ridiculous," Dane said, though something dawned on him distantly.

"I know you're mad at me," Logan said. "I know I've been ignoring you this last month, and I know I've been a jerk to everyone, and I know this stupid Hailey thing is *really* bad timing. But you and I have to work together now."

"Forget it, tightwad," Dane said, and he moved to retreat into his den.

"They're kidnapping you tonight," Logan said desperately. "At the battle of the bands."

"How would you even *know* that, Logan? Even if it weren't the stupidest thing I've ever heard, how could you possibly know that?"

"I've been trailing them," Logan said. "Me and Erin. *That's* why I've been so weird this month. We think they've been spying on us . . . and we think they've been spying on you too."

"So the man with two girlfriends is *also* a superhero, huh? Secret Agent, Man of Mystery!" Dane laughed at the thought of it.

"Hardly," Logan said. "I'm just in over my head. And I'm sorry, but for whatever reason . . . you are too."

"Get out of my house or I'm calling the cops."

"Please, Dane. Don't go to the concert. They're after you. They're bagging you tonight!"

"Right," Dane said. "Bagging. What does that even mean?"

"It means throwing a black bag over your thick head and dragging you away like they did Meg!"

"Okay." Dane laughed. "Let's all see how gullible Dane is. It isn't enough to take Hailey——"

"*This has nothing to do with Hailey!*" Logan yelled. George appeared now in the hallway, watching. "I'm trying to help you."

"Well, thanks," Dane said. "I really appreciate it."

"Think about it, Dane. Have you noticed anything out of the ordinary recently? Anything unusual? Anything at all? For me, it was noises in the nighttime, strange signs that someone was there . . . I tried to ignore it for the longest time, Dane, but it's real."

Dane thought about the flowers from a few weeks before. He

thought about the phone call, and the DOME number he'd been given.

"You know what this sounds like to me?" Dane said. "This sounds like the most pathetic prank I've ever heard of. George, bring the phone! I'm calling the cops. Logan here is trespassing with criminal intent."

"You know what, Dane? It's your funeral," Logan said. And he pushed past George and into the night.

┐

"Call DOME," Logan said. "He wouldn't listen to me. The Dust is gonna get him."

"Don't you think we can stop it first?" Erin asked.

"No, I don't think we can stop it," Logan said.

"Well, I'm not calling DOME."

"We don't have a choice. We need help."

"Logan—everything we've been up to, everything we've done . . . you honestly want to *invite* DOME's scrutiny upon us, at this stage of the game? You want to *ask* them to take a good, hard look at what we've been doing? 'Cause to me, that seems like an awfully good way to get us both arrested—"

"Oh, stop it! Forget worrying about yourself for two seconds! We were never supposed to be the heroes. We were never supposed to be taking on the Dust all alone. We were *supposed* to get a *tiny* amount of evidence and turn it over to DOME. We should have done this right from the start, and you know it! I think you just like playing spy—and it's going to get Dane kidnapped or us killed. Now make the call."

Erin gave him a cold, hard stare. "You make it," she said. "If you're so sure."

"Fine." Logan placed the call.

⊟

"Mr. Arbitor, sir?"

"Yes, Johnson."

"A moment?"

"Yes, Johnson."

Agent Johnson walked forward, a tablet in hand. He unfolded it and began tapping its surface to shuffle the documents on its display. "We just received an anonymous tip. Seems Peck is planning another abduction—tonight."

Mr. Arbitor made no attempt to hide his alarm. "Of whom?"

"Boy named Dane Harold. He's playing a concert at the Spokie Community Center within the hour."

"Gather all agents on duty. I want this casual, though. Until Peck shows himself, we're just faces in the crowd, you got that?"

"Loud and clear, sir."

"Get to it, then."

"Will you be coming with us, sir?"

"I'll be stationed here, ready to act if this turns out to be a false alarm . . . or a diversion."

"Sir, there's reason to believe it's neither of those things." He glanced anxiously at Mr. Arbitor. "In fact . . . there's reason to believe this caller is in some way associated with the vigilante we've been hunting."

"All the same," Mr. Arbitor said.

But Johnson carried on. "There's even reason to believe, sir, that this caller was travelling to the event *with* our vigilante, and that our vigilante might be headed to the community center to fend off this attack . . . herself."

"So what!"

"So, sir . . . by all reasonable estimations, that would put her in a fair amount of danger."

"Then keep your eye out!" Mr. Arbitor yelled. "Do your job!"

"I think you'll want to be on hand for it, sir."

Mr. Arbitor stopped cold. "What are you getting at, Johnson?"

Agent Johnson held his breath. "I believe . . . I believe I've traced the identity of the vigilante in question."

"Fine, then—who is it? And does this conversation have to happen now?"

Agent Johnson looked more nervous still. "Well . . . sir . . . first . . . let me just say . . . since the missing equipment came from our own Umbrella, there are really only two reasonable explanations for who could possibly have been on Peck's trail to begin with."

"I know that, you—"

"The first is that one of our agents was either doing it themselves, or else smuggling equipment to an unknown party in order to farm out the effort."

"I said I *know* that, Johnson—"

"But since the vigilante in question appears to be working *with* us, I can't, for the life of me, see—if that scenario were, in fact, our explanation—why that hypothetical agent wouldn't have come forward with his or her actions and intents—"

"I agree, Johnson. You're wasting my time."

"I'm not, sir. I'm making sure we agree on the basis of my

investigations, so that we might increase our chances of agreeing on their conclusion."

Mr. Arbitor narrowed his eyes.

Johnson cleared his throat. "So then it stands to reason that if a DOME agent wasn't responsible for the missing equipment and . . . playground tape . . . well, then, only a visitor could have been." .

"There've been no break-ins," Mr. Arbitor said. "The security record is clean. And it hasn't been tampered with—I've already made sure of that."

"You're right, sir, on both counts. No break-ins. All visitors have been green. Nevertheless . . ." He hesitated. "There *was* a visitor on the day our equipment went missing . . . She just happened to have clearance."

"Go on."

"And I believe this person is now directly in harm's way."

"I said, out with it!"

Johnson flipped the tablet so Mr. Arbitor could see the entrance log. When he said it, he couldn't bring himself to look Mr. Arbitor in the eyes. "It's your daughter, sir."

NINE

DANE HAROLD'S QUIET ENCORE

1

LOGAN AND ERIN ENTERED THE GYMNASIUM just as the Boxing Gloves went on. They had followed Dane to the community center with no signs of trouble, but they'd spent the last few minutes keeping watch on the sidewalk for anything suspicious, just in case. The waiting was silent and awkward. Erin was still angry with Logan for calling DOME, and there was nothing he could do about it.

"Remember, Logan, whatever they're planning for Dane tonight, they could just as easily do to you. Part of me thinks we're walking right into a trap," she said curtly, and she reached into her pocket and handed Logan two flash pellets and a smoke bomb. "I'm keeping the pepper spray for myself."

Logan knew she was right about what they were diving into, but that didn't make him feel any more comfortable about smuggling tactical espionage weaponry into a community center event. "I get it," Logan said. "I'll be careful."

Inside, Dane stood center stage with his wailing mitts and swung them in wide circles to get the sound he wanted, punctuating the low drones of one with the fast riffs of the other as he pulled the mitts' various rings with his fingers. Primo wailing. Logan was impressed.

The community center was dim inside except for the black lights that glowed from lamps hung haphazardly along the walls, illuminating the nanodust from all the Marks in the crowd and giving the room a crystalline sparkle. Some of the new Pledges even used the trail of dust coming from their wrists to form a kind of ribbon dance to Dane's music. Logan walked through the shimmering air and wondered what it was doing to him to breathe the stuff.

"Some crowd!" he shouted to Erin, though it was barely audible over the music.

"I know." She frowned. "Easy to hide in."

Logan knew Erin was right. Spotting anyone suspicious here would be next to impossible. Half the audience was made up of total strangers, and in the disorienting light and music, everyone looked sinister. Logan saw Hailey halfway across the room, and even she looked like she was up to something.

"Hailey!" Logan yelled, and she turned to him, smiling without looking directly at him. Logan slid through the crowd until he was at her side. "Cool show," Logan said. Hailey nodded at the ground.

"Hey, Erin," Veronica said. "Logan."

Logan hadn't seen Veronica standing there with Hailey. She didn't look at him. "Hi, Veronica." Tom was there too, as was most of the Spokie Middle crowd. Nobody else said hi.

"How long's the set?" Logan asked.

Hailey shrugged.

"Half an hour," Tom said. "Then the band with the most support gets an encore."

Logan felt his mouth go dry. That was a long time for something to go wrong.

"Let's take a loop," Erin whispered. "See who else is here . . ."

Logan suddenly noticed Hailey staring at Erin, the way Erin
was whispering into Logan's ear. Hailey looked hurt. Logan pulled
away.

"What's the matter?" Erin asked.

"Nothing," he said. "Let's go." And he frowned and shrugged
at Hailey before slipping off into the crowd.

2

Outside, in the shadows, Tyler and Eddie were flipping cards, taking turns punching each other in the face.

"If I win this round, I get to bag him."

"Two out of three," Eddie said.

And Tyler said, "Hey, Blake, whaddo we do once we bag him?"

Blake had been keeping a lookout for agents or, worse, Logan
and his miserly friend Erin. The last thing he wanted was another
playground-type disaster. "Knock him out." Blake shrugged. "Don't
you know how to knock someone out? You practically do it to your-
selves all the time."

"Yeah, but we never *actually* do it," Tyler said, as Eddie punched
him in the face.

"Well, whaddaya want me to say? Clock him in the head with
something. I don't know."

"I'm afraid I'll crack his skull. I'm afraid I'll kill him."

Blake rolled his eyes. "Fine. Use this, if you have to," he said, and he handed Tyler a vial.

"What's chlor . . . chlor . . . chloro . . ." Tyler struggled to read the side of the glass.

"Chloroform, stupid." Blake tapped the label. "Just drip some on the front of the bag." Blake snapped his fingers. "It'll knock 'im right out."

Tyler uncapped the vial and started waving it around Eddie's face excitedly, announcing the rules of his "new game."

"Careful with that!" Blake said. "And don't waste it!"

"Where'd you even get this?" Tyler asked, wide-eyed.

Blake let out a small laugh. "Think of it as a gift. From our good friend Trenton."

"Last we'll be getting from him!" Eddie laughed.

"Shut it, skinflint."

Tyler stared reverently at the liquid. "Still won't be easy," he said.

"Well, that's why you're a professional," Jo butted in, exiting a side door of the building. "So start acting like one. And clean up your stingy nose."

Tyler sniffled and realized he was bleeding out both nostrils.

"I won!" Eddie said. Then in childlike singsong, he added, "*I-I-I* get to *ba-a-ag* him!"

Tyler wiped his nose. "Fine, but I drip the juice."

"So what's the situation?" Blake asked Jo.

"Dim lighting, loud music. Easy to hide."

"That's good," Blake said.

"Yes. But he's got a ton of friends in there. Once he's in the crowd, it'll be impossible to get him alone."

"You'll have to be creative," Blake said.

"You gonna wait out here?"

"Yeah. Make sure the coast stays clear. You come right out this door, okay?"

"Where's Meg?" Jo asked, looking around.

"At the Fulmart. Tied up."

"Why the Fulmart?"

"That's where we're headed. You'll need a wheelbarrow to get Dane all the way to the warehouse, but I sure wasn't about to bring one here." Blake looked at his watch. "Concert's almost through. You know what that means."

"Showtime," Jo said. And she slipped back into the building through the emergency exit, pulling Tyler and Eddie along with her.

∃

"This is impossible," Erin said to Logan. "I can't see. Anything could be happening in this crowd."

The room was hot and humid with sweat, and dozens of arms and shoulders knocked Logan violently as he walked through the mosh pit. The music was so loud it pressed against his chest, and very little of what Erin was saying had registered.

"No sign of the Dust," she yelled. "That's good, at least."

"That's worse," Logan said. "That means they're outsmarting us."

Just then the members of another band, still waiting to perform, passed through a side door and into the gym, scowling at the Boxing Gloves as they did. Logan realized he was looking at the backstage entrance. "This way," he yelled, and Erin followed. "We'll meet him the second he comes offstage."

But getting there wouldn't be so easy.

"Can I help you kids?" a man shouted, stepping out from the crowd and blocking the door in one swift motion.

"Just like to get through," Logan yelled.

But the man shook his head. "No can do, kid. Sorry."

Logan stood for a moment, stumped. "Look, I'm not really asking you," he said, finally. "I'm telling you." As far as Logan could see, this guy had no real authority whatsoever, and Logan didn't have time to waste.

The man narrowed his eyes at Logan. He wore a dull knit sweater and khakis, and by this point he stood with his legs spread and his arms folded, practically daring Logan to push his way through.

"Hey, why don't we take a walk," Erin whispered, suddenly but calmly, right into his ear. "Just walk with me for a second, okay?"

But Logan wasn't having it. "Look, mister. My friend's up there in that band onstage. He's about to finish his set, and I *need* to be back in this wing when he does."

The man stared at Logan, more intensely now, and as Erin stood there, he began eyeing her too.

Erin leaned in to Logan and grabbed his arm with both hands. "Logan," she pleaded. "Can you *please* come over here with me?" And she pulled him aside and into the crowd without letting him refuse.

"This is ridiculous," Logan said. "We need to get back there, and I don't care what some volunteer chaperone has to say about it!"

"That's no chaperone," Erin said. "That's DOME." Logan peered at the man, disbelieving. "I'm sure of it," she said. "I'm *sure* of it."

"Okay . . . ," Logan said. "Well, that's good, then! That means they responded to the call! Look, maybe . . . if you're right, maybe we can tell them everything—just . . . confess to everything, right now." Erin could see the wheels turning in his head. He was getting excited now. "Yes. Erin, this is great. They can work with us. Erin, they're gonna help us!"

But Erin looked at the man by the door. She studied his expression, watched the way he mumbled into his collar. "Logan, I'm not so sure there's much left to confess," she said. And now several other men, just as large and weirdly average-looking, stepped ominously from the crowd and moved directly toward her and Logan. "And no, Logan . . . I *don't* think they're about to help us."

4

Onstage, Dane played the final tune of his set—his new song "Comet"—and let the music envelop him. He sang into the microphone and wailed with his hands to his sides, gazing out into the crowd of classmates and friends who screamed and clapped and jumped up and down, like a tidal wave summoned by him. By his music. By his words. And Hailey in the front row. It was perfect. It was his moment.

And even when the Boxing Gloves left the gym and turned the stage over to the next band, even when the glow and applause and sparkling air faded completely behind the harsh fluorescent light and cold, cinder-block walls backstage, Dane *still* was flying so high off adrenaline and endorphins that he could barely feel his feet on the ground.

"We'll for sure get the encore," Dane told his drummer as they walked off. "We're *for sure* gonna win."

The excitement continued well into the wings, where Dane and the rest of his band walked back through the hallway, slapping one another on the shoulders and laughing. In the midst of the commotion, Dane almost passed right by the tall girl and her two friends, who were standing, waiting for him, bouncing a little, eyes wide and thrilled and eager, just a short way down the hall.

"Dane Harold?" she asked. "Are you *the* Dane Harold? Of *the Boxing Gloves*?"

Dane laughed. "Uh . . . yeah, that's me."

"Dane, I am your *biggest* fan!"

Dane smiled at his bandmates. He didn't know he had *any* fans, let alone a biggest one.

"Can I have your autograph? Please, Dane? *Please?*"

"Of course!" Dane said. He felt around in his pockets. "But I don't seem to have a stylus on me . . ."

The Boxing Gloves' drummer rolled his eyes. The bassist crossed his arms and began tapping his foot impatiently.

"That's okay, you guys. Go on ahead. I'll catch up with you in the crowd."

When they left, Dane saw his bandmates walk past two grown men who sat, slouched against the wall, sleeping. *How odd*, Dane thought. He wondered how anyone could sleep in all this noise, or why they would want to.

But that didn't matter. Right now it was just Dane Harold, lead singer of the Boxing Gloves, alone in the wings with his three biggest fans.

5

In the gymnasium, Mr. Arbitor pushed his way past kid after sweaty kid. He hated rock music. He hated crowds. And right now, he especially hated teenagers.

His daughter was an exception . . . but barely.

He cleared the worst of the moshing now, and walked toward the circle of his men, camped outside the crowd and in front of the side door. There she was, in the middle of it. Erin. And her stingy friend, Logan Langly.

Standing among the DOME agents, Erin looked up with a horror Logan had never seen on her face, not in all their adventuring, and that frightened him worse than anything else.

"Hi, Dad," Erin said. "Like the show?"

Mr. Arbitor gazed down upon her with an authority that was absolute.

"Snooping through classified documents. Breaking and entering into government property. Grand theft of weapons-grade materials. Taking the highest laws of the A.U. into your own hands. And playing a monthlong game of chicken with a known serial kidnapper. Just for fun."

"It wasn't for *fun*. It was self-defense!" Logan said.

"I'm not talking to you, boy."

"Dad," Erin said. "I can explain."

"Oh yeah?" Mr. Arbitor said. "And what exactly do you think I don't already know? What, precisely, is it about this situation that eludes me? Because if there's anything—anything at all—that does, then you have my word—I'll retire right here and now."

"Dad—"

"Because to me, this is the simplest cut-and-dry case in the books. To me, this is a little girl who found a boy she liked . . . and decided to make a little adventure for herself."

"Peck's after me," Logan said. "She saved my life—"

"*I know that, boy. I'm not talking to you!*"

"You know it now!" Erin yelled suddenly. "You know it because of me! Because of us! *We* led you here! *We* did this. We deserve a medal!"

"Mr. Arbitor," Logan butted in. "With all due respect, whatever punishments you have in store for us—they *have* to wait."

"Was that an order, Logan Langly?" Mr. Arbitor laughed at the thought of it.

Logan gulped. "Yes! Actually, it was! My friend is back there and he's in danger! Now either stop wasting your own time or stop wasting ours—because *one* of us has to help him!"

Mr. Arbitor smiled. "Your selflessness is admirable, for someone carrying so many treasonous charges."

"Please," Logan begged, feebly now.

"We have two men back there," Mr. Arbitor said. "If you're right about any of this, they will be more than capable of handling it."

"Just like you've handled everything else so far?" Erin shot back. "Because it seems to me that we're the two best agents you've got!"

But something about that statement struck a nerve. Mr. Arbitor didn't look angry anymore—he looked crazed.

"Cuff them, Johnson. Cuff them both."

The smaller of the two boys jumped up and down, and his voice echoed in the quiet hall. "Ooh! Here's a pen! I have a pen!" The girl took it from him and handed the thing to Dane. It wasn't a stylus. It was an actual pen. Dane couldn't remember the last time he had held one like it, if he ever had.

"Uh . . . so where'd you like me to sign?"

"I don't have a tablet," the girl said. "So how about just signing right here?" She held out her hand, strangely, and pointed to her wrist, which was blank. Dane looked up at her face. This girl was a teenager. There was no doubt about it. This girl was a Markless.

Dane cleared his throat. "Right . . . uh . . . right there, huh?" He took the girl's hand and held the pen above her wrist, right above where the Mark should have been.

"What's the matter?" she said. "Don't you wanna Mark me, Dane?"

Dane glanced uneasily at the men asleep down the hall. His own hand began to shake.

The girl frowned at him. "I'm sorry about this," she said.

"Oh, don't be!" Dane laughed, nervously now. "I can catch up to my bandmates in just a minute, it's no problem." And he put his head down to scribble his signature onto the girl's wrist.

"No, I'm not sorry for keeping you," she said.

Dane looked up and met her eyes. They were very sad.

The next several things happened quickly. The world went black behind a thick, dirty pillowcase, and an awful sweetness filled Dane's nostrils as the pillowcase went damp. Dane flailed wildly.

"You screwed it up!" one of the boys said.

"Then you try!" said the other.

"It's not as easy as it looks!"

"Why won't he pass out?"

All the while, a rotten aroma was stifling every breath Dane took. Three . . . four . . . seven . . . ten of them, shallower and shallower. Weaker flailing from Dane. Knees beginning to buckle. Hyperventilating now. Hard to breathe.

"He's tougher than the agents!"

"That's 'cause we're trying not to kill him."

"It isn't like the movies!"

"Pour some more on!"

"Blake said not to waste it!"

"You suck!"

"Let me try!"

"You just did!"

More flailing. Swinging dizzily into blackness. Not connecting. Weaker and weaker.

Then the girl's voice. "It's working." Another breath. Stars inside the bag. Euphoria. Bright white fireworks.

"You killed him."

"I didn't kill him."

"Jo wins."

"It wasn't a game."

"Everything's a game."

And Dane slipped off into a happier place.

╗

"There was shouting. I heard shouting!" Logan pushed against the agent holding him, trying desperately to peek around and through the doorway.

"I'm gonna have to ask you both to come with me," the man said. He pulled a pair of electro-magnecuffs from his pocket.

"They're taking him," Logan shouted. "They're *taking* him!"

"Our men back there will handle it, Logan Langly. Now calm down or we will calm you by force!"

There wasn't time to negotiate. There wasn't time to think. Whatever was happening to Dane, it was happening *right now*.

"Okay," Logan said. "I understand." He took Erin's arms and pulled hers up with his, so that all four of their hands were in the air and surrendering.

"Very good," Mr. Arbitor said. "Johnson—the cuffs."

But before anything else could happen, Logan closed his eyes . . . and he threw his flash pellets onto the ground.

The light from them was staggering. Screams from the crowd. Everyone in the vicinity went blind. Even Logan, eyes squeezed as tight as they were for the burst, was having trouble seeing in the aftermath.

But he did see the silhouettes of the men in front of him, Mr. Arbitor included, hunched over and clutching their eyes. They were yelling, Logan thought, but he couldn't see their mouths, and it was impossible to hear over the sound of the band. Logan pulled Erin by the arm and led her quickly through the doors.

The hallway in front of them was empty, save for two more DOME agents slumped against the wall. "We're too late," Logan said. "Follow me."

Beside him, Erin was crying. Purple tears flowed down her face, a reaction to the nanotech in the flash, but Logan could tell that the sobs were real.

"What have you done?" Erin was saying. "Logan. *What have you done?*"

⊟

Moments later, Logan was at Erin's rollerstick and using her Mark to turn it on. She stumbled blindly beside him. "I'll drive," he said. "Hold on tight."

Logan had always imagined that maneuvering a rollerstick would be difficult for him. He didn't like high speeds. He didn't even like the thought of them. He especially didn't like being in control of them.

But tonight, the way things were, riding a rollerstick was the least of Logan's worries. He moved it intuitively beneath him, and without thought or fear, he was soon flying down the Spokie streets.

"The flash isn't permanent, right? You'll get better, right?" Logan called back to Erin as he swerved along the sidewalk.

"I don't know!" Erin yelled. "I have no idea what those things do!"

"Then why'd you give them to me?"

"I didn't think you'd actually *use* them!"

But within a few minutes, Erin admitted she could see shapes and movement.

"That means DOME can too," Logan said. "They'll be after us soon."

"Oh, you think?" Erin said. "Because I was guessing they might just call it a night."

"We need a plan," Logan said. "Where are we going? We don't even know where they're *taking* Dane, let alone what they're doing to him."

"Take my tablet," Erin said. Logan slowed, and she handed it to him. "Pull up the map. See if your tracker's still working."

It was the first stroke of luck either of them had had all night.

"Fulmart! They're at the Fulmart!"

"Pull up my old video feed. What does it show?"

Logan did, and he almost fell off the rollerstick when he saw it.

"What's the matter?" Erin asked, her eyes still squeezed shut. "What's happening?"

Logan looked on in horror. There, in the black-and-white fuzz of the video, was Dane, dragged along the floor by the Dust and dumped horribly into a wheelbarrow.

9

By the time they arrived at the Fulmart, Erin's sight had returned, but her face still shone purple in the moonlight from her flash pellet tears.

Logan pulled the rollerstick to a stop, and he and Erin leaped from it, a coordinated tactical team, needing no words or gestures between them, running furiously across the parking lot and into the store.

"We're here, we have weapons, and we're done messing around!" Logan yelled across the empty air of the store, holding his smoke bomb up at his side. Erin had her pepper spray out and ready in one hand. In the other, she held her tablet. No one on its security feed any longer. No one that she could see.

"It's over, Dust! No more hiding in the cracks. Come on out, hand him over, and we'll all go home." Logan didn't mention the DOME agents, whom he guessed couldn't have been more than a few minutes behind.

There were no words in the aisles. No murmuring or whispers or footsteps. Nothing.

And then, from behind them, out from between the rows of

shopping carts, Blake pounced, using one hand to pin Erin's arms behind her back and wrapping the other tightly around her neck.

"Let her go!" Logan yelled.

"I'm not gonna hurt her," Blake said. "She has nothing to do with us. She shouldn't even be here."

"But I should," Logan said.

"Yes. You should. Logan, there's a lot we need to talk about."

"Give us Dane and I'll consider talking."

"Put down the smoke bomb and I'll consider letting Erin go."

Somehow, the fact that Blake knew Erin's name was enough to send Logan into a brand-new state of panic.

"Please," Logan whispered, and laughter erupted from the aisles all around him. Kid laughter. Crazy laughter.

"We're winning!" someone squealed. "Four points for Blake!"

Shaking, Logan lay the smoke bomb on the ground.

"Now I'm gonna tie Erin up," Blake said calmly. "I'm not gonna hurt her—if she agrees not to struggle. I'm just gonna tie her up and let her dad come and get her. Okay, Erin?" he asked.

Erin spat at his hand.

"No deal," Logan said, growing angry. "Let her go or nothing else happens. DOME's on its way. I can wait here all night."

"We can make this happen faster," Blake said, and as if on cue, Tyler and Eddie appeared, Tyler with a screwdriver and Eddie with an old saw.

"You're monsters," Logan said.

"No." Blake shook his head. "Just desperate."

And right at that moment, smoke burst from the ground and filled the store with astonishing speed.

"You little miser!" Blake cried.

But Logan shook his head. "It wasn't me," he said honestly.

Green laser points cut through the smoke.

"Everybody freeze!" a man yelled, and DOME burst through the windows and into the Fulmart.

10

It all happened at once. Tyler and Eddie disappeared. Blake let Erin go. And Mr. Arbitor pinned Blake to the floor.

Everyone was a shadow in the thick gray air.

"Where's Peck?" Mr. Arbitor demanded. "Where is he? Answer me *right now!*"

"You can kill me," Blake said. "But I won't tell you." He was limp and calm.

"Do you have any idea what that boy has done?" Mr. Arbitor asked.

Blake laughed at him. "Do you?"

And suddenly, from out of a tent in the "outdoor adventure" section to the right, Meg Steward ran forward, growling and wild, lunging at Mr. Arbitor and leaping onto his back, pounding his head with a frying pan and a cooking pot she must have found in the kitchen aisle. She giggled madly as she hit him, and Mr. Arbitor yelled through each bang in head-swimming agony, swatting at her like some terrible fly, and releasing Blake in the process. Erin lay, stunned, on the ground. Logan stared in shock. The other agents were paralyzed by confusion and surprise.

After several seconds of clanging, Meg dropped the cooking pot and took the frying pan in both hands like a bat. One swing was all it took; Mr. Arbitor slumped to the ground.

The other agents ran in, but too late. Blake and Meg were

gone, invisible in the smoke after just a few steps. Mr. Arbitor groaned and held his head, yelling, "What are you waiting for? Follow them!" But the Dust knew the store too well. Even in the fog, they navigated the aisles easily, outrunning DOME despite its agents' high-tech gadgetry and heat-vision goggles. Somehow, the Dust had won, and DOME had lost.

"Go, go!" Mr. Arbitor cried into the smoke. And the agents did even though it was clear that the kids would not be caught that night.

Mr. Arbitor looked at Erin with disappointment, and at Logan with a seething hatred.

"Come on, kids," he said, swaying a little as he got to his feet. "Time to debrief."

TEN

STREET CLEANING

1

LOGAN WAS SITTING, SLUMPED AND TIRED, IN a cold metal folding chair in the waiting room of the Department of Marked Emergencies Center next to the Umbrella, just across the street from the building he'd visit in November for his Pledge. If he wasn't shipped off to jail first.

Logan's parents sat on either side of him, not saying a word. They rested like statues, Logan's father leaning forward, his elbows on his knees, his eyes to the ground, his hands clasped together and contemplative, and Logan's mother sitting straight up, with perfect posture, staring wide-eyed into nothing, hands resting idly on her lap. Neither had even said hello when they arrived after Mr. Arbitor's call.

Erin was off in a side room, being questioned separately. They wanted her story first. No doubt Mr. Arbitor planned to use hers as fact. Logan's would have to try and measure up.

After what seemed like an endless wait, Erin finally returned and stood sheepishly in front of Logan. Her arms were crossed and she was shaking a little, as if she were very cold.

"They're chalking it up to temporary insanity," she whispered. "Just the flash pellet part. Because I begged them to. The rest . . . you're on your own. But I think we're gonna be okay."

Logan's father turned to Erin as she spoke, but he said nothing. Logan's mother did not move or flinch. Logan wondered if she was even breathing.

"That's good," Logan said. "Thanks."

"I think they realized they need us," Erin said, and she couldn't help smiling, just a little.

Mr. Arbitor entered. His cheeks were still stained with purple streaks, and his head was wrapped with an ice packet. "Logan Langly," he said. "Please come with me."

Logan sat with his hands cuffed and resting on the table in front of him. The room was dim, and bare, and freezing. A floor-to-ceiling mirror took up one entire wall, and Logan wondered how many people were watching from the other side.

"We now know," Mr. Arbitor said, "that Peck is working with a group. Do you know the name of this group, Logan Langly? What they call themselves?"

"The Dust," Logan said.

"Any ideas why Peck would have chosen that name?"

Logan shook his head.

"Then I will tell you. Because it is important that you know what we are dealing with, here. It is important that you know the stakes."

Logan nodded.

"You see, Logan, 'Markless' is . . . a newer term. More . . .

politically correct. In the early days, the Markless were known, simply, as *Dust*."

"Why 'Dust'?"

"The discarded people, Logan. Invisible. The ones who'd slipped through the cracks . . . and gathered . . . forgotten."

"Why would Peck take on a name that insults him?"

"Because Peck is a *symbol*, Logan Langly. Of a movement that exists in this country. And I believe he and his friends have taken that name, *Dust*, along with all the others we've given them—*miser*, *piker*, *skinflint*, *tightwad* . . . to remind us that they are *not* forgotten. To tell us they are not afraid.

"They are a counterculture, Logan. One that believes in the eradication of the Mark Program started by General Lamson and Chancellor Cylis after the Unity. One that stands against *everything* we've been working toward."

"Why?" Logan asked.

"I'll ask the questions from here on out."

Mr. Arbitor paced now, like a predator eyeing his prey.

"Tell me, Logan. When did you first meet my daughter, Erin Arbitor?"

"Almost a month ago," Logan said. "The first day of school at Spokie."

"Go on."

"I met her at lunch. She wasn't much interested in me. But then we shared a class at the end of the day. I walked her home."

"Why? You barely knew her."

Logan blushed. "I thought she was pretty, sir."

"She is pretty." Mr. Arbitor nodded. "Glad to know you intend on telling me the truth."

"I do, sir." Logan shifted uncomfortably, embarrassed.

"And at what point did you convince my daughter to commit the treasonous act of searching through my private home files?"

Logan cleared his throat. "I didn't, sir. I didn't convince her to do anything."

Mr. Arbitor raised an eyebrow, suggesting that this had not been the right answer.

"What I did, sir, was tell your daughter about my sister."

"And what about your sister did you tell her?"

"I'd noticed Erin's Mark. I'd noticed it was new. I told her I was Pledging myself in November." Upon seeing the look on Mr. Arbitor's face, Logan added, "Or . . . at least I plan to. Anyway, I told Erin I was nervous about the whole thing. Because my sister . . . she was what I guess you call . . . a flunkee."

Mr. Arbitor was still. Logan wondered how much Erin had already told him. He wondered how much Mr. Arbitor had already figured out on his own. Logan hoped he was saying the right things.

"It killed her. I never saw her again. An accident, DOME told us. I guess it happens sometimes."

"Rarely," Mr. Arbitor said. "Very rarely."

"So when I told Erin I'd been a little paranoid ever since, that I heard footsteps at night, that I felt followed and watched . . . she was curious." It was clear to Logan that Mr. Arbitor was curious as well. "Erin said it sounded like . . . she said it sounded like the work of a Markless named Peck."

Logan continued the story of the burning note that night, how everything had suddenly seemed so real and urgent, how Erin was afraid of involving DOME since their suspicions alone betrayed her first treasonous act with her father's files.

Logan described what had happened at the playground, how it was his suspicion that he would have been abducted that night, had it not been for Erin's help. He described their visit to Slog Row, how they'd encountered the Dust without even knowing it, how the Dust responded by retreating to the stadium, how they only knew that much because of Erin's ingenuity with the security cameras and the tracker. In all of it, Logan admitted, he had never once seen Peck. Had never once known where the boy had been. Everything was smoke and mirrors, and no matter what he or Erin or the Dust did, Peck was always one step ahead.

He explained Erin's trips to the stadium without him, that she had learned of another member of the Dust working silently at Spokie Middle, and how that member remained unidentified. He told how Erin had learned of the Dust's plan to take Dane, and how that had convinced Logan to call DOME.

"Did it not occur to you that Dane's abduction might have been a trap?" Mr. Arbitor said. "A setup? For you?"

"It did," Logan admitted. "But if so, then it was *also* a trap. I don't think it was *just* a trap. I think Peck wanted Dane for Peck's own reasons."

"And what might those reasons be?"

"I'm still trying to figure that out," Logan said. "Your guess is as good as mine. Anyway, that's why I called you, for reinforcements. I knew I might be a target too. I figured I needed your help." Then Logan grew angry. "It hadn't occurred to me that you might actually get in the way."

Mr. Arbitor frowned. "That was our error," he admitted. "We underestimated Peck. We knew very little about the Dust."

"I would have stopped them," Logan said, trying to contain his frustration. "Dane would have been saved."

"I have two hospitalized men who would beg to differ."

"Are they okay?"

"Concussions. One with a cracked skull. It sounds worse than it is. They'll be all right."

"I'm sorry," Logan said.

"If we'd have let you through those doors, it would have been you in the hospital."

Logan frowned. "I don't think so."

"Oh yeah? You think you're more equipped for hand-to-hand combat than my own men?"

"No," Logan said. "I think the Dust wouldn't have hurt me like that."

Mr. Arbitor laughed. "The Dust has killed. The Dust has kidnapped. Under Peck's orders, the Dust is planting the seeds of a rebellion. And you think they'd show mercy . . . to you?"

Logan shrugged. The truth was that he did.

"I don't like you," Mr. Arbitor said. "If I had my way, I'd lock you up the rest of your life for what you put my daughter through this month." He paused. "But somehow, Logan Langly, . . . I'm afraid you've emerged as my top agent in this case."

Logan held his breath. This was going better than he had expected.

"And right now, I need your help more than I need my revenge. So I'm going to make a deal with you."

Logan listened carefully.

"If you help me apprehend Peck and the remaining members of the Dust, I will personally clear you of all wrongdoings and current charges against you."

"Can I have that in writing?" Logan asked.

"No. But I am a man of my word."

"And what if I refuse?"

"Then I will lock you up in this center, tonight. I will delay your trial indefinitely. With a couple of phone calls, I could make sure you never got one at all."

"In that case, I accept," Logan said. "What do you want me to do?"

"Get a good night's sleep," Mr. Arbitor said. "Tomorrow will be a long day."

2

"Here, batter, batter, batter, *swing*, batter, batter, batter—" Eddie chased Tyler to the pitcher's mound while Tyler threw one of a few baseballs he was holding toward Meg at first base.

"Okay, but if you can't hit me with the bat before Meg and I tag each base with these balls, then I get to have it, and it's your turn to see if you can outrun me all the way to the outfield." Tyler had never seen a game of baseball before. He assumed it went something like how he was describing it. Meg ran from first to second base and actually appeared to laugh.

Jo hopped onto the field from the lower stands and walked toward Blake, who was watching the game from behind home plate.

"She's coming out of her shell," Blake said.

"A little bit," Jo agreed, distractedly.

"Peck was right about her. She just . . . needed awhile. She's a good kid, Jo. Look at her. She'll be fine."

"She's autistic, Blake. And it's severe. You can't fix that with patience."

Blake shrugged. "No. But you can have patience with it."

Jo handed him a bag of chips for lunch.

"We can't stay here, can we?" Blake asked.

"I'm amazed you risked coming back at all."

"I bought us some time, left the tracker I'd found on Tyler back in the woods." He frowned. "The kids were going crazy in the cornfields, Jo. None of them slept last night. They needed to play. To be somewhere they know, even for a little while. Who knows what's next for us." He shrugged. "I figured an hour here couldn't hurt."

But Jo's thoughts were somewhere else.

"How's Dane?" Blake asked.

"With Peck. And our contact. He's fine."

Blake nodded.

"I assume you haven't heard." Her voice was shaky, but Blake ignored that.

"Heard what?" He pointed to Tyler and Eddie. "Boys' new game . . . this one's a doozy." In the outfield, Eddie smacked Tyler repeatedly in the legs with his bat. Meg laughed and jumped at their side.

"Blake, I was just at the Row for supplies—"

"Thank you, Jo. I really don't know what we'd do without—"

But immediately Jo began sobbing into her hands, and Blake realized their conversation had nothing to do with the supplies, or Dane, or anything else Blake could have predicted.

"What's going on?"

Between breaths Jo said, "DOME. The Row. Blake—they're cleaning up!"

"Cleaning up? What do you mean, cleaning up?"

She wiped her nose on her sleeve and coughed into her hands. "I heard it from Mama Hayes. After last night, DOME says there's probable cause to sweep out the whole block. They insist they're just looking for us, but it's obvious—everyone's gotta go."

"Because of Dane. Because of the scene at Fulmart."

"Dane . . . Peck . . . Meg and the frying pan . . . all of it. They're fed up. We all knew DOME's been looking for this excuse a long time. Now they have it."

"But this is *our* fight. No one on the Row had anything to do with it!"

"I know." Then Jo cried too hard to keep talking.

"Maybe if we got Dane from the warehouse, twisted his arm into making a statement—"

"No." Jo sniffled. "It's too late."

"They can't do this. We can stop them—"

"We can't, Blake. It's done."

"How? How is it done?"

"DOME's there *now*, Blake. Some of the girls from the Row were arrested this morning just for walking down the street. Mama Hayes said DOME agents were laughing, harassing them, bragging about what they were about to do all along the Row. How this was just a preview. And they were rough. People are going to die."

"Are the rest of them fleeing? Are they getting out of there?"

"Most haven't heard. Mama Hayes just happened to be there as it was going on . . . I ran into her right after."

"Then we have to tell the rest! Sneak them out before DOME can make the full sweep!"

"Where would we bring them if they knew?"

"We'll bring them here!"

"Oh, come on, Blake! We can't hide everyone in here—we'd all be sitting ducks!"

"I'm going."

"You can't, Blake. DOME wants us more than anything. We're the pretense for the whole thing! If they bagged you they could justify everything they're doing!"

Blake cursed under his breath. "I have to help them."

"You can't. Please, think of the Dust. Tyler, Eddie, Peck. Think of me—"

"I have to help. I have to try."

"You're gonna choose them over us?"

"I'm not *choosing* anyone."

"Then why risk it?"

"Because they're *people*, Joanne!"

"It's suicide. Blake, they have Logan and Erin *with them* to point any of us out. It'll take them two seconds to recognize you. If they see you, you're dead. They're not playing games with us."

"And what do you think they'll do with all the rest of the Markless? Huh? Give them homes? Give them work? Somehow I'm not seeing it."

Jo threw her arms around Blake. "Please don't go," she whispered, begging now. "Please don't. I can't do this without you." She dropped her face into her hands.

"I'll come back. I promise I will."

When Jo looked up, Blake was already running fast across the field, out of the stadium.

ᗱ

On Slog Row, the sun was bright and the air was warm. "I don't like this," Logan whispered to Erin. "This doesn't feel . . . *right* . . . to me."

"These people made their choice, Logan. They made their lives what they are. They had plenty of time to turn themselves around."

Ahead of them, DOME agents were storming into house after house, dragging people out in electro-magnecuffs. Some were screaming, thrashing, cursing. Others just kept their heads down.

"Maybe they didn't see it that way," Logan said. "Maybe they were happy here."

"Stop kidding yourself. Everyone on this block had to have seen this coming. In Beacon, it would have happened a long, long time ago. They should have gotten the Mark. It isn't any more complicated than that. I can assure you, Logan—life, with it, is good. These people must be pretty dim not to have seen the obvious solution here."

"Maybe they're standing up for something," Logan said. "Maybe they think we shouldn't have to Pledge in order to be contributing members of society. There was a time when we didn't, you know."

"Yeah, before the *States War*. When everyone aligned themselves *randomly*, to whatever idols they wanted, *killing* each other over the differences between them. That sound like a better system to you, Logan?"

"I'm just saying—"

"Do you even hear yourself? You're suggesting these people deserve A.U. benefits without being members of the A.U."

"*I'm* not suggesting anything. I'm telling you what I think their point might be."

"Their *point* is not worth thinking about. It doesn't even follow logically. They're angry at a government that is perfectly happy to give them full benefits and rights and pursuits of happiness as soon as they pledge allegiance to it—which they could do at any time—for the sake of everyone's safety and quality of life. I don't see the injustice here."

"Except for the ones who Pledge and don't come back. Except for the flunkees."

"You can't blame Lamson and Cylis for accidents, Logan. Now will you stop? If DOME hears you right now, it's straight back to the Center for both of us. You sound like a lunatic. You sound like one of them! Now walk with me. We have to *try* to find the Dust. We have to. That's the deal."

Logan began to walk with her, but he couldn't help looking back the way they came, to the firehouse. He heard screams from inside. Yelling. Shuffling. Then quiet.

Two DOME agents emerged from the crumbling front door. They were holding a man by his arms and feet, stretched between them. The man was thin. He had yellowing skin. His mouth hung open and he was missing most of his teeth. His hair was long and pulled back into a ponytail behind him. He was clean shaven.

Logan knew the man. Logan had fed the man. The man had smiled at him, had hugged him, had looked into Logan's eyes with gratitude.

Wallace.

Wallace was dead.

4

"DOME," Blake called quietly. "DOME coming! Street cleaning! Everybody out!" He ran in and out of houses, warning all the

Markless he could, shepherding everyone he found through back doors and alleyways, toward safer streets and better odds.

The Row was crawling with DOME. Agents flooded every house, rounding people up, beating them, insulting them, humiliating them. Years of pent-up frustration and anger and resentment, all flooding out in one horrible burst.

Blake had been through a dozen homes before he found him. The boy he'd known from Fulmart. Rusty. Cowering in a closet, sucking his thumb, clutching a towel he seemed to think of as a teddy bear.

"Oh no," Blake said. Not the boy. Not the kid. He tried to imagine DOME's strategy in handling the son of a Markless, and he guessed it didn't involve adoption, or foster homes . . . or mercy. "Okay, Rusty. Come on, now. Time to go." Blake picked the child up and carried him like a baby downstairs. But when he got to the back door, Blake realized there wasn't a direction on the compass that would lead this kid to safety. And there wasn't time to think of a better plan. So he pulled the boy's towel over both their heads, held Rusty tight, and made his way out of the building.

5

"Where are they, kids? Help me out, here!"

Down the block, Mr. Arbitor was yelling at Logan and Erin.

"We haven't seen anyone yet, sir. We don't know."

"We're looking," Erin said. "No signs."

"Mr. Arbitor, don't you think . . ." Logan hesitated. "Don't you think it's very unlikely that any of the Dust would be caught dead on this street today? They know how badly they're wanted. They're probably hiding as far from here as possible."

"Spoken like a true thinking agent, Logan, but we're a step ahead of you." Mr. Arbitor smiled. "The Dust didn't live alone, kids. They lived with these fine folks on the Row. These skimps you're looking at?" He swept his arms out and gestured to the dozens of couples, parents, grandparents, children . . . all magnecuffed and led away in cars and buses . . . or stretchers. "These skinflints? They were the Dust's community. They were the Dust's friends. This—was the Dust's neighborhood. So today"—Mr. Arbitor smiled—"today we're seeing how heartless those little pikers really are. Can they stand by and watch their fellow misers lose their homes, their families, and their miserable little lives? Or will they come back . . . to take a stand?"

"That's quite a long shot, Mr. Arbitor," Logan said.

"Is it? Well, today it's our best option. We followed that tracker you kids placed on the Dust. Turned up loose in the woods. So it's out with the old tricks and in with the new. And this here's all win-win anyway, as I see it. Worst-case scenario, Spokie gets its block back. Of course, best case . . ."

And just then, out of the corner of his eye, Logan saw him. Blake. The boy from his window. The boy who'd left the note. The boy who'd taken hold of Erin last night. The boy who started it all, and who wouldn't let go.

Blake. The enemy. Logan was here to fish him out, and there he was, right in front of him, right in Logan's line of sight, under the warm, sunny sky, clear and certain as anything Logan had ever seen.

He carried a boy in his arms. A boy with red hair. A towel covered both their heads.

And Blake saw Logan too. Logan was sure of that, now. The two of them made eye contact, and held it for some time. Blake had stopped cold. A deer in the most ferocious headlights he'd ever seen.

Blake's eyes bore into Logan. They *saw* him. And something about them pleaded.

This was Logan's chance. To give Blake to DOME . . . Logan would be a hero. His charges, gone . . . his parents, proud of him again . . . all would be forgiven. All would be over. *This* was Logan's chance.

"So keep an eye out, Logan Langly," Mr. Arbitor said cheerfully behind him. "Keep 'em peeled, keep 'em ready. Keep 'em out for the Dust!"

And Logan turned to him, suddenly, nervously.

"Sir—" Logan said. And he paused. "If I see anything . . . I'll be sure to let you know."

ELEVEN

THE MEETING OF
THE MINDS

1

LOGAN DIDN'T SEE ERIN MUCH AFTER THEIR day together on the Row. At school, she avoided him. After school, there wasn't much to talk about. The Row was clean now, vacant, but the Dust had not been found. Logan and Erin both were on probation, walking the streets with official DOME files to their names, which would never go away until the Dust was finished and Peck was in a cell.

The halls at Spokie were quieter now that Dane was gone. Students would pass through them, crying softly. Classes were slower. Teachers pulled back on the workload. Logan stopped worrying about whoever it was that was spying on him. There was nothing left to spy.

Logan's father had stopped escorting him to school, and he stopped meeting him on the lawn when classes let out. Nothing was said to Logan about any further punishment. Nothing was said to Logan at all. After the night Logan snuck out, after the night at

DOME headquarters, his parents just seemed to give up. They let him live in their house, but they never called him to dinner. They never woke him up in the morning or fixed breakfast for him. They never said good night. DOME had Logan's house guarded by two agents, twenty-four hours a day. Logan wasn't quite sure if it was to protect him from Peck or Spokie from him. Either way, his parents washed their hands of him. Logan figured they thought of their job as done.

In one month, Logan's life had collapsed around him, and he realized now how fragile all of it had been. Everything he'd ever known, he had taken for granted. But none of it had been promised. None of it was owed to him. Logan saw that now.

There was one thing left for Logan to look forward to, and he did with all his heart. One thing left to think about as he floated through classes and hallways in which no one would say hi. One thing left to think about as Logan lay in bed each night, unable to sleep.

It was his date with Hailey. The only person at Spokie Middle who still noticed when he passed. The only person in his life who hadn't just called it quits and moved right along. It had taken them until November to do it, but with Logan's punishment being somewhat more . . . *nebulous* these days, he and Hailey had finally gotten around to setting it up. She had suggested Wednesday of next week, the day before Logan's birthday, as a sort of early celebration, and Logan was all too happy to take it.

It was on that Wednesday that Erin found Logan in the Amazon Wing.

"I hear you got a date tonight," she said. It was the first time she had stopped him for any real conversation since their day cleaning up the Row.

"Sort of," Logan admitted. "If you wanna call it that."

"Doesn't matter what I call it," Erin said. "It is what it is."

"Like you care," Logan said.

Erin looked at him very sadly. "You never got it, did you?" she said. "Through all of it, you never actually understood."

Logan wanted to ask just precisely what that meant. He wanted to jump inside Erin's head and know right then exactly what she was thinking. But he didn't, and he couldn't.

In the projections behind Erin, a monkey swung into the trees and looked at the two of them. It picked at a leaf, chewing and swinging a little and laughing. Bugs swarmed, and Logan could see the underbelly of a tarantula as it crawled across the virtual pane of glass. Logan had time to look at all of this because Erin had walked away.

2

After school that day, Logan walked the streets of Spokie for a long time before heading over to Hailey's house. He didn't want to go home. Without the Mark, he couldn't hang out in a mall or a store. So he walked, just like he'd do with Hailey when he picked her up, and he used the time to think.

It only barely registered to Logan that tomorrow was his birthday. It only vaguely dawned on him that tomorrow was his Pledge. He wasn't afraid of it anymore. There was nothing left to be afraid of.

When Logan made it to Hailey's door, she had it open before he could ring the bell. She smiled in a way he'd never seen from her, and in a way he hadn't seen from anyone in weeks. She was happy to see him. He loved her for it.

"Hi," Logan said.

Hailey still couldn't quite make eye contact. She never could. But her voice was sincere. "I'm glad you came."

They walked through all of Spokie. They walked for hours. They walked under the trees in Old District; they walked through the playground in the park; they walked past the school, past the shops, past the Umbrella and the Center surrounding it.

They chatted idly. It was just nice to talk.

"There's a place just outside of town," Hailey said. "A really neat old building. I like to go there sometimes to think."

Logan smiled.

"You wanna see it?"

"Of course," Logan said. He had nowhere else to be.

The sun had long since set when they crested the hill far out of town. It was dark and calm under the stars. But there, in the distance, in a glade between the trees of the undeveloped land well beyond Spokie's borders, stood an old, white building, still beautiful despite the graffiti and dirt on its walls. A steeple rose from its side with a bell at its top.

"What is this place?" Logan asked. "I've never seen anything like it."

"I know." Hailey smiled. "It's a warehouse. I think you'll like it here."

ヨ

From the shadows behind Hailey, a boy emerged. And then another. The second one laughed a little, maniacally. Logan recognized them instantly.

"Hailey," Logan said, grabbing her arm, his nerves taking over. "We have to get out of here!"

But Hailey stood still. She didn't look afraid. She just stared.

"Hailey, I know these guys," Logan whispered urgently. "Trust me when I tell you, we have to leave *now*!"

Hailey took his hand.

"Good," Logan said. "Follow me!"

He turned to run, but Hailey planted her feet firmly on the ground. Logan stumbled a little against her weight. He turned to her. Slowly it dawned on him . . . something impossible . . . something that could not be.

"Hailey," Logan said. "What exactly is going on here?"

"I'm sorry, Logan," Hailey said, still frozen, and even her lips seemed not to move.

So that was it, then. After all the games, and discoveries, and fears, and revelations, at the final hour, Logan had let his loneliness blind him.

The spy at Spokie Middle was Hailey.

He didn't feel betrayed. He just felt empty.

"You've done well, Hailey," Jo said, stepping out from the shadows. "Perfectly, in fact. Thank you."

Something in Logan snapped. He pounced before anyone knew what had happened. Immediately he was on Tyler, punching him, clawing at him, the two of them rolling on the ground, cursing, bleeding. It took all the strength of Eddie and Jo and Hailey together to hold Logan back, and when they finally had him, everyone in the yard was bruised and cut and out of breath. Tyler had both knees on Logan's chest now, and Hailey held his head with her fingers pressed firmly on the brows above Logan's eyes. She held him so he looked straight up into the sky, so that he could see when out of the darkness Blake emerged and towered above the tableau. The small redheaded kid from the Row stood by his side, holding Blake's hand.

"I saved you!" Logan said. "I let you go! We're done now! You've ruined my life! Just leave me alone!"

"No can do," Blake said. "Sorry."

Jo stood and joined Blake by his side. "Logan," she said. "Thank you for coming." It was the oddest possible thing for her to say, so unexpected that Logan stopped struggling altogether. "And just in time too." She knelt down to put a hand on his shoulder, looking into his eyes with concern and gravity. "You are in terrible danger." She frowned. "Please come in. There's someone we'd like you to meet."

4

Inside the warehouse, the Dust escorted Logan through a maze of crates and boxes, beyond which glowed the aura of candlelight from a stage cluttered with the strange sight of books and paper. At the center of that stage stood a person.

"Peck."

"Logan. We're so glad you're here." Peck smiled. "After all the trouble. I'd offer you a drink if I didn't suppose you'd assume it was poisoned."

Logan looked into his eyes, searching Peck's face. What he saw confused him, because what he saw was not the face of a killer. His were not the cold, sinister eyes of a criminal. They were empathetic. They were warm. They were of a boy no older than Logan's sister might have been, had she lived.

"You must have many questions for me," Peck said.

It's all part of it. It's all a trap. Don't be fooled! Logan reached for his tablet and found it gone. He spun quickly to see Hailey turn it off just before pocketing it. She shook her head slowly. *You're alone,* the gesture seemed to say. *No phone calls. No cries for help. You're playing by our rules now . . . if you ever weren't.*

"I'd just as soon you talk first," Logan said. "You seem to be the one to have called this little meeting."

Peck nodded. "Fair enough. First, then, I'll apologize for all the secrecy, and for our invasion of your privacy. I hope you understand why I couldn't simply . . . invite you to the party."

"But I *don't* understand," Logan said. "I don't understand you people at all! If you're aiming to kill me, take your shot! You've won, all right? You've won!"

Peck looked disgusted, offended, even. "*Kill* you?" he said. "Logan." Peck assumed the look of a man choosing his words so carefully that none even came out.

"Then what?" Logan asked. "What is this?" A wave of relief flooded through him, but he tried not to let it show as any sign of weakness. One way or another, this remained a matter of life and death.

"Surely by now you know what this is about," Peck said. He looked genuinely convinced that Logan must.

"I know you kidnap Pledges. I know you kill the Marked. And DOME agents—"

Peck shuddered at the accusations. "You can't honestly tell me you risked so much to spy on my friends just to come to *those* conclusions?"

For a moment Logan felt a tinge of self-doubt. "I'm not sure what I've concluded," he said. "I admit it doesn't all add up."

"No," Peck agreed. "It doesn't."

"Which makes you even scarier!" Logan said, ashamed and not looking at anyone now. "I can't stop you if I don't know what you're after! You're better than me. I give up."

Peck frowned and was thoughtful for a moment. "I am . . . a bad person," he said, finally. "I'm a bad kid." He sat at the edge of the stage now, deflating in front of everyone. "All growing up, I was . . . the problem child. I cheated on tests, I'd lie to my parents, I wouldn't listen, I'd fight . . ." Peck laughed. "My last few years at school, I spent more time with the principal than I did in class . . . more time at home than in school . . . and I was a bully." Peck shrugged. "So no. I have a long ways to go before I am better than you, or anyone." He stood and began pacing around the stage. The whole thing seemed rehearsed, as though spoken many times to many kids.

"So you refused the Mark," Logan said. "And now you're taking it out on everyone else."

Peck sighed. "Hardly," he said. And then he paused. "Surely, after your sister, you know a thing or two about . . . flunkees?"

Immense anger rose inside Logan now. "*What do you know about my sister, you miser?*" He cocked his fist and lunged, but Peck easily deflected him, and Logan fell to the ground.

"We'll get to your sister, Logan. First I want to know what *you* know—about the ones who don't return."

"I know some kids die in the Pledge. I know accidents happen. I know it's rare. That's all I know."

"So you *don't* know, then, that the rate of flunkees has increased every year since the Mark Program began?"

"No . . ."

"And you *don't* know, then, that there seems to be a pattern among the kids who don't come back?"

Logan recoiled. "What are you talking about? What pattern? It's random failure. Procedural risk!"

At this, Peck laughed a hearty, tired laugh. "I don't know everything," he said. "But I do know this: Flunkees are *not* random failure. Flunkees are calculated. Flunkees are chosen."

"That's ridiculous—"

"There is no such thing as 'procedural risk,' Logan. There is only judgment. Judgment from people with no right to judge. Judgment over the ones who pass . . . and the ones who don't."

"That's crazy, Peck. That's an absurd conspiracy theory."

"It is crazy," Hailey said. "But it's true. At least . . . we believe it's true."

"And you expect me to believe this—coming from a wanted murderer?"

Now silent tears began to roll down Peck's face. He didn't speak.

"Peck didn't kill Jon," Hailey said, finally. "DOME did."

"That's absurd. Why would DOME do that?"

"To frame him, Logan. To cut off his support. They had a dozen reasons. Jon was our Dust on the inside. He could live the life we couldn't. He could help us."

"Trenton too," Blake said. "And DOME had the same plans for him. Would've worked if I hadn't caught on . . . and if Peck hadn't stopped them first."

Logan looked from Dust to Dust. And despite himself, he started to believe them.

"I can't prove what I'm saying," Peck admitted. "I've tracked kids who've gone on to call me insane . . . worse . . . who've laughed at me and Pledged and lived happily ever since. There's no science to what I'm doing here, and I'm probably wrong as often as I'm right." He frowned. "But I don't think I'm wrong in your case."

"*My* case?" Logan felt a chill run down his body. "What are you talking about, 'my case'?"

At this, Peck took a deep breath. "Logan. It is my belief that if you Pledge tomorrow, you will never return."

5

Logan felt tunnel vision closing in on him now. His head pounded, and he feared he might faint, so he found a chair on the stage and sat, limp, his arms hanging off its sides.

"But I have to Pledge," Logan said. "My appointment is set. My parents need me to—" His voice caught. "I'm already hated by everyone I know. If I don't Pledge, I'll be a pariah, I'll be nothing, I'll be . . ."

"Like us," someone said. "You'll be like us." It was Dane. He stepped from the darkness between the crates and walked delicately toward Logan, standing before him in the chair. "I know the feeling."

"Dane!" Logan jumped from his seat, having half a mind to throw a hug around him, but stopping just short. "You're alive."

"Thanks to Peck," Dane said. "I believe that's thanks to Peck."

Peck walked to them now. "When I went Markless, Logan, it

was my belief that I could run from it. From the pattern I'd seen. From the reality of it, and the horror. It was my belief I'd be free of it. That I'd washed my hands clean, that I could make it out on Slog Row, fending for myself, forgetting about the rest." Peck stared off, distracted for a moment. "But I wasn't free of it, Logan." He shook his head. "I wasn't free at all. Because every time I heard whispers of another Pledge not coming back, I knew it could've been me . . . *should* have been, perhaps. And it was a guilt that would not let me go."

Logan tried to follow. "What pattern, Peck? What reality? What horror? What is it you and the Dust know that the rest of us don't?"

Peck looked across the warehouse, across the crates of books and stories. "It started with teachers, cops . . . idle threats to 'Make sure you behave, you little brat! Or you just might not come back from the Pledge!' At first, it sounded to me like the boogeyman, waiting to take me away at night if I'd been a bad boy. But it planted doubt. It planted suspicion. So I began looking. 'Any flunkees today?' I'd wonder. 'Who were they? What were their stories?' Finally I started to believe the threats the authorities didn't believe themselves. Finally I realized the myth . . . might be true. That maybe it wasn't just an empty threat."

"You're kidding yourself," Logan said. "Of course it was."

Peck thought for a moment, then sighed a deep sigh. "We live in the American Union, Logan. Soon to be Global. But true unity is not in a name. It's a way of thought." He went, now, to the podium. He planted his hands on the sides. "When the Mark Program began, it was the intention that the Pledge would bring us together. Would create peace. That our allegiance to Lamson and ultimately to Cylis would bind us—give us a common ground from which all ideas could grow, together. Compatibly. After the Total War, the Mark was to be a symbol of our commitment to honor this goal. A constant reminder of our loftiest intentions." Peck laughed. "But DOME soon realized that a promise was not enough. That words were only so binding. That allegiance forced was no allegiance at all. And it never would be." Peck gestured across the space, past the stage and into the stacks. "This is a warehouse of books, Logan. Banned books. I live in a house of ideas nobody wanted us to have. And I've had a lot of time to read." He smiled. "These days, Logan, the Mark is many things. But chief among them, it's a sorting process. A pruning. They're swiping kids, Logan. Kids who, once grown, might not make for a . . . more perfect Union. Kids who might grow up not to get along. Kids who might grow up to be sick. Kids who might grow up to be criminals, yes, but also kids who might grow up just to think different. Who might grow up to *question*. To *doubt*. They're weeding us out, Logan. So that all who remain . . . may be . . . *unified*."

"That's . . . not true," Logan said, but some part of him knew it could be. "I'm the last person you'll ever meet to defend the Mark Program, but it is *not* some sort of . . . selection process."

"Oh no? You don't think? Then tell me, Logan, why it is that, in some way or another, *all* the kids who don't come back—*all* of them—are . . ." He searched for the word. "*Off*."

"Off?"

"The bad kids, Logan. The . . . *troubled* . . . kids."

Suddenly Logan seized on Peck with a defensive, passionate hatred. "My sister was not *off*!" he yelled. "She was not *troubled*. My sister was *perfect*!"

"I know," Peck said quickly. He was mournful now. Apologetic. "I am so . . . fully aware of that."

The admission struck Logan dumb. He squinted at Peck in the candlelight. Was it possible? Did Logan . . . recognize him? "You . . ." Logan tripped on the words. "You were her friend. Daniel. You were there on the morning of her Pledge. Your name is Daniel Peck."

Peck swallowed and pressed on. "DOME saw something in your sister. Something that scared them. Something they didn't quite like. Maybe some part of Lily questioned Lamson, or Cylis . . . or could grow to someday. Maybe a part of her thought too deep, saw too much . . ."

"So they killed her," Logan said. "For a crime she didn't yet commit."

"Yes and no," Peck said. He looked into Logan now with sadness and support, preparing him, bracing him.

"What? What is it?"

"Logan. Your sister is alive."

ᗡ

His sister was alive. It was impossible. She couldn't be—could she? Logan was anxious now, filled with a hope he hadn't felt in years, but he couldn't quite allow himself to believe it.

"How can you know that?" he said, narrowing his eyes. "How could you possibly . . . ?"

Peck frowned. "Because I've spent the last five years figuring it out," he said sadly. "Why do you think DOME is so afraid of me?"

Slowly, Logan allowed himself to accept the possibility that this was true. "We have to save her," he said. And somehow, stating the words aloud gave them weight, and truth. Logan exploded. "We have to do something!"

"If only," Peck said, unmoved. "If only we could."

"What is that supposed to mean? Where is she? What have they done to her?"

Peck frowned. "We don't know."

"*What*? How can you tell me all this and not know? What kind of cruel trick is that?"

"No trick, Logan. Just the truth. Our suspicions, our investigations . . . they can take us only so far. We're dealing with secrets so deep now, I'm not sure they belong to anyone anymore."

"Well, *someone* must know. At least enough to put us on the right track!"

"You'll kill yourself chasing her, Logan. There's no way."

"So what, then?" Logan yelled. "You expect me just to run, like all of you? To just leave her behind and not look back?"

"What I'm doing is giving you a choice. I'm saying that if you'd prefer not to suffer your sister's fate . . . that we will help you."

"Forget about my suffering! I'm going to save Lily! And don't tell me you don't know how to do it!"

Peck sighed. "It is true there might be a way. But I can't in good conscience allow—"

"Tell me! Tell me, you miser!" Logan was on top of him now. Peck didn't deflect him so easily this time.

"The Markers," Peck said, pinned but not afraid. "I don't believe they know much, but the Markers must at least know where flunkees are sent."

Logan rose. "Then I'll get my answers from them."

"It isn't that easy, Logan. Markers are anonymous. The Marking floor of the Center is impenetrable, and once a Marker leaves it, they can't be traced. The only way even to *talk* to one would be to Pledge."

"Then that settles it." Logan turned toward the door.

"Oh, don't be a fool, Logan! Whatever crime those skinflints saw in Lily, they *will* see it in you! I knew her too well—I've watched you too long—not to be sure of that."

"I'm going. It's worth the risk."

"Logan, if you walk into that Center tomorrow, all of this—*all of it*—will be wasted. I am giving you your life, Logan—at great cost to all of us. Do *not* throw it away on some pipe-dream reunion!"

"And what? Stay here with you? Live as a fugitive, scaring Pledges and letting parents think I'm kidnapping their kids? Wondering forever where my sister is and dreaming horrible dreams about her, just to wake up in this nightmare with all of you? How can we fight what's happening here if we don't even know what's going on?"

"We're not fighting, Logan. We're retreating. It's all we have the power to do."

"Then I'm different from you!" Logan said.

"Logan, come to your senses! I won't let you walk into this trap."

"I'm finding my sister," Logan said. "Kill me if you won't allow it."

The Dust looked at him, horrified, desperate.

But no one stopped him as Logan fled from the warehouse and into the night.

⌐

Logan ran on overgrown paths back to Spokie and wondered what to do next. He was reeling from all Peck had told him, but undistracted and resolute.

It wasn't until he made his way back into town that Logan realized he couldn't face tomorrow alone. He had to see her. The one
person he could trust, unconditionally.

Erin.

When he rang the bell to her apartment, it was Mr. Arbitor
who answered the door. His expression was blank, bored.

"What are you doing here, Logan?"

"I came to see Erin."

"She's studying."

"Please, sir. I Pledge tomorrow. I just need a friend to talk to."
Logan heard himself. He had intended to lie, but what came out
was the truth.

"Come on in," Mr. Arbitor said.

Erin was lying on the bed with Iggy when Logan knocked on her
door. Her legs dangled off the edge, and she kicked them idly, staring up at the ceiling and petting her iguana. "How was your date?"

"Erin," Logan said.

She sat up and was surprised when she saw him. "Hm," she
said. "Rough night, I take it?"

Logan wondered what his expression must have been. Tired?
Afraid? Determined?

"How could you tell?"

Erin shrugged. "Your eyes."

Logan frowned. "Listen, Erin. Tomorrow's my birthday,
and—"

"Happy birthday," she said. Her voice was quiet and thin.

"Thanks. Anyway, I'm scheduled to Pledge in the morning—"

"That's great."

Logan hesitated. "Erin. Can we go somewhere to talk?"

She took him to the ice-cream parlor a few blocks away. Mr. Arbitor agreed on the condition that he could wait for them on the sidewalk. Through the glass, Logan could see him cup his face and peer into the store periodically, but Logan knew his words here would be private.

Erin bought them a fudge sundae to share, having made a point of smiling at Logan as she swiped her Mark under the cashier's Markscan. *See how great?* her smile seemed to say. *See how comfortable and easy life will be?*

It wasn't until they sat in their booth that Logan broke the news.

"Hailey was the spy."

Erin dropped her spoon. "*What?*"

"I know."

"Do you have proof?"

Logan laughed. "Yeah," he said. "I have proof."

"Well, let's go!" She pointed to her dad. "Let's tell my dad right now!"

"Wait," Logan said. "It's not that simple."

"Why not? What happened?" Erin's face was bright and alive in a way Logan hadn't seen since Dane's battle of the bands.

"Erin," he said. "She brought me to Peck."

Erin sat, speechless for some time, her mouth hanging just slightly open. "Where?"

"A warehouse. Far outside of town. Some old, converted building. We'd been walking a long ways . . . I never suspected a thing. I should have."

"How'd you escape?"

"I didn't." Logan shrugged. "That's the thing."

"I don't understand."

"He wasn't out to get me, Erin. He's not out to get anyone. Peck was trying to warn me."

Erin laughed a mean laugh. "That's ridiculous."

"And yet, he let me go."

"Well, warn you of what?"

Logan's eyes darted back and forth between hers now. He didn't quite know how to tell her this. "Of DOME," he said, finally. "Of Pledging."

"You don't think there's any truth to what he—"

"I don't know," Logan said. "But it made sense to me."

Erin narrowed her eyes. "What exactly did Peck say?"

"That my sister was no accident. That if I Pledged, I'd end up like her."

Erin had trouble hiding her frustration under the veil of her sympathy.

"I am sorry about your sister, Logan. But . . . I mean, seriously, you can't possibly believe—"

Logan shook his head. "He had a pretty compelling argu—"

"Of *course* he had a compelling argument, Logan. He's a killer. He's a traitor, and he's a fugitive. I'm sure he's thought of a hundred different alibis a hundred times over! I'm sure it all checks out perfectly! Have you forgotten completely that this is the kid who's spent the last five years *spying* on you, leaving a trail of bodies and disappearances along the way? I mean, have you lost your *mind*?"

"He had me," Logan said. "He let me go. If his plans had been sinister, then why'd he let me go?"

"Well," Erin said harshly. "Maybe because he wasn't too stupid to realize that if he killed you right then and there, he'd have all of DOME—led by your best friend, Erin Arbitor—busting down his door in, like, oh, I don't know, *four seconds?*"

"Peck believed what he was saying," Logan said. "Think of it what you will, but Peck and the Dust believe it. Hailey believes it . . . Dane believes it."

Erin inched closer to Logan and put her hand on his. Suddenly she spoke with softness and a patience that had never been there before. "Logan, I know the Pledge is scary. But it's not scary because of some conspiracy behind it. It's scary because it's a milestone. As of tomorrow, you'll be an adult. You'll be independent—as independent as you want to be. Childhood will be . . . over. And I know that's a frightening thought. But you can't let yourself confuse that anxiety with these crazy delusions of—"

"Do you remember?" Logan asked. "Do you remember what it was like? The first thing about it, even? Your procedure?"

"Not really," Erin said. "You go in, it's a clean room, they give you a spoonful of nanosleep, and while you doze off, they ask you a few questions about—you know, the . . . test, or whatever. Then you wake up and you're Marked. People get nervous for it, sure, but honestly, people get nervous over any big event."

Logan stared for a moment. "You really can't explain it, can you? No one can. Everyone gets this treatment, and no one can tell me what it's actually like."

"I just did. I just did explain it."

"Not really," Logan said. "You described a sterile room and a foggy haze. You have no idea what they actually did to you in there."

"That's because it doesn't *matter*," Erin said, suddenly impatient again. "It doesn't hurt; you never think about it again . . . the specifics aren't important."

"How can they not be? Doesn't that seem weird to you?"

"What seems weird to me is the idea that DOME would waste their time or money with anything more than a numbing shot and a nanoink tattoo."

"So there's a shot?"

"Well, yeah, in your wrist, so you don't feel the Marking, but you're already so dazed by that point—"

"And what other details are you leaving out?"

"Nothing! Seriously, Logan, why do I feel like you're interrogating me? Just get the stupid Mark and I'll see you when it's over!" She dug into the ice cream now, distractedly.

"There's no question I'm Pledging," Logan said. "That's . . . mostly what I came in here to tell you. That I am going in for it, despite Peck's warnings."

Erin relaxed a little. "Good." She nodded. "That's good news, Logan."

"But . . ."

"What? What now?"

Logan swallowed. "Lily's alive, Erin. My sister is alive."

Erin stared at him.

"Flunkees don't die during the Marking," Logan said. "They're swiped. They're sent off—"

And Erin banged the table with both hands. Their spoons rattled against the sundae's cup. "And here you go again! With this crazy conspiracy stuff! Do you hear yourself?"

Logan pressed on. "The only people who know where they're sent must be the Markers. And there's only one way to talk to a Marker."

"Logan, no. This *cannot* be what you're Pledging for. This cannot be your plan."

"I guess I shouldn't count on your help, then."

"Logan, what could I even do?"

"I don't know." Logan shrugged. "Hack into the system. Get me out if you had to."

Erin stared at him sadly.

"I need to find my sister, Erin. You have to understand." Tears filled his eyes quickly now, unexpectedly. "I miss her so much, Erin . . ." He wiped them with the back of his unmarked hand. "I've missed her so much . . ."

Erin was quiet for a moment. "Logan," she said as gently as she could. "Peck is manipulating you. He found your weakness, and he's using it to manipulate you into doing something rebellious against DOME. Against *Lamson and Cylis*, Logan. He's tricking you into doing his dirty work."

"I am *not* being manipulated," Logan said. "These are *my* choices. *My* beliefs, now."

"Please," she begged. "Don't do anything stupid tomorrow. Go in there and *behave*, Logan! Or else you really *will* be in danger! You're on thin ice with DOME as it is! It's all they need for you to act out during your Pledge! Going off on some conspiracy rant, interrogating some poor Marker—"

"If I'm wrong, I'll know I'm wrong, and I can bury Lily for good. I'd still come out ahead."

"In a jail cell!"

"And if I'm right . . ."

"Logan, promise me you'll go home and think about what I'm saying. All I want—*all* I want—is for you to come home to me tomorrow, smiling and Marked. And for us to enjoy Spokie as full A.U. citizens in Lamson's name. In Cylis's name. Together."

Logan smiled. In another lifetime, that would be all he wanted too.

"I promise I'll consider it," Logan said. And he took her hand. "But I want you to promise me something too."

Erin waited for him to speak.

"Don't say anything about Peck to your father. Not about the warehouse, not about the other kids . . . let's just . . . wait 'til after the Pledge to sort all that out, all right? They aren't a threat to me now, and whatever's really going on with them, let's just . . . let's just sleep on it, okay?"

Erin frowned. Then she nodded.

"Say okay."

"Okay," she said. She was looking at her reflection in the spoon. It was upside down.

Erin smiled as she and Logan stood up from the booth. But when they went out to meet Mr. Arbitor on the sidewalk, she walked to her father without looking back, and the two of them left without saying good-bye.

TWELVE

PLEDGE

1

THE MORNING OF LOGAN'S PLEDGE, THERE WAS no cake, no extended family gathered around the table, and no celebration.

Logan ate a piece of toast, and his mom sat next to him silently.

"Big day," Dad said, coming into the room. "You, uh . . . you want me to walk you there, or anything?" It was the most his dad had said to him in a month.

"I'll be fine," Logan said. "I know the way."

"You know . . ." His dad was clearly trying his hardest. "It's really going to be great for us. For your mother. And maybe a nice, steady, after-school job would . . . would do you some good."

"I know." Logan finished his breakfast. "I know all that."

And still, Mom didn't say a word. She just stared at Logan's plate, at the crumbs he'd left on it, sitting perfectly upright, hands at her lap, vapid . . .

"Oh, I know, I know," Dad said. "I'm just . . . just excited for us. A new start and all. Today's a good day." He placed his hands on

Mom's shoulders, and it was only the faintest glimmer in his eyes that said anything different.

"Well, I'll be off, then," Logan said, not making a longer moment out of any of it than he needed to. And as he entered the elevator, he wondered when, or if, he'd see either of them again.

Logan stood in front of the Center for almost an hour before going in. He watched Pledges come and go, he watched staffers punch in for the day, even watched some leave again for lunch. He wondered which were Markers. And he knew there was only one way to find out. He watched the sun move a good ways across the sky, until the large spire of the DOME Umbrella cast him in shadow, and the windows of the Center to its side reflected bright, painful spots of sunlight into his eyes. Logan breathed the air and stood, calm and still, less frightened than he'd been in as long as he could remember, because today would be the end of all of that. His dad was right. Today would be the start of something altogether new.

2

"Just complete these two forms, please." Logan took the tablet and stylus from the lady at the desk. "Last ones you'll ever need to fill out," she said with a wink, and Logan thought of that unmistakable standard-issue Government Smile.

"You'll call me in?" Logan asked, finding a seat in the waiting area.

"Oh yes. Your reservation's in our system, so it won't be long."

Logan went to work on the forms.

The room surrounding him was dotted with nervous kids fidgeting on felt seat benches, half a dozen in total. Each celebrating his or her birthday, like Logan, alone in the sterile, white room among the chatterbox televisions of the DOME Center for Pledging and Treatment. One frame projected a woman talking excitedly about all the many daily uses of the Mark—access to shopping, banking, health services, transit services, worker's eligibility, no-hassle security clearance, voter registration . . . the list went on and on. Another frame projected a man discussing outreach to those who didn't yet have the Mark, and welcoming those Markless who had finally decided to make The Right Choice and Pledge Today.

Those words flashed across the screen as the man said them: "The Right Choice" and "Pledge Today."

And indeed, perhaps as many as twenty Markless sat in the waiting room at this very moment, men and women of every age, all of them filthy, hungry, putrid, scratching themselves and jittery, antsy, looking constantly around the room as though any moment someone would sneak up behind them, whisper, "Gotcha! Ya filthy, stinkin' skinflint!" and clasp an industrial-grade pair of electro-magnecuffs around their abhorrent, Unmarked wrists.

"Logan Paul Langly?" a nurse called from halfway behind a swinging door.

Logan stood, head held high, and went in for his Pledge.

3

The nurse led Logan through a labyrinth of hallways and stairways and elevators, and he tried to count the turns. Left, right, straight, left, left, right, up, right, elevator—thirteenth floor, straight, left, right . . . but he couldn't keep track. It turned out his visit to the Center across the street, with Erin's dad after Dane's concert, was just a preview. He'd never walked so deep into a building so big and so swallowing.

"You ever forget where you're going?" Logan joked to the nurse.

"Constantly," she said, and she swiped her Mark under a scanner mounted to the wall, above which a floor map appeared and dotted a line to their destination, like the world's worst imitation of Pac-Man.

The room she finally brought Logan to was featureless and unassuming. In its center, against the far wall, was a chair like you'd see in a university lecture hall, with its right side flattening out into a small surface big enough to rest an arm against. Along this surface and at its end were stirrups—one for the upper forearm just below the elbow, the next for the back of the hand— and five rings for the fingers. This was Logan's guess; the nurse explained none of it.

To the side of the chair was a machine, roughly the size of a refrigerator, stacked with disk drives and exuding a tangle of wires leading to a monitor. Logan followed with his eyes the wires to their ends. They looked to be designed specifically for attaching to flesh, and Logan felt his heart rate rise.

"You can sit right there," the nurse said, and when Logan did, he noticed a wall-length mirror to his right. He saw himself in it, remembered his interrogation with Mr. Arbitor after Dane's concert, and immediately wondered who was watching from the other side. "Your Marker will be in shortly to officiate your Pledge and conduct the procedure. I will be prepping you for it in the meantime. Do you have any questions before we begin?"

"Yes," Logan said. "Can I do it without the nanosleep?"

The nurse smiled at him as if he'd asked her to drill a hole in his head. "Trust me when I say you wouldn't want that," she said.

"Do I not have the option?"

"I've been prepping Pledges here for nine years," she said. "No one's ever done it without the sleep." She held the spoon out. Pooled on it was a thick, silvery serum. It looked to Logan like mercury, and just as poisonous. "Open up."

"I'd rather know what you're doing to me," Logan said, and a look of righteous anger flashed across the nurse's face.

"I'm sorry," she said. "It's . . . a requisite part of the process. If you need more time to consider the benefits of the Pledge itself, I can reschedule your appointment for a later date. But between you and me"—she glanced almost imperceptibly toward the mirror at Logan's right—"I'd take the sleep."

Peck's warnings began buzzing through Logan's mind like mosquitoes. *You will not return from the Pledge*, they hummed. *Whatever crime they saw in your sister, they will see it in you.*

But Logan *had* to see a Marker. Five minutes alone with one— that's all he needed. It was worth the risk. So Logan opened his mouth, and in went the nanosleep. It tasted good, icy and thick like a gelatin. The nurse waited for him to swallow, but he did not.

"Whah if ah own'd wagup?" Logan asked. The dose crackled on his tongue like soda and Pop Rocks, electric in its reaction to his mouth.

"You will." The nurse laughed. "I promise you'll wake up."

"Buh whah if ah own'd?"

The nurse smiled. "When it's over, I give you this." She wielded a syringe from the countertop beside her. "It'll perk you right up."

Logan weighed his options a final time. But there was no

avoiding it. The choice had been made. Logan swallowed the nano-sleep.

"Good," the nurse said. "In a moment you'll feel the first wave of the sleep, and from there we'll have a few minutes for questions and answers before you nod off and I make way for your Marker." The nurse smiled, as if this were all the simplest thing in the world. "And when you wake up, it'll all be over! May I?" She brushed Logan's hair back and began attaching wires with cool, wet suction cups to his temples and scalp and the nape of his neck. He shivered at her touch. "Logan, do you have any professional goals? Career plans? Aspirations?"

The question caught him off guard. "I wanna make a difference," he said. "I guess I never thought much about how."

The nurse nodded. "And what do you like to do for fun?"

"I, uh . . ." Thoughts of Erin flashed through his head. Flying down the streets on her rollerstick, his arms around her. Tablet calls late at night with exciting news. Lunches spent planning the evening's adventures. "I like reading," Logan said. "I like music." The machine to his right flashed brightly in several places.

The nurse eyed it. "Mm-hm."

Panic surged through Logan's brain as it fought the encroaching effects of the nanosleep. Imagining believable lies to the nurse's questions became much too complicated, much too confusing. As she probed deeper and deeper into his family history, his childhood, his schoolwork, his thoughts on the American Union . . . it became impossible to think of anything but the truth. He watched himself speak, some part of him cringing at his own answers, recoiling at the display of flashing lights on the machine. If he hadn't been so determined to fight the onset of his medication from the start, he doubted he would have known what he was saying at all.

"When'sa Marker gettin' . . . ?" Logan slurred. There was urgency now.

"Just a few more minutes," the nurse said. "You're probably feeling a little light-headed by now, but don't worry. That's normal." She looked nervously to the machine, now, to his right. Her voice was distant and tinny. Euphoria swept over Logan, and he found himself suddenly giggling and at the same time furious with himself for it. He was rapidly losing control.

Logan thought hard, trying desperately to calculate when he'd swallowed the nanosleep and figuring he had no more than a couple of minutes until the stuff took intractable hold of his consciousness.

So Logan took a deep, sharp breath.

Better make 'em count.

4

Logan had to move fast if any part of his plan was going to work. He had to move fast if he was going to make it out of this building on his own terms. It took supreme concentration to fight even the preliminary effects of the nanosleep, and Logan knew those were merely the lazy shadow of what loomed ahead once the dose was fully metabolized.

His vision grew spotty and dim, like an old, yellowing photograph, and Logan's very self seemed to bubble up through his head and out of his skull in fizzy, carbonated gurgles. It was painful, but it was a pain he'd never imagined. A pain that made him laugh.

Now Logan felt his lungs hyperventilating in some kind of last-ditch effort to jolt his brain back into gear, and he found another part of his self noticing with ultimate, lame indifference that the nurse had already locked his arm in place on the stirrups of the desk, and that she was currently injecting his wrist with a shot of something he could not feel.

Bemused and vacant, Logan watched with faraway eyes as the nurse pressed an intercom button on the wall . . . and called his Marker in.

It was done before he knew he was doing it. With the nurse across the room and distracted, Logan had leaned far over to the countertop at his left. Still locked into his stirrups, his reach had dragged the legs of his desk across the floor with a grating screech he hadn't heard. The nurse turned back his way in alarm, but Logan had already grabbed the syringe of whatever-it-was and lodged it firmly into his shoulder, pressing its trigger all the way down before she could make it back to his corner to tear the needle out. The world snapped back into view, skipping like the bad frame rate of an old, distorted video, but there and present nonetheless.

Logan was groggy and slow and confused, but he'd regained enough of his self to know he had one chance to react. With the nurse leaning over and tending to the dark swelling that had popped up on Logan's shoulder, he saw an opportunity that wouldn't come again. Logan swung his free arm in a wide circle, catching the wires still anchored to his body and wrapping them tightly around the nurse's head and neck. He would not hurt her. But she couldn't know that yet.

A man stormed furiously into the room, wearing a uniform unlike Logan had ever seen, part military and part medical. This man was Logan's Marker.

"I already know I'm a flunkee, so save your breath!" Logan said. The man paused, waiting for what might come next. "Five years ago, my sister came in for the Mark like every other kid her age—"

"Now, Logan—"

"*Why?* Why didn't she come back? You tell me that!"

"Mr. Langly, we need you to calm down." It was the first time anyone had ever called Logan "mister." Titles like that were reserved for the Marked. Logan looked at his wrist in a confused, hazy horror. It swam in front of him, fading in and out like everything else, but it was still Unmarked.

"I'm no mister," Logan said. "I have no Mark." He couldn't tell to what extent his words were slurred. In his head they were crystal clear.

"But you will, Mr. Langly. You are here to Pledge your allegiance to General Lamson and Chancellor Cylis. You're currently having an adverse reaction to the nanosleep, but if you'll just calm down—"

"*I am calm. This is calm. Now, what happens to flunkees?*" Logan demanded.

"Mr. Langly, as we've already informed your family and documented extensively in official DOME records, Lily Langly was a casualty of the Marking procedure—"

"Meaning *what?*" Logan asked.

"Meaning that the procedure didn't *agree* with her—"

"You're gonna have to be more specific than that," Logan said, and he pulled more tightly on the wires around his nurse's neck. She didn't struggle.

"Mr. Langly, consider the consequences of what you are doing—"

"I want my sister back! Tell me where my sister is!" He could hear whimpering from the nurse in front of him, and he hated himself passionately for it. *Why won't you just tell me? Tell me where my sister is so this can be over!*

"Mr. Langly, what you're asking for is highly classified information."

"Then she *is* alive! You know where she is!"

"I didn't say that, Mr. Langly. But if you let the nurse go, I promise—you and I can have the private chat you're looking for."

"We chat first!"

The Marker lowered his shoulders. The tension left him. "Mr. Langly . . . look at yourself."

Logan paused. He let the wires slack. The nurse rubbed her neck and stood up, not looking at Logan as she rushed out of the room. Logan slumped in his chair, his arm pressing uncomfortably against the stirrups. And Logan wept.

5

"I'm a monster," Logan told his Marker. "I hate myself."

The Marker handed him a handkerchief. "You're not a monster. You're just desperate."

"You could have stopped me sooner. You could have overpowered me."

"Yes. But then in your eyes I'd be still be the enemy. And I am not the enemy, Logan. Your nurse was not the enemy. DOME is not the enemy."

"I'm the enemy."

A shrug.

"And I'm a flunkee, aren't I?"

The Marker sighed. "Usually they aren't so lucid when we tell them so."

"What will you do to me?"

"I can't tell you that, Logan."

"Do you even know?"

"My piece of it, yes."

"Will it be the same thing you did to Lily?"

"It's always the same."

"If I'm a lost cause anyway, you might as well tell me, right? What do you have to lose?"

The Marker laughed. Logan waited for him to speak, but he didn't.

"They're coming for me, aren't they?"

"Yes, Logan."

"Right now."

"Yes, Logan."

"Will I be punished? Will I be tortured?"

The Marker suddenly took an interest in his own hands that were resting on his lap. "Yes, Logan."

"Where will I go?"

The Marker smiled thinly. There was silence.

"Do you like your job?" Logan asked.

The Marker frowned for some time. "I don't," he said, finally. "Between you and me."

"Then why do you do it?"

The Marker chose his words carefully. "When I began, it was for the cause. I believed in peace, Unity, Lamson and Cylis . . . I believed in the symbol of that cause. I believed in what it meant. For us to come together, one people, one mind-set . . . content."

"And then?"

"I still believe in that cause, Logan."

"And if you think anyone doesn't—or might ever not—you swipe them. You nip them in the bud."

"A stitch in time . . . ," the Marker said. He laughed at himself, sadly.

"I was excited for the Mark," Logan said. "As a kid. It was all I wanted. When my sister Pledged . . . I couldn't have been happier for her." His Marker listened intently now. "My sister was a wonderful girl," Logan said. "My first memories are of her holding me and kissing me with a bright smile. I think she adored me. Though I couldn't have seen it in those terms at the time. Of course, she adored everyone. She listened. She cared. She had great big plans . . . But DOME didn't see any of that, did it? DOME saw blinking lights on a machine, and DOME shrugged its shoulders, and DOME snuffed my sister out. Just as they will me, just as they do anyone else, when they so choose."

Logan's Marker stared at him. He walked to Logan, still strapped into the chair. He rested his hand on Logan's shoulder, and he spoke calmly, but very fast.

"Four men will arrive shortly to take you away. I don't know for certain what they will do to you. I don't know yet where they will take you. It could be a number of places, and that won't be disclosed to me until you are dispatched. I can't stop them, Logan, and I never could've." The Marker looked fearfully over his shoulder now, to the door behind him. "But I can tell you what you came here to learn."

"Thank you," Logan whispered.

"Your sister is in Beacon," the Marker said. He fingered a charm hidden around his neck as he spoke. "God forgive me. God forgive us all."

ᄂ

In a far-off room, Erin sat at her father's computer, breaking the rules one final time. She hacked under his account through DOME's deepest, safest channels. She hacked straight into the Center Marking computer that hosted Logan's name, and she played the recorded scene of his Pledge from its beginning. It was clear, the choice Logan had made. It was clear what Erin had to do.

ᄀ

Four men arrived now to take Logan away. The first two were nurses, looking frightened and apologetic. The other two were officers, looking anything but.

By now, Logan was accustomed to the DOME agents and policemen of Spokie's streets. But these two men before him were a class altogether new. Together, they must have weighed five hundred pounds. They wore helmets with visors that came down past their eyes; their shadowed faces were like stone. Each wore a belt and shoulder straps holding equipment and weapons. And they came holding the two biggest and sturdiest pairs of remote-controlled electro-magnecuffs Logan had ever seen.

Logan's mind raced and his heart pounded. His Marker hadn't known all the details. He had known very few, in fact. But in their last few minutes alone, he had told Logan what he knew. He had done for Logan what he could. And Logan forgave him for the rest. "Now we're even," Logan had said.

"No. But maybe now I can sleep at night."

The Marker watched as the officers locked Logan into the

electro-magnecuffs—one pair for his wrists and one for his feet. The nurses flanked them on either side, nervously. Together, the men walked Logan from the room.

In the hall, each officer followed Logan with a weapon close to his back. But the nurses kept their distance up ahead. One of them swiped his hand under a Markscan on the wall, and the same map display appeared from before, with a new dotted line pointing the group along their way.

"That's odd," the nurse said. "Why would we take *that* route?"

"The system has its reasons," the other said. "Lead the way."

The officers pushed Logan into an unmarked side door, where instead of plaster-white and clean, the walls were concrete-gray and forgotten. They'd followed the system's directions into the Center's unused, innermost halls.

"You remember where it said to go?" the first nurse asked.

The second pointed. "The map said this way."

"I've never been this way."

"Me neither."

"Maybe it's faster. Maybe it's a shortcut."

Logan shuffled silently between officers as the nurses second-guessed themselves and circled deeper and deeper into the Center's bowels.

"Down there," one said. "Another Markscan. See where we are."

The other walked forward and swiped his hand under the scanner on the wall . . .

. . . and immediately, all the lights in the windowless passage-way went out. Simultaneously, Logan's electro-magnecuffs turned off. They went slack and fell from his wrists and feet, clanging on the ground and echoing through the hall. The darkness surrounding him was complete. There was shouting and anger and confusion between the nurses, and empty, frustrated clicking from the weapons and tools the two officers carried. Nothing worked.

"What did you do?"

"I didn't do nothin'!"

"You busted the whole system!"

"No, I didn't!"

"Well then, why's it *broke?*"

And Logan stumbled blindly through two doorways and down three flights of steps before anyone knew he had gone.

"Erin," Logan whispered as he barreled through an emergency exit and out into the setting sun. "Thank you."

⊟

Logan was free, but he could not think of where to go. He could not go home. He could not go to Erin's apartment. He could not go into town.

Logan saw Spokie's streets through the eyes of a wanted man.

There was one place he could think of that would take him in. One place DOME wouldn't immediately know to look. One place where he would be welcomed. With open arms. Celebrated, even, with any luck.

The warehouse. Peck. The Dust.

After an hour of running along side paths and shadows, Logan was relieved to be rounding the final section of woods toward the hide-out, far outside of town and away from the countless authorities Logan was sure were after him, even if he hadn't seen any since leaving the Center, even if that *had* seemed a little odd.

And as Logan went, the warehouse steeple rose up higher, higher over the crest of the hill, and relief washed over him.

But something about it was wrong.

Smoke that didn't belong.

A glow that couldn't be.

"No," Logan whispered. "No."

Logan's sanctuary was burning.

He ran faster now, until the full view of the warehouse loomed before him. Last night, something about it had struck Logan as so beautiful, so peaceful . . . as if from another world far greater and grander than his own.

Looking at it now, the building was anything but peaceful. Logan watched its roof collapse in on itself, watched its bell tower lean precariously and fall. Windows burst and shattered in the heat. The whole facade buckled under the torment of the blaze.

Logan made it to the bottom of the hill, where pages from books flamed and floated in the wind. Embers popped and wood crackled, and the heat from the fire was overwhelming, even at this distance.

Logan sank to his knees. *What now?* he thought. *Please. What do I do now?*

And as if on cue, from behind a fiery scaffold, a familiar face appeared. Erin. Her expression was blank and calm.

Logan stood, and she stepped closer to him. He went to speak, but she shook her head. There were bright tears in her eyes that flickered in the fire's light, and her lips quivered, but she made no noise.

"Erin," Logan said.

She leaned in and hugged him, gently, sweetly. And he hugged her back. They closed their eyes, and the two of them stayed in that moment for as long as they could.

Then Erin pulled away. "Peck and his Dust escaped. My dad is after them, with the rest of DOME. They will be caught." She took another step back. "A second wave is on their way from the Umbrella. They know you're here. They know everything."

"Do they know you helped me escape?"

"No."

Logan shook his head. "Why did you bother? Why save my life just to leave it like this?" He swept his arms around the scene.

"I helped *you*, Logan. But I won't help your cause. Today you picked the wrong side of history." Erin looked toward the hill. "You don't have much time."

But Logan stood, paralyzed, staring into the wreckage. "You did this," he said.

Erin nodded.

"You promised," Logan said. "You made a *promise*."

"We both made promises, Logan."

"But my sister . . . ," he said.

"I know." She pushed him weakly. "Go."

Logan stepped back, his eyes darting between Erin and the warehouse, its flames dancing against the sky, as if celebrating the glory of the stars. Two tears rolled down Erin's face in a single line, one right after another. She made no motion to brush either of them away.

"It didn't have to end like this," she said. "You made it this way. Remember that you made it this way." She shook her head, swallowing hard. "You're alone now, Logan. I can't help you anymore."

Logan stood an arm's length away. He didn't speak. He didn't reach out for her.

Instead he turned, down the hill and into the woods that led to who-knew-where.

And he ran. Faster and faster, away from the wreckage. Away from the betrayal. Away from Erin and his parents and his school and his home . . . away from everything he had ever known and everything he had ever come to expect.

And still the flames lingered in his mind.

I am on my own, he thought, pressing on, one foot ahead of the next, in the darkness and stillness of the soft, forest night. *But I am not alone.*

I have my sister. I have Lily.

And if it means tearing Beacon down brick by brick, I am going to save her.

Because I am Dust.

Because I am not afraid.

ABOUT THE AUTHOR

Evan Angler is safe, for now. He lives without the Mark, evading DOME and writing in the shadows of Beacon.

As a kid he was quiet and well-behaved, having grown up in a town not unlike Spokie, where he enjoyed music, drawing, hover-dodge, astrophysics, hiking, virtual reality . . .

None of that matters now.

Swipe is Evan's first book. But if anyone asks, you know nothing about it, and you didn't hear anything from him. Don't make eye contact if you see him. Don't call his name out loud. He's in enough trouble already.

And so are you, if you've read this book.

Evan Angler

Look for book 2 in the Swipe series, *Sneak*, in Fall 2012!

Five years after Logan's sister disappeared, he's finally ready to leave his fears behind and track her down. But after Logan reunites with the Dust and makes it all the way to Beacon through the secret network of the Unmarked, he comes face-to-face with some disturbing surprises . . . will taking a leap of faith be the answer to their problems, or will it ruin the Dust's chances of ever being free?

By Evan Angler

www.tommynelson.com
www.evanangler.com

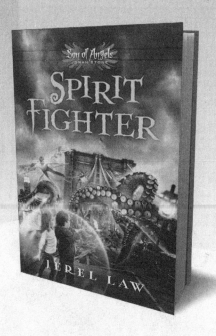